A Love to ~~Die~~ Kill For

by

Stephen B King

Copyright Notice

This is a work of fiction. Names, characters, places, and incidents are either the product of the author's imagination or are used fictitiously, and any resemblance to actual persons living or dead, business establishments, events, or locales, is entirely coincidental.

A Love to Die Kill For

COPYRIGHT © 2024 by Stephen B King

All rights reserved. No part of this book may be used or reproduced in any manner whatsoever including the purpose of training artificial intelligence technologies in accordance with Article 4(3) of the Digital Single Market Directive 2019/790, The Wild Rose Press expressly reserves this work from the text and data mining exception. Only brief quotations embodied in critical articles or reviews may be allowed. Contact Information: info@thewildrosepress.com

Cover Art by *Tina Lynn Stout*

The Wild Rose Press, Inc.
PO Box 708
Adams Basin, NY 14410-0708
Visit us at www.thewildrosepress.com

Publishing History
First Edition, 2025
Trade Paperback ISBN 978-1-5092-6039-3
Digital ISBN 978-1-5092-6040-9

Published in the United States of America

Dedication

This book, my first to be set in New York, is dedicated to my good friend and editor, Melanie Billings. Mel makes my stories readable, my grammar acceptable, and my characters believable. I love you to bits, Mel.

"To love abundantly is to live abundantly, and to love forever is to live forever."

"You will find as you look back upon your life that the moments when you have truly lived are the moments when you have done things in the spirit of love."

"The people who influence you are the people who believe in you."

Henry Drummond 1851 – 1897

Chapter 1

Betrayal

"And all men kill the thing they love. By all, let this be heard: Some do it with a bitter look, some with a flattering word, the coward does it with a kiss, the brave man with a sword."
Oscar Wilde

Wednesday

Dave Margolis was having a bad day; in fact, it was, without a doubt, the worst day of his life to date. The incriminating pictures staring back at him from the top of his desk were terrible enough, sickening even, but something had transpired, so he was forced to delay his plans to confront his wife. He would typically finish work in forty-five minutes when he intended to face Lynne. But a call just came in for him to attend the Medusa Plaza building downtown, and as the only other negotiator was on sick leave with COVID, Dave had no choice but to go. Inevitably, that meant he would be late and lose the opportunity to have the confrontation before other events that he had put in place occurred.

Ordinarily, being late for dinner was something Lynne, his wife of eleven years, and their two children, Ben, aged eight, and Molly, five, expected, if not as the norm, at least semi-regularly. With Dave being a New

York detective who specialized as a trained negotiator, he was often called into hostage situations that could drag on for hours or, on serious occasions, days. Dave attended numerous domestic violence situations that spiraled out of control, usually at night when a drunken husband abused a long-suffering wife, which would result in overtime. Domestic incidents sometimes dragged on for hours and were the hardest for Dave to deal with, especially if children were involved and had witnessed their mother being hurt.

In the past three months, Dave had attended four high-rise buildings or bridges to try to talk someone out of jumping to commit suicide. He wondered if the post-COVID times in New York had led to a higher incidence of depression, which fueled more than the usual rate of suicide attempts.

The dispatcher had informed Dave that another potential jumper was the cause for tonight's call to work late. A woman, name unknown, sat on a fortieth-story ledge at the Plaza, refusing to talk other than to threaten to jump if anyone tried to stop her. The officer at the scene reported that she wanted to be left alone, seemingly until she found the courage to take the last leap of her life at sunset.

In the five and a half years since becoming a negotiator, Dave had lost count of the number of jumpers he had spoken to but knew it was more than fifty. His success rate of talking people out of taking their final, irrevocable step was, he was told by his superiors, extraordinarily high, though sadly, it was not one hundred percent. During training, his instructors predicted it would be because Dave had an uncanny ability to relate emotionally to other people. They postulated that his empathy would assist in making him an exceptional negotiator and a good husband and father. Dave always believed the latter was true until his world fell apart when he discovered Lynne's infidelity.

With the car's emergency light flashing and siren blaring on his way to the Medusa Plaza, Dave cursed the lousy timing. That night was to be when he confronted Lynne and demanded why she was throwing their marriage away. Now, he didn't know when he would be home. He pressed the Bluetooth dial button for her cell, and she answered almost immediately in a subdued, nearly miserable, if not depressed-sounding voice. "What's up, Dave?"

"I'm going to be late home, Lynne. I have a jumper at the Medusa Plaza, and I'm on my way to try to talk her down."

Her sigh was audible. "Yeah, you do what you're best at, Dave, caring for strangers."

He would have argued, yelled, and ranted that he knew about the affair with her boss, Marlon Flanders, but the phone was already dead because she'd hung up. *Well, that's a conversation we'll have later,* he thought, though Dave hadn't decided what he would say or do when the truth came out. All he knew was he would not be Lynne's cuckold, and he doubted he could forgive and forget even if she was remorseful and begged for a second chance, which remained to be seen.

The problem was that Dave loved Lynne and had since high school. He didn't relish a life stretching ahead into infinity without her and his children to share it. He knew many divorced cops who got to see their kids every other weekend, if they were lucky, and lived in rundown one-bedroom apartments because, after the property settlement, alimony, and child support payments, they could ill afford anything else. Most shared that miserable, worn look as if life had just passed them by. Sometimes, depression, fueled by booze, caused them to end their lives. The suicide rate among NY police officers was high for many reasons, but divorce was frequently thought to be a significant factor.

Dave glanced at his wristwatch and gave a sickly smile. By now, he imagined the fireworks were well and truly ablaze in the Flanders household. Mitch, the private detective, had provided a thumb drive containing pictures, making it easier to email them to Dorothy Flanders-Gibbs, CEO of Bond Enterprises Corp. She was the brains and money of her marriage, and along with her father, owned a string of blue-chip businesses, including the public relations company that had installed Marlon Flanders as CEO, who shortly after taking over, promoted Lynne Margolis as his assistant, and then seduced her.

****

Dave stopped beside three police cars, angle parked in front of the Medusa Building, switched off the ignition, and opened the door in one practiced fluid motion. He flashed his badge to the uniform cop on duty at the automatic doors and ran to the bank of elevators. Another cop awaited him as the doors swished open on the fortieth floor.

"You're the negotiator?" he asked in a gruff voice. Dave nodded and once again showed his ID. "Frank Casey, Sergeant Frank Casey, she's this way," the cop murmured, turning on his heel and speaking over his shoulder. "Her name is Susan Bodinski, and she works as a freelance editor. This afternoon, she had a visitor, and shortly after he left, she climbed out of her office window and crawled along the ledge. She's just sitting there and hasn't said anything other than to tell us to stay away from her; otherwise, she'll jump."

Dave nodded thoughtfully. "Any idea who the male visitor was?"

"Yeah, we believe her husband. We've been unable to locate him to get him to come and talk to her. His cell phone is turned off, and he isn't at their condo or his place of work; he's a high school teacher."

Another cop stood by an open office door, and Dave grabbed the sergeant's arm. "Please don't let anyone go near that window. I need to talk to her, which could take some time, and I don't want interruptions or anyone listening. I need to gain her trust. Are we clear on that?"

The cop nodded. "The street has been cleared underneath, so she's all yours."

****

Dave slowly leaned out of the window, turned his head to the right, and saw her. He was stunned by the view so much he couldn't speak for a moment. In profile, she was so achingly beautiful he felt like someone had thudded him in the chest with a hammer. She sat with her long, lithe legs, covered in a long business skirt, dangling into the void. The evening breeze gently blew her impossibly thin shoulder-length blonde hair around her face. Her skin was pale, her nose perfectly shaped to suit her face, her lips were ruby red, and he could tell she was curved in all the right places by the way her matching jacket clung to her upper body. As she gazed at the approaching sunset, it dawned on Dave that he was looking at one of the most beautiful, if not the most beautiful, women he had ever seen. He guessed her age to be around thirty, and he was sure that if he could make her smile, her face would light up a room.

"Hi," he said softly, not wanting to make her jump in fright. "Do you mind if I join you?"

She turned to him, her face showing the abject misery she must be feeling to have decided that her life was no longer worth living. Dave smiled his best; *I'm not here to talk you out of this,* smile. Without waiting for a reply, he hoisted his body onto the window ledge and crawled through, breaking one of the golden rules in the suicide negotiator's handbook: not to put himself in danger. It was a fact that sometimes, when a jumper changed their mind and came to their senses, they panicked and grabbed hold of the person trying to save them, and they both fell into the next world.

"Please don't," she said with a note of urgency in her trembling voice. "Please, just leave me alone."

Dave tried to read the tone of her voice to decide just how serious she was about killing herself, and with a sinking heart, recognized the hopelessness in the way she had uttered those few words. "It's okay, Susan, no need to panic. Oh, sorry, you don't mind if I call you Susan, do you? I'm Dave. Dave Margolis. Don't worry; I'm not coming too close, and I'm not going to talk you out of whatever you decide to do. I do this for a living, and I have a wife and two children at home waiting for me. So I won't do anything rash, I promise. But as you might be aware, in situations like this, there are some formalities we need to get out of the way before…well, you know, before you decide to end things." He turned so he was sitting as she was, back thrust firmly against the rough concrete wall, hoping the ledge would take his weight, scared but somehow exhilarated to be in such a magnificent woman's company forty floors above the sidewalk. The danger of his predicament only seemed to add to his minor sense of euphoria, and suddenly, he realized he had stopped feeling as much rage about Lynne's affair as he had ten minutes earlier.

"What formalities?" she asked, and Dave felt gladdened that there was a subtle change in her voice. Interest or annoyance, he wasn't sure which, but it was at least a change, and any change was for the better.

"Oh, you know. Things like why you're doing this and any family members you want me to talk to after you've gone. Sometimes, for the loved ones left behind, the worst thing for them is not knowing why. Wow, that's some view. Is this your office?" He deliberately changed the subject mid-conversation because he felt it would help put the woman at ease.

She nodded cautiously, only six feet away, but too far to grab, not that he would usually, as that would ensure they both tumbled into the void. But she was so incredibly beautiful. He could be tempted, if only for the chance to touch her. Then Dave instantly regretted the thought. His married life as he knew it was likely to end once he got home and confronted Lynne, yet he was mesmerized by another woman he had only just met and who was intent on killing herself. He shook himself mentally and told himself to get back to work. "Well, you know what? If I had a view like this out of my office, it would constantly remind me how beautiful the world can be. Me? I work out of a basement with no view, and let me tell you, we are fed the worst coffee in the world, bar none. Maybe you and I should swap offices." Dave grinned and watched for a reaction that didn't come. "So, who would you like me to talk to after? Well, you know…" he nodded toward the setting sun.

She raised her hands to cover her face, and her shoulders shook as she cried in a soul-wrenching and pitiful way. For no reason he could understand later when he remembered, Dave was suddenly overcome with his marital problems. Before he could think or stop himself, he recalled that he was about to lose his wife, children, and home, and he felt a wave of sadness as tears sprang from his eyes. Dave sobbed loudly. He couldn't stop himself. For days, he had kept his suspicions, rage, and hurt inside, waiting for the proof that had arrived that afternoon. He'd had no one to confide in because he was just too embarrassed to admit to family or friends that he was so inadequate his beloved wife had felt the need to find sex with her boss.

"I thought you were here to help and talk me out of jumping. It seems to me we should both go together." She murmured, and Dave thought her voice had a wry touch of humor.

Dave wiped tears away using the thumb of his right hand and took a deep, cleansing breath. "I'm sorry. That wife at home I mentioned earlier. I just found out she's been having an affair with her boss. While I minded our two children on Monday nights, she saw him at a motel. Then, of course, because he's her boss, they've probably been at it in his office too during lunch breaks."

"What will you do?" Susan asked, and through his pain, he thought her voice had changed again; she seemed genuinely interested.

Dave shrugged. "God knows. This afternoon, I was sent pictures of their last tryst." He turned to her and continued, "Nice word that, isn't it, tryst? It makes it sound almost dignified. Anyway, I emailed his wife the pictures late this afternoon because I thought, well, if my marriage is over, why shouldn't his be too? Then I intended to confront Lynne about it tonight, around the same time Mr. Flanders' wife threw him out. But I got the call to come here, and well, here I am. By the time I get home, you can bet he will have been on the phone bitching to Lynne about what a slime-ball I am for ruining his marriage. She will, of course, agree because it couldn't possibly be their fault for cheating." He shrugged again and glanced at her, and the next moment, they both burst into near-hysterical laughter.

When they stopped, they looked at each other again and laughed again. "Is this how you do it? She asked.

"Do what?"

"Talk us pathetic creatures out of killing ourselves by coming up with some cockamamie story to make us feel more sorry for you than we do for ourselves."

Dave shook his head. "Nah. Let me tell you two things, Susan. Firstly, unfortunately, every word I said was true, and secondly, if you told my boss what I'd told you, I'd lose my job and have to take counseling before they ever let me have it back."

"Well, your secret is safe with me. I will take it to my grave." He saw her shrug. "Sorry, but I'm still going through with this." She sighed loudly and mournfully."

****

Dave felt a real terrifying fear that this beautiful goddess would throw herself off the ledge and plummet forty stories, and there wasn't a thing he could do about it. "Why, please at least tell me why. As I said, anyone who cares about you will want to know that, and a part of my job is to try to explain it to them."

"You said your name was Dave, didn't you?" He

nodded. "Well, Dave, everyone who knows me will understand why without you telling them. I'm such an ugly freak; even my husband could no longer stand to be with me. He told me today he was sorry, but he was leaving. Oh, he tried to be nice about it, but I could tell that he could no longer stand to look at me, let alone touch me, so in an instant, I knew I had to handle this nightmare by myself. And I'm just not strong enough to do it alone."

Dave stared at her, disbelieving his ears. *What on earth is she talking about? She is the most beautiful woman I have ever laid eyes on.* "Susan, I have no idea what your problems are, but any sane man would agree you are a stunningly beautiful woman, and I can tell your personality matches your looks. If your husband decided to leave you, it's not because you're a freak; it's because he is mentally defective."

They both stared into each other's eyes briefly before she smiled sadly. "You're a lovely and caring man, and your wife must be mad to swap you for cheap sex in a motel, no matter how exciting she must have found it. But unfortunately, you're mistaken. You're only going by what you can observe, and my husband, Mark, could see what is hidden under my clothes. At least he used to be able to before he got so sick at looking at me that he moved into the spare bedroom."

"Sick at looking at you? What is wrong with him, Susan? I swear if I weren't married, well, I'm not likely to be married for much longer, but I mean, if I were your husband, I'd consider myself the luckiest man alive to be looking at you every day. Especially, *especially,* if you didn't sleep with your boss behind my back."

She gave the faintest smile again, reinforcing to

Dave that she was staggeringly beautiful. "Maybe if we'd met before we ended up with the wrong partners, things would have tuned out differently for both of us. But then again, maybe not. I would never fool around behind my husband's back; the idea is abhorrent to me. But I'm afraid, sooner or later, you would have become just like Mark and couldn't bring yourself to look at me naked, let alone make love to me. I'm a freak, as ugly as sin. If I lived a hundred years ago, I'd have been a circus act, or two hundred years ago, burned at the stake as a witch."

Dave shook his head violently. "What are you even talking about? *You are not ugly.*"

She gazed at him and sighed. "Goodbye, Dave. Thanks for trying to talk me out of it. It's time for you to go and try to save your marriage now. I'm a lost cause." She turned back to stare at the evening skyscape and wriggled her bottom forward on the ledge.

All of Dave's training went out the window when he had crawled out to the ledge; Dave realized later when he thought back. There were so many things he could have said and should have said if he had followed procedure, but at that moment, he knew they wouldn't work. Yet what he did say, without any conscious planning, did. "Please don't, at least not now. I don't want to go home and face my cheating wife, not yet, anyway. Let her stew on what she's done to our marriage and children. I'd rather spend some time with you, please, let's talk. I can't stop you if you want to end your life. And even if you spent a few hours with me, you could always come back here tomorrow and jump. I have a choice between going home to have an almighty fight with Lynne, packing, and going to a motel or staying with you for a while to talk. If you permit me, I choose to stay with you."

She stopped bare inches from oblivion and turned her head back. "Why, Dave? Why do you even care?"

He sighed as a memory of his mother came unbidden to his mind long before they took her to the nursing home, where she slowly deteriorated from dementia. "My mum's favorite music when my brother and I were kids was sixties and seventies rock, and I remember a line from one song that seems so appropriate right now: *'We're just two lost souls swimming in a fishbowl.'* That's us, you and me, two lost souls, yet we've met and found each other. I feel so gutted now, and when I think about what my life will be like after the divorce, it's like just total blackness stretching ahead for me for years to come. So, Susan, I will jump right after you if you jump. Here's the weirdest thing: I came here to try and save your life tonight, but instead, you could try to save mine. I like you, and I think you are beautiful, and I'd like to spend some time with you and find out why you think you're so ugly. Maybe, just maybe, if I try to help you, you can heal my suffering, too, so I can come to terms with my wife's adultery. And." He shrugged. "If we can't help each other, we can just do this another time. What do you say? Let me get rid of all the cops and come and have dinner and a drink with me; let's talk. Please, I really want to."

Susan paused for what seemed like hours but was less than a minute. "I'm not dumb, you know. I know a suicide attempt like this means you will take me to a psychiatric hospital for evaluation, and I don't want that. They can't help me because my problem is physical, not mental."

"Susan, one thing I know, and trust me in this job, I am pretty accurate in assessing people, is you are far from dumb. I don't know your problems, but I want to know. Your timing is perfect and lucky. It's the end of the shift for the cops down below who are holding back the crowd of morons who are waiting for you to jump. All the cops want is to finish work and go home to their loved ones. So, if we end this now before it drags on for much longer, I can tell them I will look after you and take you to a family member who will be able to help you, and we can avoid going to the hospital. Trust me, these guys have had a long day and would love me to do the paperwork so they can go and be with their families."

"You're pretty good at this, aren't you?" She said with the ghost of a smile.

Dave laughed. "Susan, believe me, none of what I've said is out of the training manual. This is the real me, genuinely interested in you and dreading going home."

After a lengthy pause, Susan spoke. "I think you're a good man, and your wife is stupid, whereas I can't blame Mark for abandoning me. Most, if not all, men would run away in the same situation. Do you promise me you're telling me the truth? Because Dave, I'm serious about this. If this is just some game to you, and you're just a guy doing his job, then all you are doing is delaying the inevitable. No amount of psychobabble will fix me. Nothing can, well, let me rephrase that; nothing short of around three hundred thousand dollars can fix my problem, and I don't have it. So, honestly, if this is all just an act, please stop and let me be. I've got more problems than anyone should have to bear."

"Let me prove it to you."

She looked startled. "How can you do that?"

"Two ways that I can think of. One, let me sidle over to you and hug you. I think you desperately need one, and let me tell you, I know I do. I'd love to hold a beautiful woman right now. Second, in my pocket is an envelope; if you doubt my honesty, I can show you the pictures of my wife with her lover given to me today by the private investigator I hired."

"I don't even know you. Why would you think I'd want to see pornographic pictures of your wife or want to hug you?" She asked, but Dave could see her whole demeanor had changed.

"Sure, you know me. I'm just like you. Suicidally lonely, with a lousy life partner and desperate for someone to care enough to cuddle."

She burst into spontaneous laughter, and as Dave grinned and stared at her, it dawned on him that he was falling in love, and his earlier thought was correct. When she smiled, she could light up a room. "Come on, let's go inside; what do you have to lose except one more night on this earth with a guy who thinks you are the most beautiful woman he's ever seen?"

In an instant, the smile disappeared. "Okay, you win, one more night, but Dave? You're going to discover I am not as beautiful as you think. I will hug you; I'd enjoy that, but if I were naked, trust me on this, you would not want to touch me. You'd run a mile."

Dave slowly and emphatically shook his head. "Susan? Technically, I'm still married, and until we break up, I would never be unfaithful to Lynne, no matter what she's done to me. But I promise you, once I am separated, which I expect to be later, if you took your clothes off, I'd want to do a whole lot more than touch you."

"Oh, Dave, where were you before all this mess started? I think just maybe you wouldn't have run off as Mark has, but I warn you, my story is not a pretty one, and I am most definitely ugly. You know the old saying, don't you? 'Looks are only skin deep.' Well, in my case, my skin is the problem. But you win, lead the way, take me back inside, and if you keep me out of the hospital, you can buy me a last meal, a red wine or two, and you can hug me as much as you like."

"Deal. I need to go back in first, but promise me, Susan, that you won't jump after I do, will you? If you do, I will never speak to you again." Without waiting for a reply, he swung his legs up, turned, and crawled back to the window. Once there, he turned his head and watched as she took one last look at the now-darkening sky; then, she wriggled her body to bring her knees up under her into a crawling position. She nodded at him. "It's fine, Dave, I'm coming in. Suddenly, I want that hug."

The senior cop helped Dave climb back inside. "You're fucking mad for going out there; they could never pay me enough to do what you guys do," he grunted.

Dave's legs felt shaky when he stood on them, and he knew Susan's would be worse. "Sergeant, you can stand everyone down. I will take care of her from here; she will be fine."

"What about the report?"

"Leave everything to me. I'm going to take her to her family. I will file the paperwork in the morning. You guys go home; she's going to be okay."

Dave turned on him and leaned back through the

window. Susan had arrived, and he reached through with one hand to take hers while his other touched her back to help guide her. She flinched so suddenly and abruptly that he thought she would fall, and he tightened his grip on her hand. Her eyes appeared wide and frightened, and she shook her head frantically. "Don't touch me there; you don't want to touch my back."

"I'm sorry, Susan, I didn't mean anything by it. I was trying to help you. I don't want you falling because of a cramp now we've come this far." Dave worried she might have thought he was inappropriate by touching her back. True, he had felt the clasp of her bra strap, but she couldn't believe he was that much of a sleaze, could she?

It was as if she suddenly realized that was what he thought, and she managed a frosty smile. "I didn't mean to sound ungrateful or accuse you of anything…it's just that, well, my back is where my problems started, and when I said you don't want to touch me there, I meant it. If you knew what was happening to me, that is the last place you'd ever want to touch me. My legs feel like they've turned to lead, and I will need your help to get back inside without falling, so touching me is fine, Dave. I didn't mean what I said to sound insulting or ungrateful. Forgive me if I came across that way."

He smiled the best smile in his repertoire. "It's fine. We've both had a stressful day, but no harm was done. Now, let's get you inside. Frank, can you help me please?" Together, the two men got her back through the window, and Dave helped her to her leather swivel chair behind the desk and sat her down. "Give me a couple of minutes to stand down the troops," he said softly, then stood and nodded to the sergeant to follow him outside the office.

Once in the passage, Dave wearily leaned against the wall. "Frank, as you can see, I've talked her around. I'm going to spend some time with her and try to find out what made her suddenly try to kill herself, and then I will take her to a family member or check her into the psych ward. You can leave everything to me; you lot can go home."

"You sure?"

Dave nodded, silently wishing the uniformed officer would go away quickly because he desperately wanted to learn about Susan, but he knew the cop would want reassurance. Dave was intrigued and attracted to her. If he was honest, he couldn't even understand why, but his heart ached to be with her, touch her, and even care for her. It wasn't in a sexual way; no, he was sure he didn't want to have sex with her, though he had to admit she was gorgeous. No matter how beautiful or even sexy he found her, Dave considered himself still married, which counted for a lot in his world, unlike Lynne's definition of *'forsaking all others,'* obviously. No, his fascination and attraction for her was more that he wanted to wrap his arms around Susan and never let her go. Something dreadful had happened in her relationship to make her think she was ugly, but what? He couldn't wait to find out.

Eventually, the uniformed cops left with Dave's assurance they were no longer required.

****

Susan directed him to a small Italian restaurant called Romero's, within walking distance from the office block. "Sorry," she'd said as they entered the dimly lit doorway. "It's the only one I know locally. Mark and I came here sometimes because they do a spectacular veal scaloppine."

He glanced at her when she said it and was pleased that though she clearly remembered happier times, those memories didn't make her break down and cry. *Maybe there's hope for her yet,* he mused. "Well, I'm a demon for good veal scaloppine, especially if it's served with angel hair spaghetti."

She stopped in her tracks. "No, way, no freakin way, how did you know that's how that I have mine served? They tell me that no one ever orders it like that except me! Even Mark used to shake his head with disgust and eat his with creamed potatoes and spring vegetables."

"Well, if you'll forgive me for saying so, that further proves his lack of good taste." Dave grinned to show he wasn't overly serious but wanted to make a point and realized he had. "Lynne, my wife, was horrified too when I ordered it just like that. Maybe they should have gotten together. They'd have made the perfect dinner partners, which would have saved you and me a lot of angst."

Before she could reply, a middle-aged hostess wearing a black apron approached. "Table for two? Did you have a booking? We're very busy tonight."

She didn't sound Italian with her broad Bronx accent. Dave flashed his badge. "Yes, just the two of us, and no, we didn't book, but I'd take it a great personal favor if you could squeeze us in."

She turned her attention to Susan. "Haven't seen you here for a few weeks, Mrs. Bodinski. Where's that delicious husband of yours, working late?"

Dave groaned inwardly, wondering how Susan would handle her inferred infidelity with him as her dinner partner. Rather than see the probing question upset an already fragile woman, Dave took control. "My brother is Susan's husband, and he's away in Pensacola for the week on business, so I thought I would take the opportunity to see if what these guys have always told me is true: you guys make the best scaloppine this side of the Hudson."

"Both sides of the Hudson," The hostess replied with a smile that showed she approved of Susan's companion. "I think we can fit you in; come this way."

****

They sat together in a booth in the farthest corner from the front door. Dave wondered how to start a conversation for two minutes before Susan spoke suddenly. "Why did you lie to her, and where did you learn to lie so convincingly?" she asked.

Dave smirked. "Well, why I lied should be obvious: I wanted to protect your reputation." He shook his head to stop Susan's inevitable interruption. "Susan, I know you still intend to end your life, and I know I can't stop that if that's what you intend to do, but…I hope you won't. And, if you don't, I didn't want you to be embarrassed to return to your favorite restaurant just because you brought me here. I am not your lover, so that woman should not be allowed to think I am. Who knows, your husband may come to his senses and return to you; he's stone-cold mad if he doesn't, in my opinion. If he did, I don't want the staff here to give you strange glances in front of him. As to how I learned to lie so well, well, I'm not sure how to answer that except to say I hate lying for selfish reasons, but when you lie to help someone you like or care for, then, well, I think the end justifies the means, don't you?"

"I still don't get it with you; why do you care about

me? Aren't you taking your job too far? Dinner with a suicidal woman while your unfaithful wife waits for your return. I just don't get it. You should be at home talking to her; she's far more important to you than me."

"I hardly get it myself, except, Susan, there is something between us beyond coincidence. God knows what, but you're right; I don't know you, but it seems like destiny. On the worst day of my life, I met a woman I think is the most beautiful I've ever seen, bar none, having the worst day of her life. And we end up here, in a romantic little restaurant, but wait, and there's more, we both have a weird love of a bizarre meal." He laughed and was thrilled to see she laughed, too.

A thin, pretty waitress with black hair appeared. "Still or sparkling, and can I get you folks a drink? Your usual retsina, Mrs. Bodinski?"

Susan nodded, and Dave replied, "Still is fine for me, if it's okay with you, Susan. I will have a light beer; I'm driving. We don't need a menu; we will have the scaloppine with angel hair pasta, thanks. I'm told it's sensational."

They remained silent until the waitress served the drinks—a glass of red wine and a chilled bottle of Italian beer for Dave. He took a loving sip after chinking the side of her glass with the neck of the bottle. "*L'chaim,*" he said quietly, and she giggled.

"You're a funny guy; how can you seriously wish me 'to life' in Hebrew when you successfully talked me down from a forty-story ledge where I'd gone to kill myself? Tell me, Dave, why do you think your wife started screwing around? You are a guy most women would give their eye-teeth to be with."

He snorted. "I'm no catch. If I was, why would

Lynne screw around with her boss? No, I'm not the kind of man you mistakenly think I am. I'm a loser; at least, that's how I feel about myself since I realized she was being unfaithful. But I am very keen to hear why you think you're ugly; Susan, you are definitely not."

She took a sip of her wine, savoring it momentarily before swallowing. I will tell you my story. I owe you that, but only after we eat." She shrugged. "If I told you now, you might lose your appetite. In the interim, though, I am serious in my question. To repay you for your kindness, you might benefit from a woman's perspective, so why do you think your wife ended up screwing her boss in a hotel?"

Dave stopped to think for a minute and realized the one thing he hadn't done was wonder why. Was he in some way responsible? Was he a terrible lover? Did he not satisfy Lynne? A hundred questions rattled around in his head, and suddenly, he was grateful for the offer of Susan's thoughts. "Are you sure you won't find this boring?"

She shook her head and sipped again from her glass. "No, Dave, I'm genuinely interested. Sure, if this was a date, then probably the last thing I'd want you talking about was your ex, but it's not. You said it best earlier: our meeting is like karma. Maybe fate thrust us together to help each other through a dreadful time. Talk to me because I think maybe that's one of the problems in your marriage; you don't open up to her."

Dave shifted on his chair uncomfortably. "I don't think it's that complicated. It has to be for the sex. Maybe he is better equipped than me; he's undoubtedly rich. Or he is a better lover, more exciting, which wouldn't be hard because we have two children, and we've been together a long time. The gloss must have gone for her. Her boss looks better than me, and he's changed her from a boring mom and wife. He's shown her excitement like she's dating all over again."

At first, Susan stared at him, and he squirmed under her scrutiny. Finally, she sighed. "Yes, I sensed that was what you thought. Dave. I hate to break it to you, but most women aren't that shallow, especially those who've been married for a long time with children to consider. I don't know your wife, and maybe she is a woman who can't keep her legs closed, but I think I know that you are a kind, caring, and considerate man. Else, why do you have such an awful job? If your wife was the type of person who lived for sex with a multitude of partners, I don't think you'd be with her in the first place. So, in my opinion, this isn't about sex. That is the result, yes, but not the cause. I think she wasn't getting what she needed from you emotionally. Maybe you both took each other for granted. Too many late nights home from work and tired nights with you both working, and your love life dropped off with quality and frequency. She works and then looks after children when they finish school, and she does much of the cooking, cleaning, and mundane things women do in a family situation. Not enough romance with you both, and maybe when you did arrange date nights occasionally, you had to work late, so she didn't get to have them. She didn't know it, but her life became humdrum, and you didn't see the signs. She was screaming for help from you, and you didn't hear because you thought you were safe and secure in the cocoon you wove around your marriage. Let me ask a question: Have you ever hosted a BBQ for family or friends?"

"You're saying it's my fault she's screwing around?" he asked in an irritated voice.

"No, not at all. But Dave, it doesn't matter how good a dancer you are; it always takes two to tango. You can't possibly think it is *all* her fault, either. Answer the question, do you host BBQs at home?"

He shook his head, unsure where she was going with her question and feeling annoyed with her criticism of him. "Yes, as it happens, we do. I love to cook outdoors."

Susan smiled. "Yes, I thought you'd be the kind of guy who likes to act the chef, and I bet you get the steaks just right, don't you?"

What is she doing? First, she insults me and then compliments my cooking skills; what is her point? Dave wondered, then shrugged and sipped from his beer bottle. "Yes, I think I'm a good cook, and most everyone enjoys it."

"Yep, I thought so. So, you hang out around the BBQ with the guys, drinking beer and cooking up a storm. Lynne makes the salads, baked potatoes, prepares the corn?"

"Yes. Lynne makes fantastic salads. Where are you going with this?"

"Bear with me; I'll get there. Before the guests arrive, she has cleaned the house from top to bottom because she's a house-proud woman and wouldn't want anyone to see a dirty bathroom or toilet, right?"

Dave's heart began to sink as he suddenly realized what Susan's point would be. He nodded and tried to cover his embarrassment by sipping again from the bottle. "Your friends arrive; she has made little snacks and canapes, and while you're firing up the BBQ and getting the coals just right, she is serving everyone, ensuring their glasses are full. Meanwhile, she sets the table, gets everything ready, being the perfect hostess, and you are with the males, having more than a few beers, knowing you're going to grill up a storm. You cook, have a few laughs, and tell a few bawdy jokes while Lynne brings you drinks because what you're doing is so important. She makes sure all the guests are looked after, brings plates and cutlery out, and eventually, you serve the perfect meats. Everyone compliments your cooking skills, and you have a great night. Later, she does most of the cleaning up and loads the dishwasher. Then around eleven o'clock, you've had such a good night, you're horny, but she isn't, and you get mad at her because she is exhausted. How am I doing?"

"You're grossly exaggerating."

"Am I?"

"Well, maybe not grossly."

"The point is, all your friends congratulate you for a great barbeque because you cooked the steaks and hamburgers, but do you ever appreciate her workload so you can get the credit? Do you ever offer for her to sit down and relax while you clean up at the end of the night?"

His face glowed red, but before he could respond, the meals arrived. Dave looked down at his plate and became aware of an aroma full of richness, garlic, and chili, and his mouth instantly watered. When the waitress left, Dave said, "Okay, point taken, I see what you mean; perhaps with the years we've been together, yes, I accept, I could have been more considerate, loving, and affectionate. But the fact I wasn't didn't give her the right to screw someone else." The inner rage he felt had returned. "She could have spoken to me, told me she was unhappy, given me a chance to try to improve."

"Are you completely, one hundred percent sure she didn't? Or, possibly, when she tried to communicate with you, you thought she was nagging and not appreciating what you were going through at work. Dave, trust me on this: good women don't stray for sex; they stray because someone is paying them a lot more attention than their husband, assuming they were happy in the early days. Try the veal before you answer, and please, don't get mad at me. I'm not here to criticize you; just give you a female perspective and help you see things you might otherwise miss with all the rage and anger you feel inside."

"But I get frustrated too. What if I got bored and slept with another woman on the side? How would she feel then?"

"Good point, ask Lynne that, see if she can see your point of view. Now that her secret, exciting world has collapsed around her shoulders, Lynne will realize what she is about to lose. In a way, I feel sorry for her because you know the old saying, don't you? You never know what you've got till it's gone, and if I read you right, you're gone from her life when she needs you the most. She doesn't know it yet, but Lynne will go through hell, with her friends and family ostracizing her for doing the dirty on you. Whatever you do, Dave, please take my advice; hold on to your temper when you confront her. Now eat, I've said enough."

Dave deliberately didn't reply immediately because she had hit the nail on the head in many ways. He knew that, but it didn't ease the pain of betrayal, the loss of trust, and the sheer agony of imagining Lynne in the throes of sleeping with another man. He cut a piece of the meat, twirled his fork around some pasta, and popped it in his mouth. It was delicious. His mouth was assailed with the cream Marsala flavor, and the homemade spaghetti had been cooked to perfection while the meat was so tender it almost melted. He put the cutlery down; while he loved the quality of the meal, his stomach felt like it was knotted with tension. "I can't just turn a blind eye to her infidelity. Surely you're not suggesting I do?"

"Nope. I'm not suggesting that for a moment. Consider this, though: before you met Lynne, I'm guessing you both slept with other people, yes?" She asked as she took a mouthful of cream-dripping pasta.

"Yes, what's that got to do with anything?"

"Nothing in terms of her betrayal of your trust, but if you took that out of the equation, and imagine you met her for the first time tonight, and she told you she had been having an affair with her married boss but was ending it, would you still want to begin a relationship with her?"

It was a stupid question; he knew that. Dave had always hated hypotheticals. He dealt with facts, and the reality was Lynne had been sleeping with her boss for God knew how long, and he failed to see how that was his fault. True, Susan made some excellent points, and he had to admit he had been taking his wife and comfortable life for granted, but that didn't give Lynne the right to step outside her marriage vows. Though Dave had lost most of his appetite, he ate more of the veal, which was cooked to perfection, and as he ate, he found his temper ebbing. "Let me ask you this, Susan," he asked as he dabbed his mouth with the napkin. "What if you had discovered Mark was having an affair? Would you feel the same way?"

"She grinned at him, put her fork down, and picked up her wine glass, saluting him. "I am many things, Dave, but a hypocrite isn't one of them. You can't compare my situation to yours because not only would I understand if Mark had slept around, but when the extent of my problems became known, I suggested he did. I saw the difference between love and him needing release, which he no longer desired with me. I wanted him to stay with me till the bitter end, but sadly, that is not happening. But if once or twice a week, he found some sexual happiness elsewhere, but he saved his love for me, I would have been happy."

"Look, you just can't liken, for example, you and I meeting like we have tonight, admitting that we had many previous sexual partners and then started a relationship because we would see each other based on honesty. How can I ever trust Lynne again? Without trust, there is nothing. She has been doing this in secret, and the only regret she will have is that I've found out and stopped it. Therefore, our marriage is now over, the way I'm feeling right now."

"Oh, I don't think that will be the case entirely. I think Lynne has been living in a little fantasy world where she felt appreciated and excited, and not once did she realize the consequences of what she was doing and the eventual result if caught. It's just so cliché. A married, powerful, and dominant man who has set his sights on making Lynne's life exciting. One thing's for sure: you need to listen to her if she tries to explain, that is, if you still love her. If what she has done has destroyed your marriage, and you can't accept it, so be it. Move on. Find a woman who will appreciate you for who and what you are. I suspect many will be in the queue once word gets around. Sure, divorce in this state is hard on the male." She shrugged. "That's the way it is, and I feel sorry for you for the practical side of how you will suffer financially if you go down that route. I'm saying this didn't happen for no reason, and you need to get her side of things before you throw away your relationship. If you listen without hurling abuse at her out of anger, you might learn something valuable."

Dave took the time to consider what Susan had said by taking a few more mouthfuls. Eventually, Dave almost finished his meal, realizing he had been hungry despite not feeling like he could have eaten a thing. "Okay, enough of my problems; it's time to hear your story." He pushed the plate away, picked up the beer bottle, and leaned back in his seat."

"Will you at least think about what I've said? I do think you are a good man who has been handed a shitty stick. What you do with that stick will affect yours, your wife's, and your children's lives."

"Susan, I've done nothing but worry about it. The problem is, I am still trying to figure out why she has done this, and now I've found out she has what she intends to do about us. Maybe she wants us to end so she can be with him, especially now that I've sent the pictures to his wife, and I suspect his marriage is over, too. He will want to make things permanent with Lynne because he will have nowhere to go. He's probably working on her right now to kick me out of my house so he can move in."

"Do you *really* think that?"

He shrugged. "I don't know what to think; I honestly don't. I've been blindsided, and the chips will fall where they will." Dave sighed. "I'd like to think it's not that bad and that she still has some feelings for me and the life I thought we had together. But I won't beg, and if she doesn't want to rebuild our marriage and genuinely regret what she's done, there isn't anything left to fight for."

His phone chimed in his pocket, and Dave ignored it, knowing it would be from Lynne; the time was about right. Loverboy was evicted, and he would have been straight on the phone to Lynne, possibly even blaming her. Dave gave a faint grin at that thought, and Susan noticed. "Is that Lynne? You should speak to her, forget about me, go to her; save your marriage."

Dave took the phone out of his pocket. "What's the betting she's told me not to come home?"

Susan reached out and covered his hand with hers to hide the screen. "I'll take that bet. Her message will be to beg you to go home and talk, that she feels terrible for the hurt she's caused you."

Her touch was electric, and he paused to enjoy the warmth. "If we have a bet, what are the stakes?" Dave asked softly.

"If I win, I promise to stay alive until next Sunday night, and then you have to meet me here for dinner and tell me if your marriage is saved."

"And if I win?"

"If you win the bet, you've lost your wife. So, what's left that you would want from me?"

"You to promise me not to kill yourself for one year."

He'd got her. Her face changed from a humorous, flirtatious look to genuine shock. "What?" She asked incredulously. "You realize what you're saying? If that message says what you think it might, it means that you've lost your wife. And if you win the bet, all you want is my word that I won't step out onto that ledge for a year?" He nodded. "Why is that so important to you?"

Dave paused to clarify his thoughts. "Because I care. That's it; that's the only reason. I don't want to think that Lynne and I are over, but if we are, I'd like to get to know you, and I can hardly do that if you leave here and go straight back to your office and jump out the window. Give me one year to get to know you as friends, not lovers; I'm not suggesting anything untoward. I think if you had a good friend for a year, someone who genuinely cared, maybe, no matter how dark things look from time to time, you wouldn't want to kill yourself. And that, for me, would be the best outcome I could hope for."

She held his gaze, then shook her head. "All right, it's a deal."

"You promise one year?"

"I promise." She removed her hand, and Dave pressed the home key, then clicked on the most recent text message. He read while Susan finished her glass of wine. "Let me guess; you're meeting me for dinner?"

Silently, he put the phone on the table and turned it so she could read the screen.

—Dave. I know you must be hurting. I've been stupid and done something so mad I can't believe it myself. You are a wonderful man, an incredible father, and the best husband a woman could ever hope to have. I don't know if you can ever find it in your heart to forgive me. For all I know, I've lost you for good. Please let me explain where my head was and why I went astray. What I did was not your fault; it was mine. My boss forced me into doing something I shouldn't have done,

and I am so ashamed. Please, please, please come home. I'm guessing you didn't have a jumper to go and save tonight. I think you chose not to come home to confront me, and I don't blame you. Please know I am so sorry, not because you found out, but because I betrayed your trust. If you give me a chance, I will spend a lifetime trying to show you I'm worthy of forgiveness.—

"She doesn't think you exist, Susan. That's nice. She screws her boss and thinks I'm lying about where I am. Talk about the pot calling the kettle black."

"You don't mean that; go to her; she wants you to forgive her. Are you brave enough to?"

Dave considered the taunt. *Am I brave enough? Boy, Susan knows how to cut to the chase.* He made a decision and called the waitress for two more drinks. "I'm not going anywhere until you tell me why you think you're so ugly that your husband ran out on you and you felt you had no alternative but to end your life."

Susan stayed silent while the waitress brought the drinks. When she left, she moved forward on her chair and tilted her head down so people at nearby tables couldn't hear her. "Dave, you don't want to hear this; your marriage is far more important. Go to Lynne, sort things out, and come back and meet me here Sunday night. I promise I will tell you then, and you can tell me if you've forgiven Lynne for her moment of madness."

Dave suspected she was lying and had no intention of meeting him. He believed if he left her, she would return to her office and complete the job she'd begun earlier. "No," he said calmly. "Susan, you know, don't you, that if I walk out that door and you go and kill yourself, I will lose my job for not taking you for a psych evaluation. Would you subject me to that?" She reddened, and Dave knew he had been right.

"But I promised to meet you here on Sunday," she said sadly like a child caught being naughty.

He sipped from the fresh bottle. "Well, if I'm wrong, forgive me, but recently, I've learned that there are two types of promises. There are those we keep and forget when convenient, like Lynne forgot her wedding vow to 'forsake all others.' It would be best if you let it all out, and I genuinely want to hear what's driven you to this. It's not going to hurt Lynne to wait a while longer; she's the one who took a lover, and I'm happy to let her stew on it until I'm ready to go and confront her. If you tell me about your problems and then give me your word, you will wait until Sunday to meet with me for an update on whether I'm married or separated; you will keep that promise.

Susan smiled sadly. "You're a smart man, and Lynne's a lucky woman."

"Maybe not anymore; time will tell just how lucky she is. So, enough stalling; what's wrong?"

She didn't start immediately; she took a long drink of her wine, sighed deeply, and began. "One of the reasons I love animals so much is that I can't have children." She shrugged as if that piece of news was background only and not a reason for suicide. "I thought Mark and I were a match made in heaven because he wasn't bothered about having kids either, and he loves dogs; we have three, though now he has left, he has taken our dogs too. I think he intended I fight him for visitation rights."

She stopped to blink back tears, then took another sip of wine. "He not only appreciated my love of furry friends but actively encouraged it beyond my wildest dreams. On one birthday, he adopted a panda bear for me, named Ci-Ci. A koala bear was rescued from a bushfire through the WWF in Australia the year before. We regularly donate money to animal charities and have participated in animal welfare demonstrations. Don't get me wrong, I don't love animals more than humans, but sometimes it's a close-run race, present company excepted." She smiled and raised her wine glass in salute, and Dave saluted back.

"Who knew it would be my love of animals that would kill me?"

He sat up straight. "What! How can that be?"

"You wanted the whole story; let me tell it in my way." She smiled, sipped wine, and Dave relaxed in the chair to listen. He loved the sound of her voice; it suited her, soft and melodic, in a word, beautiful, just like her appearance. He knew her personality would match her looks with her love of animals being so strong. *So why does she think she is ugly?* He couldn't even begin to imagine, but he knew he was about to learn.

"Over three years ago, Mark surprised me with the gift of a lifetime and what I thought was a true indication of how much he loved and understood me. For Christmas, when I opened my card, a sheet of paper fell out. It was an itinerary for us to take a three-week photographic safari through Africa. Three National parks, The Kruger in South Africa, the Serengeti in Kenya, and the Chobe in Botswana. Oh, Dave, it was wonderful. We saw everything, and all the wild animals were in their natural habitat. I have albums full of the most wonderful photos and a thousand memories of my trip of a lifetime. Mark and I made love every night in our tent, which I'm sure the guides enjoyed too because, well," she blushed, "I'm quite vocal when excited."

Dave laughed, amazed at her sensuality, loving how talking of the memory had lit up her face with happiness. If he could only maintain her good mood, he thought she couldn't possibly go back to wanting to end her life. "Go on, please; I'm so glad you're sharing this with me."

"It was on the eighth day. We stood under a tree watching a pride of lions only fifty yards away. They were so majestic and regal that I was enraptured with everything, and then it happened. A bug dropped from a branch overhead and fell down the back of my shirt. It somehow got under my bra strap and bit me repeatedly. I screamed, spooking the lions, and they turned toward us, but the spider, or whatever it was, kept stinging, and I kept screaming."

"Oh, my God. What happened?"

"We ran, and the lions came after us, and the bug kept biting me. Our head guide had to shoot one of the males, and while the rest attacked him, we managed to get back to the Land Rovers. Mark ripped my shirt and bra off the moment we got safely inside, but he couldn't find what had bitten me. I had over a dozen welts, like small lesions." She shrugged and sipped her wine, then shuddered as she recalled the horror of being stung repeatedly.

"I felt fine and wanted to continue the safari, though Mark wanted to get me to the hospital. The guides didn't think it was too serious; they felt the spider wasn't venomous like a snake bite or anything like that, so we continued on our way. Later that evening, we camped near a waterhole that didn't have resident alligators, and because I was so hot and sweaty and no doubt running a slight fever, Mark and I went for a swim to cool off.

Afterward, we lay on the sand because I felt better, and it was such a beautiful evening." She blushed once more. "We made love. The perfect end to a memorable day, other than the death of a beautiful lion, I thought at the time. However, dirt, animal feces, or germs somehow got into the lesions and became infected. Four days later, I felt unwell; two days after that, I was delirious, but it was still another day before they could get me to the hospital. A week later, I was better; thankfully, the antibiotics they fed me worked, and we returned home to the states with some wonderful and not-quite-so-wonderful memories. The only problem was, the infection under my skin hadn't gone away, and a few months later, it started to mutate and take hold, not that I knew it at the time."

Once more, Susan shuddered as the memory coursed through her, and Dave reached across the table and took her hand, squeezing gently. "Please go on," he urged softly.

"Several months later, Mark noticed one morning after my shower what he thought were dead skin spots or small scabs on my back because I said I was itchy. He didn't like the look of it, so he made me go to my doctor, but I put it off for a week or two, as you do, thinking it was just mosquito bites or something." She smiled grimly. "Of course, it just got worse, and when I finally went, my doctor said he'd never seen anything like it. He referred me to a specialist dermatologist, and things started going from bad to horrific. After numerous tests, he admitted he'd never seen anything like it but thought the infection stemmed from my African vacation. As that was the cause listed on his report, my health insurance company refused to cover treatment because they said it began outside the United States. The insurance company

Mark used for travel cover denied my claim, too, stating there was no causal proof that it did happen back then. Too much time had passed, they said. I hadn't claimed while we were in Africa because they had treated me as an emergency patient, and when I got better, I had no documentary proof. Trying to get records from the African hospital was a nightmare, so I was in trouble with a capital T. We could only afford the drugs the specialist prescribed to try to beat it. Still, it seems the antibiotics I'd received in Africa had helped the infection mutate, not kill it, and the fresh ones didn't work. Mark is a teacher, and I'm a freelance editor, so neither make much money because we work for our passions. We make enough, but that's all. We just had to hope the problem would improve with time. It didn't. Slowly, the scabs grew into a rash, spreading and turning into weeping sores, which kept worsening. It's now located all over my back and sides in patches and is still spreading. My shoulders are covered, and if you look at me in the right light, my back resembles a reptile or a large fish with scales. It has now spread to the top of my buttocks and left upper thigh."

"Oh, my God. Susan, I'm so sorry. Are you in pain?" Dave asked, feeling his heart would break with anguish at her suffering.

She shook her head. "No, not really, thankfully. Well, nothing so far that strong painkillers won't help. It's not so much agony, more like a creeping ulceration. But the prognosis is that it will get a lot worse with time. Sometimes, when a fresh sore appears, it does hurt, but it's not like I'm in severe pain all the time. When you touched my back earlier, I felt a scab burst, so I cringed. The worst thing for me is how I look and know the infection is spreading slowly, and soon, it will take over my whole body, not just the parts you can't see when I'm dressed. It got so bad my husband couldn't bear to look at me without the sores being covered and could no longer dress my wounds without wanting to vomit. Today, Mark told me that he needed time apart because while he still loved me, he couldn't deal with my body slowly disintegrating."

She suddenly sobbed, remembering the earlier conversation and how Mark abandoned her. She took a few moments, wiped her bloodshot eyes with her napkin, then continued. "So now I'm on my own, slowly turning into the monster from the Black Lagoon. I'm no longer beautiful and never will be again. I am without a husband and any hope of surviving because the sores are internal as well and will bring me to a slow and agonizing death. I don't want to get to where people cross the road rather than look at me as some kind of reptilian monster. I'm turning into something with scales, Dave, at least my skin is. And now you know why I chose the coward's way out because there is no future and no hope for me except a lonely life of misery and pain as I mutate into a zombie horror movie extra."

"Susan...we never had that hug," Dave said, still holding her hand on the table.

"Really? You still want to touch me?"

"Yes, I do, more than ever. So long as it's not going to hurt you, I want to stand up, wrap my arms around you, and give you the biggest hug in the world."

Susan smiled. "Perhaps not here in the restaurant, but when we leave. I will enjoy that; it's been a while since Mark could bear to touch me, let alone make love. Inside, I'm still the same person, though, of course, on the outside, I'm becoming something you might run and hide from."

Dave shook his head sadly. "You said earlier that three hundred thousand dollars could fix the problem. What did you mean by that?"

She looked across the table, her face looking suddenly sad. "Well, that's the rub. Being a high school teacher, Mark researched and found a private clinic in Germany that has done amazing work on all kinds of extreme skin disorders. He emailed them my medical notes, pictures of my back, and history, and they replied. They believe they have an eighty percent chance of helping me, but the treatment is expensive. My insurance company won't cover it, and neither of us nor our families have that sort of money, so it's like fool's gold."

Dave's phone flashed on the table. He glanced down and pressed the home button so the message was displayed.

—Please, please, Dave, come home. I am so sorry for what I've done.—

Dave saw Susan read it, too. "Susan, I have an idea. Will you promise me you will trust me for one week? I may be able to help." He held up his hand. "No, I can't tell you why, and I don't want to give you false hope, but please, please give me a chance. I will phone you once daily to ensure you stay off that ledge, and I will meet you here next Wednesday night. Just give me one week, or it could be much less. Is that too much to ask? I promise you I'm serious; I may just be able to solve your problem."

She held his gaze while she considered his offer. Her face was so beautiful while deep in thought. He believed her big brown eyes bored into him, looking for his sincerity. Dave's heart felt like it could explode from his emotion for her, but he knew he couldn't tell her his true feelings in her fragile state. "I guess one week isn't going to hurt," she whispered. "But if the sores start appearing on my face or anywhere that shows, I reserve the right to renege."

Dave smiled. He wanted to kiss her, yet at the same time, he knew he shouldn't feel that way. He took a pen from his jacket and one of his police business cards, scribbled on it, and then handed it to her. "On there is my cell phone number and my email address. I want you to call me day or night if you get bad thoughts and want to climb back out on the ledge. I also want you to email me the pictures of your skin condition and the medical report."

"If I give you a week, you have to promise me something, too; that's only fair, right?" He nodded, knowing what she would ask him, and he could hardly refuse her if it meant she would keep her word to him. "Well, it's two things. Firstly, promise me that when you talk to Lynne, keep calm and listen to what she says but, just as importantly, what she doesn't say. She will feel terrible right now, and if you lock her out, she might end up on a ledge herself."

Dave felt way too angry with Lynne to comment, but that Lynne might commit suicide from shame and regret resonated somewhere deep inside him because he hadn't considered Lynne would do that. He realized that if Lynne were genuinely remorseful, and he left her, she may take that way out. One thing was certain: until the confrontation, he had no idea what Lynne would say, so he had to have the meeting. Dave nodded. "I agree. What's the second thing?"

"Every day when you phone me, I want you to talk to me about how it's going with her, tell me how she is feeling, and how you are coping." She reached over, her turn to squeeze his hand, and a vibrant electric feeling shot up his arm into his chest.

"Susan, I don't understand. You have more problems than anyone should ever have to bear, so why do you care about my marriage?" He turned his hand over and gripped hers. Suddenly, it dawned on him what they were doing. *We are holding hands at the table in a romantic restaurant. If Lynne saw a picture of this, she would think I was the one having an affair,* he thought, but then added: *but I'm not in a motel making love, am I?*

"I could say it's because I need the distraction to keep from killing myself, or I could say it's because you care about me, so it's only fair that I care back. Or maybe it's because you spend your working life so invested in saving other people that I'm worried you might have lost sight of how to look after yourself and your wife. All that would be true, but I think the real reason is this." She paused as if gathering her thoughts. "I was going to jump when I crawled out on the ledge earlier. It wasn't a cry for attention or to make Mark feel sorry for me, and I didn't want anyone to save me. I just wanted to watch one last sunset and then say goodbye to the world and what my crappy life has become. Yet here I am, with a handsome guy who cares for me, a stranger who, while having the worst day of his life, stayed to help me. What kind of a woman would I be if I didn't try to care back?"

He grinned. Her honesty astounded and somehow thrilled him. "All right, I promise. Now I need to get all your details, not just for the report but also for me. And then I need you to tell me if I'm taking you to your home or to someone who you can stay with."

"Yeah, well, I don't want you getting in trouble with your superiors, Dave. Please take me home, and I will call my friend and ask if she can come and stay with me for a couple of days. Will that do? I have to be there in case Mark comes back." She explained: "I don't believe he will, and really, who can blame him? But just in case, I need to be there."

They stood and left the restaurant after Dave settled the bill. Susan insisted on paying half, but Dave refused. He told her that the dinner was as much about his feelings as hers. Dave was grateful for her support while suffering her own misery. He also thanked her for introducing him to the best scaloppine he had ever eaten.

Outside, away from the staff's prying eyes, Dave gently pulled her to him and put his arms around her. Being very careful not to hurt her, and at the same time ensuring he did not inappropriately touch her, he hugged her to him. Her body fitted against his perfectly; Dave felt her firm, full breasts against his chest and her tummy mold to his. His chin rested snugly in the crook of her neck, and he smelled her scent, which reminded him of spring flowers. Dave couldn't remember experiencing such a cuddle with Lynne for a very long time. It was sensual as much as sexy, and he couldn't help the erection that burgeoned inside his underwear. Dave hoped Susan wouldn't feel it pressing against her, but then his second thought was that he hoped she would. That wasn't just because it would remind her she was still a beautiful woman; he was genuinely attracted to her. Dave couldn't imagine the state of her back and hoped that if he ever did see it, he wouldn't be repulsed, though Dave worried that he might. For the moment, he felt sheer joy in being in her arms. She was, without doubt, one of the most beautiful women he had ever seen, and her big heart was full of compassion for his problems, which was a compelling combination.

He wanted to pull away and kiss her, long, sensually, and with his tongue exploring hers, but the moment that thought reared its head, he remembered he was married. He was still furious and bitter that his wife had been unfaithful, and he wondered, *doesn't that give me the right to be unfaithful to her?* But then he realized that if he gave in to those thoughts and desires, it was no better than what Lynne had done and, in some ways, worse because he was *planning it*. By not trying to take things further with Susan, he could take the higher ground and know that no matter how much he wanted to take her back to her home and try to make love with her, he wouldn't because *he was married*. He wasn't the type of man to seek revenge sex, and he didn't want to hurt Susan or Lynne by trying to do so. Susan deserved better than that, and after all their years together, so did Lynne.

"Wow," she whispered huskily. "That's the best hug I've had in a very long time. Thank you, Dave, for making me feel that I'm not a monster and still a desirable woman." She pulled away and looked down at his crotch. "And I can't tell you how good it feels to know I can make you that excited."

She grinned as he shifted uncomfortably, and he chastised himself for feeling embarrassed. "Susan, it doesn't matter that you have a skin disease; you are still a very sexy and beautiful woman, inside and out. Any man would get an erection while holding you that closely."

Her face softened as her eyes misted. "Well, just so you know, I wouldn't let any man hold me like that. Now, you have a wife to go and confront, and I have to call my friend."

Chapter 2

Forgiveness

"To Err is Human, to Forgive is Divine."
Alexander Pope (1711)

As Dave drove to his house after taking Susan home, he was conflicted with differing thoughts, all clamoring for supremacy. Uppermost was anger with Lynne, who had taken his faith and trust and flushed it down the toilet. No matter what excuse she could provide or regret she might show, his biggest concern for the future was: *can I ever trust her again?* He realized that once trust was lost, like respect, it wouldn't come back with the click of his fingers. Both had to be earned. He was reminded of the adage that a wildfire could be started with the striking of the match and didn't stop when you blew the match out.

Competing with the rage boiling under the surface was the depth of feeling he knew he had for Susan, which shocked him. Did that not in some way make him a hypocrite? Dave sighed as he realized he had to understand why she had done it before he could pass any judgment on Lynne's infidelity. Dave couldn't imagine any scenario that would make it easy to forgive and forget, but then, he only had the pictures and his reaction to them to go by. Maybe Susan was right; he needed to walk a mile in Lynne's shoes to understand what led her to seek sex with another man, especially as he had almost to fight his urge to seduce Susan earlier.

Dave turned into his street, which meant only another two hundred yards to go, when his phone chirped again. He stopped under an Elm Tree and looked at the message.

—*Dave, I don't know if you're with a jumper as you said, or you've left me because of Marlon. If you are working, I know I'm not to call you, but please phone me if you are not. I don't care what time it is. I can't sleep. The children are at Mum and Dad's for the night so we can be alone. I haven't stopped crying because I know how much I've hurt you, and you did nothing to deserve that. Please, Dave, I love you, please phone me back.*—

Dave settled back into the seat to try to get the tumble drier of thoughts and images raging through his mind in some semblance of order so that when he confronted Lynne, he knew what he would say.

Dave cast his mind back to when his marriage first appeared in trouble. Everything always looked much clearer with twenty-twenty hindsight, and when Dave first seriously suspected Lynne's infidelity, it dawned on him some of the tiny things he had missed before. For example, previously, Lynne always left her cell phone next to his on the shelf where they used a joint charging cable, and as they were the same brand, they often picked each other's up by mistake. One day, Dave noticed Lynne's phone had a blue cover fitted, so it was easily identifiable. Lynne said it was because she had left for work one day the week before carrying his phone and had to bring it back when the dispatcher called him to attend a bank in Manhattan where a robbery had gone wrong, and hostages were in danger. That delay had caused her to be late to work, and Lynne received a verbal warning from her boss, she'd told him. Innocent enough, Dave thought, but then Lynne started charging her phone at work and leaving it hidden in her handbag at night. He discovered Lynne had switched it to silent mode when Nancy, Lynne's mother, called him on his cell because she could not get hold of her daughter, sitting alongside him on the couch as they watched a rom-com movie. When he queried why the change, she shrugged it off. "Because I'm fed up with calls from people trying to sell me life insurance, steak knives, or anything else, Dave," she'd said in a tone that warned him not to question her further. Lynne told him coldly that she must have ended up on a telephone marketer's hit list, and he shrugged it off as inconsequential. After all, their marriage was sound, wasn't it? He asked himself that later that night in bed while Lynne snored softly in the adorable way she did.

Her mood had changed with him, too, he realized. Not in any significant way, but many small things suddenly seemed obvious when viewed in total. She appeared tired more frequently when he wanted to make love; she had headaches or wasn't in the mood. Then, once a week, she began to have supposed management meetings on Mondays, which meant she got home after ten. Those nights when she arrived home, she showered and went straight to bed, with barely a word to him other than saying she was tired after a very long day. Her mood seemed abrupt, as if she seemed annoyed with Dave, though he couldn't figure out why.

Because he empathized so well, Dave tried to be understanding and sympathetic. He gladly babysat their children and never questioned why the public relations firm she had worked for for four years suddenly had nighttime management meetings that required her presence when she was only the general manager's assistant.

Another thing Dave realized after the sky fell in was sometimes, when Lynne came home after work, she had a twinkle in her eye, which he recognized was the same as she used to have in their early days when building their relationship and had made love every available minute. Their sex life in more recent times had all but ceased, and Dave suddenly worried that Lynne was getting her love elsewhere, which increased the depth of his troubling doubts.

Then there was Lynne's nagging. Suddenly, Dave could do nothing right, and Lynne seemed to be aggravated with him continuously. When he asked her about it, she said he was imagining things, but Dave didn't think he was, and that was when he started to worry their marriage was now suffering a terminal illness. Police officers worldwide are, by nature, suspicious, and once Dave began to go down the slippery slope of doubting Lynne's loyalty, every nuance of her moods took on more significance in his mind.

"Lynne," he asked one night after the children had been read their story and tucked up in bed while they did the dinner dishes. "Is everything all right with us? I mean, is there anything going on I should know about?"

He saw her flinch and grip the edge of the stainless-steel sink in her rubber-gloved hands. "What do you mean by that, Dave?" She asked in an acid-toned voice.

He reached out with his hand that wasn't holding the tea towel and gently squeezed her shoulder. "You seem so distant with me these days. You're always tired and in a bad mood. It's been over a month since we last made love, and I'm worried I've done or said something stupid that you haven't forgiven me for."

She shrugged his hand loose, turned, and raised her eyes in an all too familiar look. "Maybe if you were more considerate of the pressure I'm under at work and stopped harping on about how there is something wrong with me, I wouldn't appear to Your Royal Highness to be so unhappy. As it happens, I was looking forward to you ravishing me tonight, but once again, you've ruined the mood, haven't you?" She ripped the gloves off and threw them into the soapy water in the sink, splashing him as she stormed into the bedroom and slammed the door behind her.

Dave stared at the quivering door. Part of him wanted to run after her, scream insulting words about how it was her that had changed, not him, and how dare she treat him like a roommate rather than her husband. But his more pragmatic side realized that the answer had become evident. Lynne was desperately unhappy with him. There was no doubt any longer in his mind that she was having an affair or, at the very least, was on the brink of one. Another man excited her, made her feel young and alive again, rather than the humdrum housewife and mother she no doubt saw herself with him and their children. Because of his empathetic nature, he could see it clearly, but he didn't know who she was seeing, how long it had been going on, or how deep her feelings were for the mystery man. Logic decreed it was someone from her work because she was always at work or home with him other than the late-night meetings. Did that mean their marriage was like a fire burnt out, and he was raking the ashes, or was there enough left to bring the flames back to life? He needed to know more, and so he set about finding out. Dave hired a private detective he knew through his work, and in a matter of days, he solemnly handed Dave the report and pictures, which showed once and for all that Dave's concerns were confirmed. He needed to act to save his pride and sanity, if not his marriage.

Earlier that afternoon, Dave had taken the first of what he thought of as his irrevocable steps, which he hoped would end Lynne's affair and might be the first step back to reconciliation if possible. He didn't know if he could forgive her and learn to trust again, but that could only occur if Lynne wanted his faith restored. For all Dave knew, she could already have decided to end their marriage so she could continue seeing Flanders without the deception. It seemed apparent that her boss had more money and prestige than Dave could ever have, and she had chosen to have an affair. If it came to a choice, Dave would probably lose on that basis, he realized.

Because he didn't know Lynne's intention, Dave had acted and thrown a hand grenade into Mr. Marlon Flanders' marriage and had emailed the incriminating pictures to Mrs. Flanders. They were of the two love birds entering room fourteen of The Three Mile Motel the previous Monday when Lynne was supposedly at work having her "manager's meeting." Several shots, though grainy, were taken through the window between a gap in the curtains, which showed them naked and clearly showed a part of her boss's body, which was meeting with a part of Lynne's, so maybe she hadn't been entirely dishonest. Dave had previously, foolishly, he now realized, believed that part of Lynne's body was his exclusive domain.

His stomach lurched every time he looked at the disgusting pictures the private detective Mitch Mitcham gave him earlier that day. After Mitch handed him the envelope and Dave peered at the contents, he had to run to the toilet and vomit. It was one thing to suspect infidelity, but it was something else to see photographic evidence. The woman he loved had chosen to ignore her marriage vows and screw another man in a motel. Ironically, Dave thought, it was the kind of place where she wouldn't be caught dead with her husband.

That was the beginning of Dave's conflict between rage and wanting to leave Lynne or trying to find a way past what she had been doing. When confronted, would Lynne choose to end the affair and leave Dave? He didn't know, and he needed a strategy to find out.

Dave planned to wreck Marlon's life and confront Lynne simultaneously in the desperate hope she would beg him for his forgiveness and help him learn to forget her betrayal. Regaining his lost trust would be another matter entirely, but he had hoped that with time, it would be possible.

Dave decided and pressed the dial button. She answered immediately. "Dave? Thank you for calling; I've been frantic."

"Well," he replied and couldn't keep the anger and bitterness from his voice, "you could always have called Marlon to comfort you. After all, you've been letting him fuck you."

He heard her gasp and sob. After she recovered, Lynne replied in a subdued voice: "I deserve that, but please let me try to explain. It's not what you think. I've let you down, betrayed your trust, and been a bloody idiot, but please don't abandon me. I need to explain what happened."

What does she mean by "not what I think?" He wondered, then shrugged, realizing she was doing what she did best, justifying *her* actions. He knew that was because, in the past, everything he did was wrong. Lynne was generally incapable of admitting when she was, but here she was saying *she* was the one at fault, and that was a first.

"Lynne, answer me this. What would you have done or thought if you discovered I had an affair in a seedy motel with a female colleague? I'm guessing by the time I got home and showered the smell of her sex off me, you'd have moved back with your mother, and a divorce would be inevitable. Why would you think I'd be any different and want to accept that you opened your legs for your boss or anyone else, and it would ever be forgivable? Do you disrespect me so much that you thought I would be your cuckold? You've made your choice so far as I'm concerned. Marlon is all yours now. He's better than me, makes you happier, gives you more orgasms, so go to him and forget me."

Lynne burst into tears, and just a little, his rage subsided. No matter what, this was his wife, the mother of his children; he loved her, and she was heartbroken. "Oh my God, Dave, that is so far from the truth. He didn't make me happier; the sex wasn't as good, and he isn't bigger or better—he is a pig. You are right, though," she sobbed. If I saw pictures of you having sex with another woman, I would have left you and felt just as you do now. But it's not what you think; please come home, listen to me, let me explain, and you will see how sorry

I am."

He wanted to let go, wanted to soften, but felt incapable. "I think you're only sorry because it's ended. I sent the pictures to his wife, and I'm guessing she has thrown him out. Now your boyfriend wants you to do the same with me so he can move in. If I hadn't acted and told her, you'd have carried on letting him inside your panties as often as he wanted. I'm making it easy for you now, Lynne; let him move in. You chose him over me and your wedding vows. Remember those, Lynne? 'Forsaking all others,' and to 'love, honor, and cherish.' I saw your face as you entered that motel and how he made you happy. No need to say thanks; I'm moving aside so you can be with him."

"I don't want to be with him," she screamed. "I only want you; why won't you believe that?"

"You're kidding, right? Why would I believe you only want me? Could it be the number of times you let him screw you while at the same time turning the tap off on our lovemaking?"

"If you believe nothing else, please believe this, Dave. *He never made me orgasm.* And you're right. I drew away from you because I felt ashamed of what I was doing. But I had to do it, I had to, to protect you and your reputation, as well as mine."

Dave sat up in the seat. "What do you mean, you had to do it? Are you saying he raped you repeatedly and made you smile while entering the motel room so he could do it more?"

She sighed and then sobbed again. "Please, Dave, come home, I promise, no lies, let me explain. Let me spend the rest of my life making this up to you. I've been a fool, and I'm desperate. He did phone me, you were right about that, but only to scream at me and threaten you. He said he would make us pay unless I left you to be with him. He has a place set up for us; his family owns a mansion upstate, but that is not what I want, and I never did. I am relieved it's all over because what he made me do was disgusting, and I never had feelings for him. I had already ended it last night, and I can prove it. But he now blames me for telling you about us, and his wife has kicked him out. He says he will destroy us as a couple if I don't leave you. I need to tell you the truth. Please, come home; I can't do this alone. If you let me explain and still want to separate, I will move out and leave the kids with you. You never deserved this mess I've created and don't deserve to be without them. I know how much you love Ben and Molly."

Something in her pleading voice made him forget his pain and betrayal. *He will destroy us? She is relieved it's over?* Something in her voice sounded a warning bell. "I will be there soon, Lynne; I'm only around the corner," he said curtly and ended the call.

Dave rubbed the cell phone over his top lip. Dave tried to think about what he knew and not what he thought he knew. But exactly what was that? Dave had assumed the affair had been lengthy by her change in behavior, which had been a little over a month, so far as he could tell. Then, the Monday night meetings started three weeks before. He sighed; no matter how he looked at it, whatever had been going on was more than once and could hardly be non-consensual. Lynne had lied and deceived him at worst or refused to confide in him at best. It wasn't one drunken girls' night out when her libido was in overdrive and someone took advantage of her when inebriated. Dave thought he could have forgiven that kind of straying so long as Lynne regretted it and was honest. But an affair that took planning to go behind his back was something else entirely.

Did he want to spend the rest of his life with someone who would treat him as disrespectfully as that? He wasn't sure he could overcome the loss of trust and the mental image the pictures had promoted. Dave doubted he could ever forget those.

Dave had plenty of opportunities to stray himself with female police officers and others he met while working, but he had never wanted to take it beyond harmless flirting. Dave had never once seriously considered destroying his marriage vows and like a fool, he thought Lynne hadn't either. Dave thought flirting was a good thing; it made him feel he was still attractive to the opposite sex and gave him an ego boost. He had never objected to Lynne being flirtatious with other men either. She was a beautiful woman who was fun to be around; men would try to pick her up at worst or kid around at best. He was okay with that because he previously believed she had never gone beyond playful joking around.

Images of Susan's face crept into his mind unbidden, along with a troubling thought that just possibly, with her, he *could* lose control. Susan was magnificent, vulnerable, and going through seven tons of crap in her life after her husband walked out on her when she needed him the most. Yet now, the only thing keeping her alive was her desire to know what was happening in Dave's life and marriage. He felt he was being tugged in two directions at once and was confused by his emotions.

Sighing, Dave realized he was delaying the

inevitable, and if he wanted answers, he had to go and find them. Dave restarted the car, put it in drive, and headed off to his house and the long-overdue confrontation with Lynne.

****

Dave no sooner got his key in the lock when the door swung wide, and there was Lynne, her tear-streaked face welcoming as she threw her arms around her husband and held on tight.

I haven't had a welcome like this since we were dating, he thought, then realized he was being unkind. But then again, Lynne had been screwing another man, so which of them was the unkindest? Calmly, he reached up and disengaged her arms because he was nowhere near ready to let go of his anger, and he did not want her to woo him out of his rage and inner turmoil. Dave kicked the front door behind him and walked to the living room, leaving Lynne stranded in the hall.

He sat in an armchair opposite the couch he would generally sit on when Lynne would be alongside him while they watched TV. He didn't want to be next to her, not now, and maybe never again. "So, let's get to it; how long have you been fucking him, when did it start, and are you only sorry it's over because I found out and told your lover's wife?"

Lynne sat on the couch, folded her hands in her lap, and took a deep breath. "Despite what you think, I intended to tell you everything when you got home tonight because the relationship, if you can call it that, which I had with him ended last night. I finally got enough evidence to stop him from ruining our reputations. I was so upset when I got home late last night; it was late, and you were asleep. I couldn't face waking you with what had transpired. Please, Dave, let me tell you everything from the beginning."

He nodded and folded his arms across his chest. Being a police officer, he was well versed in spotting when someone was lying to him, and he determined to watch her closely to spot the signs.

"It started innocently enough when Marlon joined the company as CEO and General Manager and asked that I be his PA, which was a big step for me. He was nothing if not proper in every way, though he was flirtatious. That said, he was no more using innuendo than any other male in the office, and as you know, I love that kind of attention; it energizes me. Working so closely together and being a complete gentleman, it's fair to say we became close colleagues, but Dave, that was all we were in the beginning. Yes, if I'm honest, I was attracted to him. He is a big, strong, and powerful man, and I know he was attracted to me; it was obvious because he always complimented me. He noticed if I had a haircut or wore a different sweater and often said how deep my eyes were and how my eye makeup suited them. But please believe that all it meant to me was the pleasure of working with a man who turned me on but respected that I was happily married with children. That was another thing I didn't cotton on to at the time, but he was *really* taken with Ben and Molly in the pictures I have in my office of you three. Slowly, though so slowly I didn't realize it at first, things began to change. He became more complimentary of me in a sexual way. The way I dressed looked hot, and I looked like *sex on two legs,* which was a phrase he used when we were alone. *He* made me feel good about myself, more feminine and, yes, sexy. Marlon's comments started to become more personal, more suggestive of what could be rather than what might be, if you know what I mean. Dave, I know you compliment me, but in comparison, it seemed like you did it because we're married, and he did it because he fancied me. Marlon Flanders is a rich and powerful man, and suddenly, it seemed like he was fascinated with not only me but Ben and Molly, too. I know you love me, Dave, but seriously, when was the last time you paid me a sincere compliment, told me I was sexy, or even ravished me anywhere outside of our bed on our regular sex nights?"

"I could easily say the same for you, Lynne. Some of the policewomen I work with pay me more compliments in a day than you have in the last year, but I didn't fall into bed with any of them. In fact, over the last few weeks, you've treated me like shit, obviously because you've become more obsessed with your lover."

She sighed, and the tears came again. When she composed herself, she began again. "I didn't realize I was mistreating you, Dave. Looking back, I can see now that I did change, but I didn't see it at the time. I was confused, maybe, enjoying his attention, and resented your apparent jealousy when nothing happened. It began innocently enough, with him insisting we shared our lunch breaks to discuss work. At first, there was a group of us, but slowly, it changed to just being us. Sometimes, he took me to a restaurant to '*get away from the office,*' he said. And then his compliments changed up another gear. Walking to the restaurant, we would pass a fashion store several times. He would pick something from the display and tell me how amazing I would look wearing it. Call me stupid, but I didn't see what was happening. I told you about going to lunch with him once, and I could tell you weren't happy, jealous even, and that annoyed me. He was my boss, and I enjoyed the job and thought I was mature enough to handle things *if* anything untoward happened, which I certainly didn't think would. I didn't tell you any more about my relationship with him because I could see you were upset, and again, nothing was going on. He then asked me to attend a conference with him, which would mean staying three days in Chicago in a six-star hotel. I mentioned it to you, and you said no, that our family should come first. I first sensed that if I went with him to spite you, I could have ended up in bed with him, and I didn't want that. Once I realized I didn't want to go with him, even though it was only business so far as I knew, I had the perfect excuse to tell Marlon the answer was no. I willingly refused to go with him because not only did I begin to worry about the direction our working relationship was heading, but there were you and our children to consider. You'd made your thoughts clear, and I agreed; three days in Chicago was too imposing on our family. I also knew you were worried about my being close to him and far from home, which also helped with my wake-up call. I know you thought I could be tempted, and I must agree I began to think so, too. Things were beginning to make sense to me, and I now believe his whole motive for inviting me was to get me away from you so that he could seduce me."

"Well, he got there anyway, didn't he?"

"Please, please, Dave, let me tell this in the order things occurred. Our only chance is for you to believe me, so I must tell you what happened and how."

"Lynne, do you seriously think you can give me any explanation that justifies you going to a motel and having sex with him?"

Her eyes bored into his. "Yes, Dave, I do. You see, I have proof. You are the only man I love and the only one I want to grow old with. Things have gone wrong for us, but I hope and pray that when you know the full story, you will realize how much I love you." He nodded for her to continue.

"I noticed a definite change in how he spoke with me after I refused to go to Chicago. Not hostile, but not as warm as he had been, and the lunches stopped. In a way, I was relieved, but I also missed the compliments because he did make me feel good about myself. I wasn't the mother of two kids and a frumpy housewife with him; I was a desirable woman, and I had enjoyed that while it lasted, though the thing I realize now I think about it was how much he spoke about our children, and how he wished they were his instead of yours.

Then Marlon told me there was to be an after-hours weekly management meeting, and as his PA, I had to attend. I wasn't happy about it because it kept me away from you and the children, but it was only to be once a week for three hours, and the other department heads would be there. That's when things turned bad, Dave." She shuddered and wrapped her arms tighter around her body as Lynne lifted her heels on the couch, pressing her knees to her breasts.

"I turned up at the board room, expecting to see others, but it was just Marlon. He had a solemn and stern look and told me to come in and sit down. He said an audit had discovered I had been embezzling funds from the company. He slid some documents across the table, supposedly from the internal audit, and it looked like money was missing by red rings written around cash amounts missing from the banking records. He refused to show me further documents, which he assured me he had, proving I was responsible for the banking on those days cash disappeared. I was horrified and denied it, but he insisted I was the only person it could have been, and he had sufficient proof for the board to fire me and inform the police for charges to be brought as a deterrent to others. He told me he was duty-bound to bring the fraud squad in and have me charged, I was being dismissed immediately, and to pack up my office and leave."

Lynne sobbed loudly and then almost screamed: "I swore I had never stolen anything in my life, but he was convinced I was guilty and sat there, smugly shaking his head. He told me he had expected me to deny it, but company policy insisted that he report it to the police. He pointed out you would lose your job too, asking how a police officer could have a wife who would be charged for stealing from her employer?" Lynne stopped again as her sobs engulfed her, and Dave suddenly wondered if his earlier suspicions had been wrong. Lynne's version didn't sound like an affair but more like blackmail or extortion.

"Dave, I was distraught. I hadn't stolen money and believed he couldn't prove I had unless someone had set me up to take the fall. I had to try to gain some time to find out who had it in for me enough to do that. And I couldn't investigate if I was fired in disgrace. There was some office animosity toward me when I was promoted to Marlon's assistant. Maybe, I thought, it was someone jealous of my success. That made sense because others wanted the position and treated me unkindly when they didn't get it, and I did. I begged Marlon for time to prove

I hadn't stolen from the company. He pointed out that the money began disappearing after I had refused to go to Chicago and that if I had agreed to go with him, things might have turned out differently. Marlon said if I had gone with him, he believed we would have been closer, and it would have been easier for him to believe in my innocence." She paused and stared into Dave's eyes. "I think that was when I first suspected I wasn't being framed because of someone else's jealousy, but possibly it was all a ruse to make me toe the line and succumb to him."

"And so that's when you became his lover?"

She didn't reply, which was all the answer Dave needed. He got up, raced to the bathroom, and only just made it to the toilet before vomiting. In an instant, she was there, rubbing his back, but the last thing he wanted was to be touched by her.

Eventually, Dave stopped retching, wiped his mouth with paper, and flushed. He went to the sink, washed his face, rinsed his mouth, and spat. He raised his eyes to the mirror and saw Lynne standing behind him, and before he could stop himself, his eyes filled with tears for his loss.

She hugged him from behind and whispered, "Dave, I'm so sorry. At first, I tried to save our jobs and reputation and let him do things to me. Yes, I had previously found him attractive and exciting because he exuded this kind of magnetism or power and made me feel special. But that night in the board room, I suspected he was the worst kind of predator imaginable. I let him take me, and I appeared willing because I needed to try to get proof of what he had fabricated to frame me. But Dave, you must believe me when I promise you, I hated every moment."

Dave turned and firmly pushed her away, then went back to the chair he sat in before. "Go on, tell me everything." He was too angry and hurt to feel much more than disgust, except, somewhere inside, he felt pity for her too because he began to believe she had been forced. Lynne hadn't wanted an affair; at least, Dave didn't think she had, but how could he be entirely sure?

"It was sex, Dave, and the worst kind of sex I could ever imagine. I wasn't raped as such, and he didn't hurt me in any way, but I wasn't a willing participant either, though I had to make him think I was. Afterward, I felt ashamed, dirty, and guilty because I had betrayed you. In my mind, I was doing it for the right reason, but I was distraught when I thought about how you would react if I told you. When I got home, I felt sure you could tell what had happened because I could feel the guilt cascading out of me. No matter how hard I scrubbed or showered, I couldn't get clean. I couldn't even bring myself to cuddle you in bed because I felt unworthy of you and your love for me."

He watched as she wiped a fresh set of tears from her eyes and waited for her to go on. "The next day, I bought a voice-activated recorder because I wanted to get him somehow talking about the embezzlement and get proof of my innocence. The problem was that I knew I had to make him think I had enjoyed the night before and wanted it to continue. Dave, that was even worse than the physical act, from which I got zero pleasure. On your worst, drunken night, you are a better lover than he could ever be on his best. But I had already debased myself, and for it to mean anything, I had to clear my name and save your job because I was so sure he had some proof he could use against me. If I got that, I could come to you; you would forgive me and help me make him pay."

Dave nodded. So far, her story was believable because he knew Lynne to be strong-willed, independent, and self-sufficient. He thought it was in character for her to try to solve her problems alone, *but to sleep with her boss?* She had agreed to let another man touch her intimately, and he wasn't sure he could ever forgive her for that, no matter what her motives had been. "And you didn't think to come to me before agreeing to fuck him again?"

Lynne sighed deeply. "He caught me on the hop, and I didn't get time to think about anything clearly before that first night in the board room. Can't you see that? Can't you think the best of me after all our years together? Don't you know me better than that?"

"I thought I did know you better, Lynne. But the problem with your deceit and lying is now that the truth has come out, and it seems it has only done so because I got evidence and sent it to your lover's wife; how can I know the truth from lies? Tell me this, was it only Monday nights?"

She shook her head, and he saw the misery written on her face. "I thought it would be, but then he called me into his office during lunch breaks, made me lock the door, and…"

"I don't want all the gory details. It's bad enough knowing you let your boss have you without knowing the specifics and what you did to please him, though I know it would have been a hell of a lot more than you've been doing with me in the last month."

"Dave, please, I'm begging you, don't think that.

Sometimes, it wasn't sex. He wanted to talk about our children and how wonderful our lives could be if I left you and he left his wife, and we became a family. The very thought of that made me want to throw up, so it was almost a relief at other times when he wanted sex. I didn't want to do those things; I didn't enjoy them, and it turned me off you because it was so horrible. I'm so sorry, but making love with you has always been fantastic because you love me. It's not about sex or you getting to come inside me. It's how you hold and kiss me and whisper in my ear. It's because you make sure I enjoy it, you take time to warm me up, and then wait for me to join you so we come together. But suddenly, a man was using my body, and while he said he cared for me, he didn't care about me being happy, only his interpretation of what he believed would make me happy. It sickened and horrified me, and yes, turned me off being intimate with you. You are the only man I've ever loved and the only man I want to spend the rest of my life with, and I hope one day you can learn to trust me again."

"Well, that remains to be seen. Go on with the rest of it. You had lunchtime loving with him, and then the next Monday's fictitious meeting rolled around again. Was that the first time you went to the motel?"

She jumped up, ran to the hall table, ripped her handbag open, and reached inside. Returning, she held out her hand, which contained a small Dictaphone. "Here, listen to it; you can hear me asking about the missing money, how he laughed at me, and how he made me act like a performing seal. You can listen to me pretending it was fun and continually asking for him to show me the proof he had. Dave, you won't like the horrible, terrible sounds of what he did, but if you have any love left for me, you will believe that I was only doing it to save your job and keep me out of jail."

He waved her outstretched hand away. "I may be able to listen to it one day, but not tonight. I want to believe you, Lynne. You're my wife, and I have always loved you. I've never strayed; hell, I never wanted to. What you've done is so painful *because I love you,* and you let it go on for so long. You didn't trust me enough to tell me about it until I ended it."

"You're wrong, Dave. I desperately wanted to confide in you, but Marlon told me if I did, he would immediately turn me over to the police. This week, he told me when we met on Monday night, he would give me the paperwork because he believed I was ready to run off with him. That was last night, our third meeting. Yes, your spy saw me going in the room with him smiling, but not because I was meeting my lover for sex. I was happy because I thought that would be the last time and I could get the proof I needed. But Marlon lied to me, Dave. He got me naked and was so sure of himself that he admitted there never was any proof. He'd made it all up because he believed all I needed was a push, and I would fall for him the way he had for me. He told me he had fallen in love with me from the first day and knew we were destined to be together *as a family.*" Lynne took a deep breath as Dave noticed she was angry and trying to stay calm.

"I got furious with him, but he insisted that because we had done it so many times, he would tell you we had been having an affair if I tried to end it. He said you would throw me out because he could describe my body in such a way you would know he had to have seen me nude. He could describe the intimate tattoo I had done for your eyes only as a gift before our wedding night so well that you would know he had seen it up close. If you listen to the second recording, you will hear him admit it. You will also hear me slapping his face, screaming abuse at him, and telling him to do his worst and that I was going to inform you anyway. I told him you would come after him, and he should be afraid, and he just laughed. That's when he forced me, Dave. The bastard took me against my will.

"He raped you?" Dave's skin crawled as his rage had another outlet. He wanted to go and find Marlon Flanders and kill him.

"The reason I was late home wasn't that I was having fun. It was because I went to the hospital and got an examination. I had the doctor take a swab test for semen, even though he always used condoms and DNA from under my nails because I scratched him. I made a formal rape allegation to the police but asked the officers, Janelle Gibbons and Joe Mastic from the sexual assault squad, not to talk to you until I could explain everything first. It was so late when I got home; you were already in bed asleep, and I was exhausted and depressed. I wanted to wake you but decided to tell you in the morning, but then I woke late, and you'd already left for work. I stayed home all day, not wanting to phone but to tell you when we were together. Then you called to tell me you would be home late because you had to go and rescue a jumper. But I'd been hyped up all day, and I wanted to be rescued by you, and before I could stop myself, I lost my temper. I'm so sorry about that. I felt terrible. Part of me thought you already knew and had decided to leave me, and another part believed that if you *were* working, that person's problems were more important to you than mine. I was so frightened and worried about what you would say when I told you, and I reacted badly when you called home."

Everything Lynne had said finally made sense. Dave believed her. For the first time, he realized the extent of her suffering. What she had done was stupid by any definition, but he knew she had intended to save both of their careers, and he felt ashamed to have doubted her. He stood and crossed the room and held her tightly, stroking her back with both hands. "I believe you," he whispered. "But I wish you'd told me earlier."

"Oh God," she mumbled into his shoulder. "How I wish I had too, and I'm sorry I didn't. I was lost and confused, and so did the only thing I could think of to save us. I was wrong. But I also knew if I told you after the first night without the proof I needed, you could have left me, killed Marlon, or both. Getting Marlon to admit what he'd done was the only thing I could think of to do, even though it meant going along with his disgusting demand for sex. I'm so sorry, Dave; please believe that."

Lynne was right, of course; Dave knew he either would have disbelieved her, and their marriage would have been over, or he would have beaten the man to a bloody pulp. He wanted to do that now but knew his first loyalty was to Lynne, and she had been through hell. She may have been misguided, wrong even not to trust him, but she had suffered at the hands of a rapist, and Dave knew his responsibility was to his wife and mother of their children. He had to look after her. Marlon Flanders could wait; *he would get what was coming to him,* Dave vowed silently.

****

Thursday

Dave Margolis didn't sleep much that night, but he didn't let go of Lynne while she did. He listened to her breathing, stroked her skin, and whispered he loved her each time she stirred. They hadn't made love. Dave believed that neither was in the mood for that. Deep down, he had two competing thoughts in a place he didn't want to visit. One was that he wanted to make love to her, to reclaim his wife and show her he should be the only man to touch her. The other was a fear that he wouldn't be able to perform because he now knew another man had used her body. Possibly, Flanders had given her more pleasure than Dave ever had despite what Lynne said. In the end, Dave felt relief that he didn't have to find out and worried if he could even have risen to the occasion because Lynne appeared not to want sex either. Dave held her and tried to show he forgave her and hadn't lost his love and respect for her, though deep down, he worried if she had been *completely* honest. He mulled over that word throughout the night: *completely*...Had she told him everything, and would he ever know? It gnawed away at him, and the devil on his shoulder wouldn't let up that he was a failure, a useless lover, and a nothing husband. While the front of his brain told him that was ridiculous, he couldn't stop the fear that it was true.

Lynne had told him that the two police officers from the sexual assault squad were coming to talk to them both in the morning to formally interview her about the statement she'd made in the hospital. They would then take possession of the original voice recording, which Lynne would not let them have before she had played it to Dave, though they had taken a copy.

Dave didn't know when or if he would ever be able to listen to the recording, though he hoped not until Marlon Flanders' trial, and even then, that could be too soon for him. The mere thought of it made his blood boil with rage. Knowing they had sex was bad enough, but if he heard the sordid details, the pants and moaning, even if Lynne was, as she'd assured him, acting? No, Dave thought it best he never heard those details because he could never be entirely sure whether Lynne was acting or genuinely enjoying the sex. Being a policeman, Dave worried that the legality of the recording could well be a problem. Dave hoped he was wrong as he had no experience with sexual assaults, but he had a fair understanding of the laws in the State of New York. After what Lynne had gone through to get the recording, he knew she would be devastated if it turned out to be useless, which he suspected it was. That she had given herself to another man for no reason could have a profound psychological effect on her as more guilt set in, which only increased the number of things Dave had to worry about.

His heart had melted utterly, and tears sprang to his eyes when she undressed, and he saw the faint bruises Flanders had inflicted on her. She had bite marks on her neck and breasts and blue finger marks on her upper arms. When he saw the marks on Lynne's body, it took all his restraint not to leave the house, find the man who had hurt his wife, and shoot him dead with his service pistol. Dave knew that he needed to put aside his rage and comfort Lynne. Besides, his training told him what the consequences would be if he assaulted or murdered Flanders. He would spend a long time in jail, and if that happened, Lynne's guilt could overwhelm her, and with him locked up, their children could suffer, and they didn't deserve that fate.

Dave didn't sleep for a long time, and when he did, he awoke before dawn. Lynne opened her eyes to see Dave, his head propped on his hand, staring at her. "What's wrong, Dave?" She asked, her eyes pleading and looking as if she could cry at any moment.

"Nothing," he replied softly. "I've always enjoyed watching you while you sleep. It reminds me how much I love you. Though you wouldn't know, I'm awake before you most mornings and watch you for a while. When you're asleep, your face is stress-free, and oh my God, Lynne, it is obvious how beautiful you are and how lucky I am that you chose to be with me."

Her eyes clouded. She reached her arms up, wrapped them around him, and pulled him down to her. "I'm the lucky one," she whispered. "Thank you for forgiving me for my stupidity. I know now I should have refused his advances and told you straight away, but I swear, at the time, I did what I did for us, and not because I wanted to have sex with him."

"I know." He accepted she was sincere because Lynne was not the kind of woman who could readily admit when she was wrong. Her stubbornness had been the cause of more arguments during their marriage than Dave could remember, so willingly apologizing spoke volumes for her honesty.

"Please know you are the only man for me, and I would die if you ever left me."

He held her tightly, and for some reason, Dave didn't understand; the image of Susan, out on the ledge, frail, beautiful, and vulnerable, came unbidden into his mind. Dave felt ashamed of the feeling that washed over him.

Long before eight, Dave and Lynne were dressed and drinking coffee, waiting for the police officers to arrive. Dave had called his boss and told him he would be taking some time off because he worked late the night before with the jumper at Medusa Plaza. At seven-fifty, Lynne's cell phone rang. She picked it up, answered, listened, and replied, "Okay, thanks." She tossed the phone down. "Sorry, Dave, the officers are running late but will be here just after nine."

****

"Detective Joe Mastic and this is Detective Janelle Gibbons," the male cop said at the front door while holding his ID. Dave turned and let them enter, then closed the door behind them. He hadn't met either before. Their paths hadn't crossed, which wasn't surprising because the Sexual Assault Squad often flew below the radar due to the nature of their inquiries, and they operated out of a different floor in the precinct to him. "How is Mrs. Margolis holding up?" Janelle asked.

Dave shrugged, unsure how to answer. "She's told me everything, and so far, she is doing okay, I think. She's pretty tough, but then she has to be, being married to a cop."

"Yeah," Joe replied. "Your wife told us you were on the job, hostage negotiator, yes? Can we speak with you both, please?"

He nodded yes to both questions and led the way to the dining table, where Lynne sat waiting. She looked up from her coffee mug, a hopeful expression on her face. They exchanged good mornings, and Dave gestured for them to sit. "Coffee?" he asked, but they both shook their heads. "You guys don't look happy, so give us the bad news." Dave sat down and reached for Lynne's hand; he had a bad feeling that his suspicions about the recording were correct.

"Mrs. Margolis, we interviewed Marlon Flanders and his lawyer early this morning. As you can imagine, he denies the rape. However, he does admit to having an ongoing consensual sexual relationship with you, which he says you instigated after he accused you of stealing funds from the company. He described in detail the liaisons you shared and how you liked him to treat you roughly while having sex."

Lynne stood angrily. "That's bullshit. You've heard the tape; what did he say about that?"

He shifted uncomfortably in his seat. "On advice from the District Attorney's office, we did not mention the recording to him. In the opinion of the DA, it would not be allowed to be introduced into evidence because it would be deemed hearsay. In New York State, for any recording to be used in evidence, both participants must be aware the conversation is being recorded. As he won't permit your recording, we can't use it against him. The trial judge would have to make a ruling on its admissibility. The feeling is that it would be denied on balance, especially as Mr. Flanders can afford an excellent attorney. Without any other corroborating evidence, the DA is uncomfortable charging Mr. Flanders because it's his word against yours, so it won't get that far. His lawyer is a very accomplished criminal attorney, one of the best, and would succeed in having the recording excluded from evidence. While the recording makes it obvious your version of events is true, without being able to use it in a court of law, the DA feels it would be in your best interest to let the matter drop.

Ultimately, it is your word against his, and those trials rarely end up pretty for the victim. Flanders has shown he will stop at nothing to destroy your reputation if it goes that far. The photos sent to Mrs. Flanders by you, Mr. Margolis, proves you believed it was an ongoing affair also; therefore, that too would make a rape charge very difficult, if not impossible, to prove." The cop shrugged and held his palms up. "Think of it this way, Mr. Margolis; if *you* thought it was an affair, his lawyer would make the jury believe it too. They could even call you as a witness as to what you believed your wife was doing, though, of course, you can refuse to testify against your wife, but even then, that would point to you being guilty, Mrs. Margolis, and only made the accusation when you knew your husband had discovered the affair."

Lynne stood angrily. "What about the bruises and bite marks he gave me and the scratch I gave him?"

"I'm sorry," Janelle replied, interrupting. "This isn't pleasant, and we wish it weren't so, but he says you were quite the wild one when you had sex, that you liked it rough, and the scratch was just you flinging your hand about in the throes of orgasm with him. You must understand, Mrs. Margolis, this is just him in an interview. It would be even worse in a trial if we cannot use the recording. He would fight very dirty so your reputation would be tarnished, and people would think *there is no smoke without fire*. Please understand we are saying this for your benefit, not ours. I want to string Mr. Flanders up by his balls and leave him there, but as I'm sure your husband will agree, most rape cases don't go to trial without corroborating testimony. When they do, the victim is treated horribly by the defense attorney. Even when there is other corroborating evidence. Things like your past boyfriends in college, any medical history, and then, of course, there is the allegation of you embezzling funds."

Dave had suspected that would be the case but still felt devastated for Lynne. Wiretaps, telemarketer's phone calls, and witness interviews fell into a grey area unless both parties knew they were being recorded. Of course, in Lynne's case, Dave understood that if Marlon Flanders knew he was being recorded, he wouldn't have said what he had, let alone force himself on Lynne without destroying the incriminating evidence first. The bottom line was Lynne had subjected herself to sexual harassment on several occasions for nothing. He turned to her and saw the horrified look on her face as the realization hit her. Dave stood and put his arm around her just as her tears came. "Is there nothing you can do?" he asked.

"Mr. Margolis," Joe replied calmly. "You are well-known and respected by your fellow officers. Because I listened to the tape of your wife's rape and knew of your reputation, I have stepped outside the law to help. Marlon Flanders insisted that Lynne instigated the affair with him and that she stole money from the company. Moreover, he says they fell in love once they began the affair and planned to be together once she left you and he left his wife. Flanders admits to having sex and giving her time to repay what she stole, and he says he now regrets that. Mrs. Margolis, he says your accusation is just your way to get out of repaying your debt and cold feet at ending your marriage to be with him, which you had promised to do. Mr. Flanders points out that even your husband thought you were having a consensual sexual relationship; hence, he hired a private detective and sent the pictures to his wife. Because you have falsely accused him of rape, he said he would get his lawyer to sue you for defamation and press charges for embezzlement. I spoke to him off the record, out of earshot of his lawyer, and advised him that his best interest would be to forget any further action. I didn't play the recording but told him of its existence. While the tape might be ruled inadmissible in a criminal trial, I pointed out that he would not be afforded the same luxury in a civil suit. In short, he could not only lose any action against you, but taking it could prompt you to make a counterclaim against him. He got the message and agreed to let the matter drop, though he says you are fired, Mrs. Margolis."

****

Dave took the rest of the day off work because he knew Lynne needed him to stay with her. He had arranged for Ben and Molly to go to Lynne's parents' house after school to give him more time to make sure Lynne was mentally stable. She had barely said a word and acted as if she was in shock after the police officers left. Dave tried to let her know he didn't blame her, that he knew she did what she did for the best of reasons, and that he loved her. Lynne stayed distant and withdrawn, and around lunchtime, he put her to bed, where she fell asleep almost immediately.

Dave sat on the swing seat on the back veranda, near the barbeque Susan had teased him about, and dialed her number. He worried she wouldn't answer because she had finished the job he'd interrupted the night before, but after four rings, he heard her voice. "Hi Dave, how did it go with Lynne?"

Once again, he marveled at how wonderful she was.

That amid the monumental health and marital issues she faced, all she cared about was the state of his relationship. He guessed it could be his problems that gave her a distraction, even if for a short while, from the issues that drove her to the brink of suicide. He told her everything, and she listened, not interrupting until he finished. "You're a good man, Dave. I knew it from the moment I met you. Lynne is fortunate to have you."

"Oh, I don't know about that," he responded, shifting uncomfortably in his seat. "The thing is, I believe Lynne's intent wasn't so much about having an affair but having sex to get the information so she could avoid an affair, if that makes any sense. I know she was attracted to him and has always been a hopeless flirt, but that's one of the things I love about her. Just because they were attracted to each other wouldn't mean she would go to bed with him, I believe that. So, he manipulated her, even blackmailed her, and the worst thing is that for all her efforts, she didn't get any evidence she could use, has lost her job, and no matter how much I forgive her, she is depressed. Also, I must admit I hate that Lynne did what she did instead of trusting me. Even if she had succumbed that first time out of fear and then come to me, I could have accepted it more readily than now. Then, I could have told her that recording their conversations without his knowledge and consent would never be admissible in a criminal trial unless we got a court order for her to wear a wire, but then he would have claimed entrapment. I am, after all, a cop and have some knowledge about things like that. But she shunned me, carried on being Mrs. Independent, having sex with the man in the misguided belief she would be able to beat him at his own game. If our marriage doesn't survive, that will be the reason: her lack of trust in me; that's what I'm struggling with."

"I think the thing you're struggling with is your pride. You see your wife now as spoiled goods; someone else had sex with the woman you pledged your heart and soul to, and no matter how justified it is in her mind, she still had sex."

Damn, the woman, he thought while biting back an angry response; she *knows how to cut to the bone.* "Are you telling me you wouldn't be angry with Mark in the same circumstances?"

She laughed, a throaty, sexy laugh. "Dave, you're missing the obvious. Being a woman, I see this sort of thing differently, not just because of the skin disease ravishing my body. Being a man, Mark would want to solve the problem without involving me, as I'm sure you would too, wouldn't you? If you're being truthful, and the answer to that question is yes, then what you suggest is sexist at best and downright insulting to your wife at worst. You're saying that if a man has sex with a blackmailing woman to get evidence, somehow, that would be acceptable. But a woman, trying to save her husband's job and reputation as much as her own, might lose the man she was trying to protect. Dave, that doesn't sound very fair to me."

"Ouch."

"Damn right, ouch. If you were here, I'd have given you a good slap or an elbow to the stomach, depending on how close we sat."

Dave suddenly had a mental image of them both laying naked in bed, talking after making love, and her elbowing him for saying something dumb. He smiled before he forced those thoughts down. They were inappropriate and unwelcome, but the mental image was still delicious. "I guess you're right, Susan. My stupid male ego is rearing its ugly head. But just because I agree logically with what you say, I can't seem to stop the negative feelings that her lack of trust in me has invoked. Hopefully, in time, I will get over it."

"Well, let's hope Lynne gets over her rape before you get over your hurt feelings."

"Yes, you're right, Susan, I'm selfish and immature."

"But?"

He shook his head, almost in despair. How could this woman he barely knew understand him so well? "But nothing, I'm selfish and immature."

"You sound petulant. Dave, you realize we share a bond. I won't say you saved my life, but you certainly extended it. I like you a lot, I mean a whole lot, probably because of my emotional instability and because I feel like I know you. So, stop hiding stuff from me; use me as a sounding board by all means, but don't be petulant. If you tell me the truth, and I don't like what you say, I will tell you what I think, and it won't make me like you any less, only more because of your honesty."

He sighed. She had him backed into a corner and realized she knew it, too. "Well, don't say you didn't ask for it. Well, the rape. Can you call it rape when she knowingly went there to have sex with him? If he had any sense, he should have kept his mouth shut until after he fucked her. Sorry, excuse the frankness, please."

"It's okay." She giggled. "I've heard the word before and am not offended by it. I'm an editor, remember? I've edited some extremely racy books written by frustrated or over-sexed authors. Seriously, you can't possibly think she went there to have pleasurable sex with him?"

"N-n-n-o, I don't think she did, but will I ever know that some of the episodes, especially in his office during clandestine lunch breaks, weren't, as you put it, pleasurable?"

"Dave, you're going through a tough time, and your emotions are clouding your judgment. I understand your frustration, disappointment, and rage for the man who's done this to her. But keep sight of what's important. Though her actions might look stupidly wrong in the cold light of day and with twenty-twenty hindsight, what you have to ask yourself is what was her state of mind when she made those decisions?"

There it was, once again. Susan had hit the nail on the head. "Yeah, I know, and trust me, I have repeatedly asked myself that. I want to support her and believe and trust that her motives were pure. I want to forgive and one day forget, but it will take time."

"Nothing worthwhile in life comes easy, and all the best things take time."

"Quite the philosopher, aren't you?"

"I studied philosophy as well as English Literature at university." He imagined her smiling indulgently. "Consider this, Dave. If I were not married and didn't have a hideous skin disease turning me into a Komodo Dragon, I might be trying to get you not to forgive her so you'd look at me as her replacement. You're quite a catch, which I'm positive Lynne knows, and I think she is in there fighting for you as best as she knows how. I know you are going to be there fighting for her, too. That's the kind of man you are."

Dave paused, thinking deeply about the flirtatious

thing she had just said. She liked him, and he certainly liked her, which made no sense. She was suicidal, and he was married to a woman who had been raped. *Time to take this back to safer ground,* he thought. "Yes, I will be fighting for her, and I will also be fighting for you, Susan. I haven't had a chance to check my emails yet, but did you send the pictures and medical information?"

Dave wondered if her lengthy pause was because he had all but ignored her compliment that he was a catch and, therefore, hurt her feelings, but he needn't have worried. "No, I haven't. Look, firstly, I wanted to make sure you were sincere. Don't get me wrong, I thought you were, but then again, you could have just been doing your job, and maybe I'd have never heard from you again. Then, of course, if I had done so, I'd have sent you pictures taken of me without my clothes on, and well, while I might think you're a hunk, and these are medical pictures, not glamour shots, you would see my breasts, and that's not so easy for me to do. Sending naked pictures by email to a man I hardly know, surely you can see how difficult that is for me to do, especially because I don't know why you want them. While Mark did walk out on me yesterday, I am still married to him, and I'm not sure that he would consent to me giving out pictures of me without my clothes on to a man I met yesterday on a forty-story ledge."

"Yes, forgive me. I didn't think of those things last night, but you're right." He chuckled. *God, I'm stupid sometimes,* he concluded. "Okay, the story is this. Some time back, I re-acquainted with an old friend from school. His name is Bart, like the famous Bart, except his surname is Chisholm. We were close all during school, best buddies, you could say, but he was always a lot smarter than me, and once we finished Wilmott High, he went off to a different college to me, and as guys do, we drifted apart. About six months ago, the dispatcher called me for a job at a specialist medical clinic. A drug-crazed addict had burst in, stabbed the receptionist, and was trying to get drugs. By sheer coincidence, the doctor and owner of the practice was Bart, and the junkie was holding a knife against his throat when I arrived. Over the next couple of hours, I was able to talk him down. It turns out he wasn't such a bad guy, an ex-marine suffering from PTSD who got addicted to drugs while in Afghanistan. Like most veterans, our government turned its back on him and left him with psychological problems, compounded after his wife left him for another man while he served his country.

"Anyway, Bart had convinced himself this guy was going to murder him and had all but given up. He was a nervous wreck, but slowly, I got the junkie's confidence. Rory O'Connell was his name, and I convinced him there was a better way and that I would ensure he got help. Yes, O'Connell was in trouble for the stabbing and was going to go to court for it. Still, I thought he could escape major jail time by throwing himself at the mercy of the Judge and bringing his army experiences and wife deserting him as justification for his descent into addiction. I told him he should get himself into rehab, and then by the time his court date came around, if he had cleaned up his act, I would be a character witness on his behalf. Eventually, he gave me the knife and let Bart go, and I walked him out.

"Bart couldn't thank me enough and promised me that no matter how long it took, he would be there if I ever needed him to help me. The practice was his, and he is a skin specialist, so I thought if I showed him your case, he might be able to help you. If Bart can assist, the debt he thinks he owes me, which, by the way, he doesn't owe me a thing, could be repaid. I believe he is one of the best in his field, and while I don't know if he can help you, as we said yesterday, our meeting was destiny. This is one more coincidence in a long line of them. So, now you know why I asked for the pictures, not because I wanted to see your boobs, amazing though I'm sure they are. If you send me your medical files and photographs, I will ask him to help you. If they are of you without your clothes on, I give you my word I won't even look at them; I will pass them on to Bart."

The silence dragged on until Dave realized Susan was crying. She was softly sobbing, and his heart melted for her pain and anguish. Dave felt ashamed because his problems paled into insignificance next to hers, and he vowed silently to himself that no matter what it took, he would do everything he could to help Susan. He knew that included finding courage, forgetting his stupid pride, and being the perfect husband for Lynne.

Chapter 3

Sacrifice

"For you and anyone dear to you, I would do anything. I would embrace any sacrifice for you and for those dear to you. And when you see your own bright beauty springing up anew at your feet, think now and then that there is a man who would give his life to keep a life you love beside you."
A Tale of Two Cities
Charles Dickens 1859

Dave was still sitting, dozing, on the patio when Lynne woke and found him. She wore one of his oversized T-shirts and shorts. Her hair was messy, and her eyes were red from crying, yet she still looked beautiful to him. Dave had decided to put things behind him as much as possible and show Lynne that he supported her no matter how deep his insecurities and fears were. He could only imagine the turmoil she was going through. The sexual assault would be bad enough, but added to her fear would be that he would leave her, believing she had enjoyed the encounters with her boss. The final irony was the police wouldn't act against the man who had blackmailed her into having sex. Susan had suggested Lynne might need counseling, and Dave agreed that could be possible.

Dave wasn't so stupid to realize that if he took his rage out on Marlon Flanders, he would face assault charges and lose his job with the police. The outcome could be much worse if Dave confronted Flanders, lost his temper completely, and killed him, which Dave knew he was capable of. It took all the self-control Dave possessed not to go and do that. What state would Lynne be in if he spent the next fifteen years in jail, he wondered? And then, of course, there were his children to consider. They deserved the right to grow up in a happy home with a loving mother *and* father. Most people in prison were those who didn't stop to think of the consequences of their actions, and Dave had promised himself after the phone call with Susan that he wouldn't be one of them.

Lynne sat on his lap and curled her arms around his neck. "I'm so sorry, Dave. I've mucked everything up, haven't I? Can you ever forgive me?"

"Lynne, you did muck up, yes. You didn't come to me for help and had sex with another man. Trust is earned, never given, and I lost trust in you because I believed you were having an affair. I didn't know the circumstances, but how could I when you didn't confide in me? The point is because I found out about the affair rather than you confiding in me; in my mind, no justification would have been acceptable. Whereas, if you had come to me and told the truth after the first time, that would have been different. Marriage should be about you and me against the world, but in this case, you consciously decided to exclude me while you had sex with another man. I guess if I didn't love you so much, it wouldn't hurt as bad, and the thought of him using your body intimately, one that I thought was exclusively mine, makes me want to vomit and kill you both. But I know you, and I know you did it for a reason you thought was best and not because you desired sex with him, and that's the only reason I want to get past this. I want to forgive and be able to forget."

She lifted her head and stared into his eyes. "I swear to you that every word I've said is true. I would never have willingly had an affair, never. It was harmless flirting with a man who exuded power and personality and paid me compliments, making me feel good about myself. There was never a single time I considered taking it further than that."

He pulled her back into him and hugged her. "I know", he whispered.

"Dave?" Lynne asked softly, still on his lap. "Please, take me to bed. I need you to make love to me, help me forget the horrible things I've done, and let me show you that you're the only man I love."

Can I? Can I make love to her and not think of what she did with that man? Before he could answer, his cell phone vibrated on the table beside him. The bell saved him. "Hold that thought, hon," he whispered, squeezing her with one hand while reaching for the phone.

The caller blocked their ID, but he answered anyway, hoping it wasn't Susan. "David Margolis," he said into the microphone.

"Mr. Margolis, this is Dorothy Flanders. You sent me some disgusting pictures of your wife meeting my husband for sex. I'm not sure if I should thank you, offer you condolences, or hunt your wife down and make her disappear. With you being a policeman, I'm kidding about the last alternative, I hope you realize?"

Dave sat up straight, taking Lynne with him. Lynne

looked startled at the sudden look of dismay on his face. "I don't know if you're aware, Mrs. Flanders, but your loving husband manipulated, blackmailed, and finally raped my wife," Dave said abruptly.

The woman gave a small guttural laugh. "Well, it sure doesn't look like that by the pictures you sent. I got the distinct impression from your email you didn't think that either. You have evidence to back up this accusation now?"

He sighed, knowing this was what people would think, that his wife was the instigator. "You're right. I did think it was an affair, but I now know it was far from that. Yes, there is evidence, a recording of him admitting it and then subsequently raping Lynne. Unfortunately, it's not admissible in a criminal case, the police believe. It's Lynne's word against his, so he will get away with it, no doubt, to do it to his next PA in your employ."

"I've already kicked him out of the house and business because I won't stand for infidelity, so if he does it again, it won't be while he is my husband or CEO of one of my companies. However, he threatened wrongful dismissal and said he would sue me and the company for defamation. He assures me that your wife came onto him after embezzling money to avoid prosecution. While he does admit the sex, he has begged for forgiveness and says he agreed only while she was paying it back, and the affair was at your wife's insistence. Your wife is beautiful, and he admits falling under her spell, so it is her word against his. If you send me a copy of the recording, it will help me enormously to get to the truth and head off any litigation. In turn, I could help your wife. You and I seem to be the innocents in this whole sordid business. I'd like to have dinner with you tonight when we can discuss this further. Perhaps you could play the recording then and let me have a copy. If what you're saying is true, it can only benefit you both."

Dave considered her offer for a moment, then reached a decision. "I'm happy to meet with you and let you have a copy of the recording, but I will bring Lynne with me. Then you can speak with her and see for yourself that she was not the instigator of the affair but the victim, and she didn't steal money from your company. Your husband fabricated it all to have sex with her after she refused to go to Chicago with him for a few days."

"All right, that sounds reasonable. Thank you for letting me have this chance to get to the bottom of everything. I will divorce Marlon regardless of the outcome because of his disloyalty, which, for me, is unforgivable. But my father and I will destroy him publicly if he has brought our business into disrepute. I will book a table at Maxine's on Broadway for seven, my treat. Just mention my name to the hostess."

"The recording is on a thumb drive, so you'll need to bring a laptop."

****

Dave ended the call and told Lynne about that night's dinner arrangement with Dorothy Flanders, though he knew she would realize from his side of the conversation. Dave then suggested Lynne ask if her mother wouldn't mind feeding their children dinner after picking them up from school again and sitting them until they could get there later that night to pick them up.

Lynne blanched at the thought of coming face-to-face with Marlon's wife and began to panic. Dave calmly explained that Dorothy Flanders had said she would help destroy her ex-husband's reputation and financial standing and remove his threat of suing for wrongful dismissal and slander if she received a copy of the recording. Dave believed it would be well to have her as an ally rather than an enemy, so it was in their interest to go and meet her and let her listen to the recording.

Dave had had another idea during the phone call, which he outlined to her. "Lynne, while I don't want to profit financially from your experience, I don't want to see your reputation ruined, which it will be if and when all this becomes public knowledge, and he carries out his threat to seek damages. I can see another benefit from going along tonight and giving her a copy of the recording."

"What that?" she asked in a trembling voice.

"Hon, we can't hide from this mess. If we try, it will only give the naysayers ammunition to think you were having an affair rather than being manipulated by your boss. If we get an attorney, I'm sure we can bring a suit against Bond Corp because your boss forced you to have sex with him and invented a case of embezzlement as a means of doing so. Okay, so we can't go into criminal court with the recording because of the rules of evidence. Still, the company has a duty of care to ensure its employees aren't molested and abused by those in authority. Employer morals regulations are a serious part of staff management, and I believe you have a case that will make them sit up and take notice. Civil court is different from a criminal trial for many reasons. Sure, it would be costly and take a long time; therefore, we would need to find a lawyer to work for a percentage. But with the recording, I'm sure we would find someone competent who would think we could win. Most corporations are insured, so they would probably want to settle before going to a jury because they would know it could cost much more if it went all the way. The recording you tell me makes it clear not only was he lying about the embezzlement to force you to have sex repeatedly, but after admitting it, he raped you when you tried to end it. Let's go on the front foot and fight rather than slink away to lick our wounds. Probably, we can force a financial settlement to stop you from taking them to court, and maybe it would be enough to go into a trust account for Ben and Molly's college education."

She stared open-mouthed while she considered his thoughts, and then a look of steely determination crossed her face. He thought *that's the Lynne I know and love; welcome back.* "Do you think we can make them pay, Dave? I mean, *really pay?*" she asked. "Because if we can, I want to make them suffer as much as we can.

"Anyone who heard that recording would agree you deserve compensation. How much, well, I don't know, but we could make Mrs. Flanders and her Board of Directors sit up and take notice. You are the wronged party here, not Marlon Flanders, who, she said, has only lost his job and can't be prosecuted. You explain everything to your mother; it's time she hears about this from you. I have to check my work emails and make a couple of calls. I'll use the study."

For some reason that Dave didn't want to think about too deeply, he chose not to tell Lynne about Susan yet. He reasoned she had enough to deal with without worrying about a suicidal woman whom Dave wanted to help. If he had stopped to investigate his motivation further, Dave would have had to admit the real reason was his attraction to Susan at a time when Lynne needed all his attention.

****

The email from Susan was waiting for him in his inbox. Dave smiled, pleased she had decided to trust him before debating whether he should open it and look at the contents or forward them to Dr. Bart Chisholm. His emotions battled for three minutes. He was more than curious as to the extent of her skin disorder, and if he was honest, the thought of seeing her body was a lure too strong to resist. He didn't see his desire for her perverted, more that he was deeply interested in saving her life if he possibly could. But Susan was a stunningly beautiful woman fully dressed and, on his computer, he had pictures of her undressed. An instant recollection from his youth made him smile as a memory flooded back.

When Dave was fourteen, he delivered newspapers on his bicycle to homes in Staten Island, where he'd lived with his parents. To get to Mrs. McGill's residence, he had to ride down a laneway, where he would toss her daily paper over a tall hedge. Dave was delivering papers on a particular Saturday, and just before throwing hers, he glanced up as the sun reflected off a second-story window. He saw her, standing and drying her naked, slender body, obviously having finished a shower, not realizing a boy sat astride his cycle, staring up at her full, round breasts.

It was Dave's first-ever sexual encounter, other than those formed in his masturbatory fantasies. At that moment, Dave knew that no matter how many women's breasts he saw in the future, he would never see any more perfect than those he was currently staring at. Mesmerized, he watched them wobble like sensual jelly as she dried them with her towel. Dave wished that when he died, he could be reborn as Mrs. McGill's towel so he could touch her that intimately. He felt a warm flush start at his groin and climb up to his face, and then he froze, terrified, as he noticed she had seen him watching her. He thought she would scream or shout at him, and if she did, he would die with shame and embarrassment. Instead, she turned slowly to face him, then lowered the towel so he could see her body perfectly. His eyes almost bled tears of youthful lust as his gaze dropped from her full breasts down to below her navel and the triangle of dark curly pubic hair. He saw her smile at him, then impishly nod and turn away from the window. She was gone. Dave realized then that he was hopelessly in love with Mrs. McGill and always would be for the rest of his life.

The question that worried him for a long time after that illicit scene was: *am I a pervert for looking at her in all her naked glory?* He hadn't felt dirty then, and Mrs. McGill hadn't seemed to mind. In fact, she'd seemed amused and encouraged him. Though he hopefully looked for her in the window every day afterward, she never repeated the act, and later in life, he realized that was as it should be. Nothing could ever match that first time, and if she had flaunted herself again, it would have cheapened the initial act. Dave was satisfied with that only viewing, and to this day, sometimes late at night after Lynne had drifted off to sleep, he remembered the occasion. Her rounded curves and extraordinarily long stiletto nipples. Especially he recalled how Mrs. McGill had rubbed herself with the towel as she watched him, watching her. The memory never failed to arouse him, so maybe that made him a Peeping Tom, though he thought his only saving grace was that he hadn't sought a reason to spy on her; it had just happened. Dave returned to the present, clicked on the email, and opened the first attachment.

Oh my God! Was Dave's only thought, repeated on a never-ending loop as he scrolled from picture to picture. Dave thought he might cry at the horrific scenes flashing across the monitor screen, and he felt his eyes cloud over, then a tear from each trickle from the corners. The first picture showed Susan naked from her white bikini panties up, sitting on a doctor's couch with her back to the photographer. At first glance, it looked like she had several jagged pieces of something like newspaper dipped in tar and stuck on her back. Each piece looked to be an irregular shape but seemed of similar size, around four to six inches in diameter. The problem using the word diameter inferred each patch was a circle, but they weren't. Some were rounded, while others had jagged edges with finger-shaped lengths, making them look like a starfish had burrowed in under her skin. The color varied from deep purple to black, and Dave had never seen anything like it and struggled not to gag in horror as he switched from one image to the next. Some close-up photos showed, in high definition, detailed shots of the lesions across her back. As Susan had mentioned, the surface seemed irregular and resembled reptilian or fish scales, though he thought she had greatly exaggerated at the time. There was some blood and weeping from some sores, while others looked like chain mail armor.

After the initial shock, he sagged back in his chair, too stunned to do or think anything coherently. Eventually, Dave opened the last attachment and tried to read the doctor's report but gave up after the first two lines. Words like Necrobiosis, Epidermolysis, and Ichthyosis seemed like excerpts from a long-dead language he could neither decipher nor understand, but they sounded deathly serious.

No wonder she is going through seven kinds of hell. And to cap it all off, her husband leaves her? Dave felt shocked. *Whatever happened to the vow "in sickness and in health?"* To counter that, Dave knew that when those vows were made, both participants were in perfect health, and there was no way that anyone could imagine how grotesque Susan's skin would become several years later. He also knew from the years spent in the police force that everyone had varying degrees of being able to deal with injury. Some people could help someone bleeding profusely at the site of a car wreck, while others turned away, vomiting as the victim bled to death.

Dave realized, with a start, that he had looked at several pictures of a near-nude woman he found to be staggeringly beautiful and didn't once look at her inappropriately and couldn't even remember what her breasts looked like. *Maybe there's hope for me yet.* He briefly wondered if he should re-open the email and look again. He decided not to. Instead, he dug his address book out of the drawer, looked up a number, and dialed.

"Skin Deep Dermatology Clinic, how can I help you?" A youngish-sounding woman asked.

"I'd like to speak with Bart Chisholm, please; this is Dave Margolis calling."

"He's with a patient at the moment. Can I ask him to call you back when he is free?"

"Sure, but can you please let him know it's me? If he wants to call me back, that's fine, but you might find he'd like to chat. I promise I will be very brief." Dave had suspected he wouldn't be able to get straight through, but he wanted to try to avoid Bart calling back when he was with Lynne. Dave thought that the timing for telling her about Susan wasn't right yet. The realization that he was being as secretive about Susan as she had been about Marlon did enter his mind, but he rationalized that his motives were pure and not at all sexual.

"Well, he doesn't like to be interrupted while he is consulting, and to do so could cost me my job." She wouldn't risk transferring him to Bart's office; that was clear, and he should have realized that.

"That's fine, I understand, and I certainly wouldn't want you to risk your job. Tell me, is your name Ilene Whittaker?"

"Y-y-yes, why do you ask?"

He laughed. "I'm glad you're back at work after your traumatic experience. I hope there were no long-lasting effects from your wounding?"

"Oh my God, that's where I know the name; you're *that* David Margolis. I'm so sorry; it's been a hectic day; otherwise, I'd have recognized you immediately. I never got a chance to thank you for saving me; the doctors told me I could have bled to death if you hadn't intervened."

Dave felt the embarrassment he always did when someone thanked him for doing his job. "Ilene, it's fine. I'm glad I was there and could get you the help you needed. Is everything okay with your health?"

"Yeah, I'm fully recovered now, thanks. No major damage: he didn't hit any vital organs, thank goodness. I heard you testified at his trial. If you don't mind me asking, why did you do that for a junkie?"

Why did he? That was a question he'd asked himself many times and one his captain thought was wrong. Dave took a breath. "Ilene, the simple answer is that I gave him my word that I would during the negotiations to free you both. Because I promised, he agreed to let me get the medical assistance you needed. When he told me his story, I realized it wasn't drugs he needed; it was help. Yes, what he did in hurting you and threatening Bart was terrible, and he had an addiction; that was true. But why was he the way he was? Before he became a marine and went to fight a war, he was fine, but when he was fighting for his country, his fiancée left him for another man, and the horrors of what he saw in Afghanistan, screwed up his head. The recreational drugs he discovered there helped him escape the nightmare his life had become, then took a stronger hold back home and spiraled out of control. I promised him if he sought help, I would do my best when he went to trial, and I did. It didn't mean I condoned his actions, but it did mean that I thought he deserved some leniency if he was serious about getting his life back on track."

"I never thought of it like that. You make me feel guilty because I wanted him locked up and the key thrown away."

Dave laughed again. "Don't worry, anyone who went through what you did would have felt the same; that's human nature. I don't blame you in the slightest. Being empathetic is part of my job, and I wouldn't be very good at it if I didn't try to understand why people do what they do in hostage situations and offer help where I can. Anyway, I've kept you away from your job long enough. Would you please pass on that I'd like Bart to call me when he can? It is important, I promise."

"Nope, for you, I'm going to interrupt him. I know he'd want me to. Hold the line, please. Oh, and by the way, thank you once again for saving my life."

"You're welcome," he replied, but she had put him on hold, and the sound of piped music filled the silence.

Less than one minute later, Bart's Eastern drawl came over the phone. "Dave, hi, great to hear from you. Is everything okay?"

"Hi Bart, I'm sorry to interrupt. Thank you for taking my call. I wonder, could I ask you a huge favor?"

"Ask away; whatever I can do for you is done. My wife as a bed partner, our firstborn child, cash loan, whatever you need, ask away. I meant every word I said when you saved me from that junkie."

Dave grinned. It was a conversation they'd had before. "Bart, seriously, please believe me when I say you do not owe me a thing. I want to ask you a favor, but not because I need to cash in something owed me for doing my job."

"Whatever, ask me, it's yours."

"Thank you, Bart. This isn't easy, but I was sent to talk a woman down from a forty-story ledge. It turns out her husband left her that day because he could no longer deal with a horrific skin condition she has that is eating her body and will ultimately kill her. She is slowly turning into a reptile or human fish. She is an awesome woman with more than her fair share of bad luck and a complaint her health insurance company won't cover because it happened overseas. Her travel cover refuses to play ball, too, so she is stuck between a rock and a hard place. I just wondered if you wouldn't mind looking at her pictures and case notes to see if you can spot anything that might help her. I made her promise not to go back out on that ledge until I got your opinion so you could say it's a matter of life and death."

"Wow, Dave, of all the things I thought you would ask me, that would be near the bottom of the list. Of course, I will take a look. There isn't a terminal skin condition I'm aware of, so you have piqued my interest. What's the background?"

Knowing Bart was with a patient, Dave briefly told him of Susan's African trip, the insect bites, subsequent infection, and the final resultant spread of the disease after an ineffective treatment of antibiotics.

"All right, it sounds serious, especially if the antibiotics have caused a mutation. Send me everything you have, and let's schedule an appointment for me to see your friend urgently. As you can imagine, I'm booked for the next three weeks, but if you can get her here tomorrow evening, I will stay back following my last appointment after five thirty. Can you make that work?"

"Bart, I will get her there and come along for moral support. I've just hit send so that you will have her doctor's reports momentarily. Thank you for doing this; I appreciate it."

"Don't mention it, I'll see you tomorrow."

****

"Well, two phone calls in one day, people will talk, you know," Susan said, answering her cell phone to his call.

"They might at that, especially now I've seen you almost naked," he teased, hoping that making a joke would ease the embarrassment he knew she would be feeling.

"Good job you're not here then because you'd see I

am blushing bright red. So this call is to say goodbye; you don't want to see the Dragon Lady again?"

"Susan," he said more abruptly than he intended. "Please don't do that. Mark has let you down, and you are going through hell right now, but whether you like it or not, I will be your friend, and we will see this thing through together. I don't mind the self-deprecating humor. I get it; it's a defense mechanism, and I can kid along about that, but please don't think I'm going to abandon you, and worse, don't say you think I will. Please remember I've been a cop ever since I left school. Yes, I'm a negotiator these days, but I did my time in the ranks and paid my dues. I've seen plenty of horrific sights, so I don't think of you as a Dragon Lady, a minotaur, or even particularly ugly. I've seen worse, much worse, believe me. I could describe some car wreck victims, battered wives, and one memorable occasion when a drunken father cooked his baby in a microwave."

Dave thought he might have gone too far and upset her, but he needn't have worried. When she spoke, he realized she was one tough woman.

"All right, all right, I'm suitably chastised. Settle down; it's my way of trying to deal with my condition. I try to be humorous to hide my fear. Don't mind me; you keep telling me off if I get too self-deprecating."

"I know what's *really* upsetting you," he murmured.

"I bet you don't."

"Okay, you're on. I bet you a veal scaloppine meal at Romero's that I get it right in one go."

She laughed; all traces of her earlier angst were gone. "This will be the easiest dinner I've ever earned. Go ahead, take your best shot."

"You do realize this is a win-win for me? Either way, I get to take you out for dinner again. Okay, what is upsetting you is that you're disappointed I haven't mentioned how amazing I think your breasts looked in the pictures."

She gasped audibly. "I thought no such thing! Besides, they are not amazing, just normal boobs. They are probably not as spectacular as your wife's, and you shouldn't even be looking."

Dave enjoyed their conversation and Susan's embarrassment so much he didn't want to admit that he had looked at the series of pictures and was so shocked he hadn't noticed Susan's breasts. Even though she was admonishing him, he could tell by the lilt in her voice that she was barely hiding her joy, which was a good thing. Dave knew if he could keep her smiling, she was less likely to climb back out on the ledge. "Well," he said slowly. "I've only seen yours, whereas I've held Lynne's, but make no mistake, Susan, yours are awesome. So what night shall we go back to Romero's? Are you free tomorrow evening? I thought we could go straight after your appointment with Dr. Bart Chisholm."

"*What,* he wants to see me *straight away*? Oh, my goodness."

"Yep, he is intrigued and agrees that the bacteria may have mutated because of the low-quality antibiotics you received in Africa. He is keen to see you as soon as possible and is clearing a spot for you at five thirty tomorrow night. "I'm going to pick you up from your workplace, take you to see him, then buy you that dinner you won in the bet."

"Dave, I don't think that's such a good idea, do you? Don't get me wrong, I'm delighted, flattered even that such a great guy is into me when my husband can't bear to look at me, but we are both married, albeit I am separated. Let's not forget you have problems at home, and I'm not sure your wife would be happy with you and me going out for dinner. I think she needs you right now just as much if not more, than I do."

Her pragmatism made Dave stop and think. He felt like she had tipped a glass tumbler full of water over him. As always, he realized she was an intelligent and insightful woman, and he knew she was right. Dave had always believed that a married person should never do anything with a member of the opposite sex that they wouldn't do if their partner were with them. "Susan, you're right, but I am not suggesting anything clandestine, and we are not meeting to have sex in a motel. Of course, I will tell her about you and what I am doing as a friend who cares. She knows me well and knows I would never turn my back on someone who needed my help. I also hope she knows I would never be unfaithful to her. If you like, I will invite her to dinner with us so she can meet you?"

"My God, this conversation is like you're telling me off as if I'm a naughty schoolgirl. I wasn't inferring you had an ulterior motive in taking me to dinner. I was trying to be considerate of your wife's situation. I must remind you that one person's perception is another's reality. By that, I mean what someone sees, they believe, even though the truth might be innocent. If we think something is true, it is, even though it might be false. Supposing someone who knew Lynne saw us at Romero's and told her what she saw when you had told her you were working late, what would she think? And if that happened, would she believe you if you assured her it was innocent after the event?"

"Susan, I'm going to tell Lynne about you this afternoon, and I will pick you up from your work tomorrow and take you to see Bart because I hope he can help you. After your appointment, I will suggest Romero's, and you can decide then if it's a yes or a no; it will be your call, no pressure, no hassle. I will see you out in front of the Plaza at four forty-five."

"Okay," she answered quietly. "Dave? Thank you. I honestly can't find the words to thank you enough."

****

Dave made the next phone call to Briony McShane, an attorney he had previously dealt with through his police work. He thought she was the fairest, most truthful, and ethical among all the lawyers he had encountered. Dave outlined what had happened, and he felt her almost climb down the phone line to take on their case for damages. He spoke with her for ten minutes, emailed her the recording, and felt good about himself when he went to find Lynne. It wasn't so much about profiteering from Lynne's rape, he told himself; it was about making the Flanderses pay where it hurt them the most; their wallets.

He wondered how Lynne would react when he told her about Susan, as Dave realized he must. Would she be jealous, and if she was, would that be a bad thing with what she had been doing with Marlon Flanders? He knew he had to tell Lynne about Susan's plight; not doing so would be unthinkable and fly in the face of his angst with Lynne not telling her about her problems with Marlon immediately. He could not and would not be hypocritical.

He found her in the kitchen making coffee and

sandwiches. When he entered, she looked up and smiled faintly, a mere shadow of her former smiles. "Mom is fine with looking after the kids, and boy, you should have heard her cuss Marlon when I explained what had happened. Dave, she told me off in no uncertain terms, too, and talking to her helped make me understand even more about how stupid I was not to come to you first. Can you ever forgive me for what I now see as my blinding idiocy?"

"Lynne, I'm not going to lie to you. I can't wipe out my mental images with you being with him. Yes, I know what your motives were, but still, you had sex with him, and the memory of the photos will live with me for a very long time. I forgive you, yes, but…" He took a deep breath. "It's going to take time for me, and you're going to have to be patient if I lose my shit at times and get angry. I don't mean to, but I am so mad that our life, our marriage, has suffered because of a man who has the morals of an alley cat, and you didn't trust me enough to ask for my help."

He saw tears form in the corner of her eyes at his words, and his heart melted. He never usually used the F word with Lynne, and since they had been together, he had never once been so angry with her that he felt the need to swear. He crossed to her and hugged her to him. "I'm sorry," he whispered. "Don't worry, in the front part of my brain, I understand what and why you did what you did. Just now and again, the back part takes over. I love you, Lynne." She clung to him, and he felt her body tremble. "We will get through this, babe, I promise you. I'm not about to leave you; I'm with you completely."

"I don't deserve you," she said quietly.

"Well, you've got me. Now let's go eat; I've got to tell you some things."

****

"One million dollars?" Lynne exclaimed loudly when Dave told her the figure Briony had mentioned as they sat at their outdoor setting eating the Pastrami on Rye sandwiches she had made.

He nodded and watched her. He was pleased to see a look he deciphered as rage and revenge rather than greed cross her face. "She didn't say that's what you would get, hon, and anyway, there are her fees to consider, which she said she'd be pleased to take on contingency so that they would come out of the settlement, but Briony says that's the amount she would seek as a minimum, but she would ask for three million. I sent her your recording, and she will call back later to let us know how to handle Mrs. Flanders tonight at dinner after she listens to it. She says there is also an *'alienation of affection'* suit she can bring that effectively means that his actions affected our marriage detrimentally. She also says any corporation these days has morality clauses, so she will sue Flanders personally and Bond Corp as Flanders and your employer for not enforcing their processes."

Lynne shook her head, seemingly confused though still with a determined glint in her eyes. "Part of me just wants to forget this whole mess and spend the next twenty years making things up to you. But another part makes me so angry, Dave, because he used me and played on my naivety, and that part wants to make him suffer. He had no right to do that to me. Does that make me a bad person and a stupid one?"

He smiled. "No, it makes you human, I think. Now,

there is something else I want to talk to you about or, to be more exact, someone. The woman I went to see last night who made me late home from work, her name is Susan Bodinsky, and I want to share her story with you, because while we think our problems are bad, once I tell you her sad tale you will realize our lives are a picnic. More to the point, I want to help her, and I don't want there to be any secrets about that."

Dave slowly explained Susan's troubles. He watched Lynne closely, trying to gauge how much to give away about his feelings over and above his pity and compassion. When he finished, Lynne sat with her mouth open, almost dazed or shell-shocked that one person should suffer so much.

"Dave, you have to help her; how can you not? Thank goodness you know Bart, and he can offer his expertise. Do you think he can save her?"

Dave sighed. As much as he wanted Bart to cure Susan, he wasn't sure anyone could, but that wasn't the point. For him, it was all about trying. Dave knew if he did everything possible and it wasn't enough, he could live with that. But to not offer everything within his power would be an anathema. Dave could no more *not* assist Susan than fly to the moon, and he was delighted Lynne agreed. "I'm not sure, but I feel that whatever it takes, I have to try, and I'm so pleased you agree. She is a remarkable woman, suffering more than any human being should. It would be wonderful if Bart could halt the spread and even better if he could reverse it, though I'm not sure that's even possible."

"Have you considered how it will affect you if your friend cannot cure her and she finishes the job she started last night?"

Dave was shocked Lynne could ask such a question in the cold-blooded way she had. He hadn't thought that far ahead. Dave realized that could be because of his feelings toward Susan and his unwillingness to think negatively. Lynne had no emotional attachment, so for her, it was easy to consider the worst-case scenario, but for Dave, that thought was too horrible to contemplate. "I don't know, Lynne, and I prefer not to think that way. I could live with that if I knew I'd done all I could, and it was to no avail. I think the problem would come if Susan killed herself and I had not done all I could. That would be a burden I wouldn't want to contemplate."

Lynne reached across the table and squeezed his hand. "You like her, don't you?"

He shrugged, unsure how to answer. Of course, he wanted to say yes, that she was terrific and, somehow, had bewitched him, but he knew that would not be the wisest choice. On the other hand, he couldn't lie either; Lynne was too smart and would see through it immediately, so he had no choice but to tell her most of the truth. "Yes, Lynne, I do. I admire her; she is a very beautiful woman, though not at all stuck-up, and is extraordinarily humble. Sure, I know trying to kill herself isn't a trait that commands respect, but she fought to survive, and then her husband decided it was too hard for him. For him, can you believe that? So much for 'better or for worse,' anyway, that was what tipped her over the edge. When we were out on the ledge, for some reason, I was so upset with you that I told her about our troubles, my fears, divorcing you, and what it would mean for our children and me. Lynne, Susan was fantastic. She not only cared but became a sounding board for me and listened. She genuinely cared about our problems and gave me some good insights into what might have gone wrong with us from a woman's perspective. That helped me try to be more understanding if that makes sense. It was like she cared so much for our marriage woes it helped her forget her troubles."

"Wow," Lynne said incredulously. "All this was on a ledge forty stories up? Is this what you do, Dave, put yourself at risk to save someone else every time?"

He shook his head and turned away to hide his embarrassment. "No, I do not usually put myself at risk, and the rules forbid me to do that. Why did I this time? Well, I guess, looking back, I didn't think about it consciously, but I felt I didn't have much to live for myself. So far as I was concerned, my wife was having an affair with her boss and was probably about to leave me if I didn't leave her first. I would lose my children and the woman I loved with all my heart, so what did it matter if I went out on a limb to save someone else? Lynne, Susan is a beautiful woman going through hell who wanted to watch one last sunset and then die. I had little to lose and went out to try to talk her down. Somehow, revealing my problems took her mind off her own. We made a pact together after I got her back inside the building and took her for dinner. We agreed that if she stayed off the ledge for one week, I would speak to her daily about what happened between us, and I would try to get Bart to help her skin condition. I phoned her and gave her a report while you were asleep."

"You took her out for dinner last night?"

Dave noted the change in her tone of voice and, for a moment, regretted telling her, but then he thought, *I haven't done anything wrong.* "Yes, Lynne, I took Susan out for dinner to talk away from a heap of cops standing around listening through the open window. I didn't take her to a motel for sex." He stared at her pointedly and watched her gasp and lower her head. "Lynne, you have to understand that our marriage was over so far as I was concerned. That doesn't mean I took her to dinner to seduce her. I did it for two reasons: first, and most importantly, to save her life. Secondly, to try to save our marriage because she offered to help, and let me tell you, she did. So here I am telling you about it, being honest, which is what you should have done a month ago."

The moment the words left his mouth, he regretted them as he watched Lynne react as if he had slapped her. "I'm sorry, I didn't mean that to sound the way it did." He shrugged. "I did warn you sometimes I might forget my self-control and say something stupid. Consider this as one of those times."

Her eyes brimmed with tears. "I get it, Dave. I should have told you, and I will regret that I didn't for the rest of my life. Did you kiss her?"

"No."

"Did you want to?"

How could he answer that? Lynne's red, swollen eyes were boring into his, her pain and fear obvious. "I hugged her. We didn't kiss. I thought she needed to know someone cared, so part of the agreement for her not killing herself was that I hugged her. And, if I'm honest, I needed one too. But listen, Lynne, it's not like you think it was. My God, her husband left her. She has a disease that's devouring her skin, and you're acting as if we hopped into bed. I like and admire her, and I think she is amazing in that she genuinely cares about you and me staying together. If she'd have me, I'd like to be a friend to her, but that is all. I have a wife already, and I want to stay married to her."

Lynne blinked rapidly. "I'm so sorry. God help me for being a hypocrite. I realize now how you must have felt when you thought about me with Marlon. Are you taking her out to dinner again?"

Dave nodded. "Yes, Lynne, I am. Tomorrow, after her appointment with Bart. But I am happy for you to come too. I think you'd like her, and I'm sure she'd like you. Susan made me promise to listen to you and not just run out and find a divorce lawyer. So she isn't about starting a relationship with me; far from it. She's a friend who cares more about keeping you and me together than breaking us up. I'd like you to come and meet her, so long as you can handle someone near suicidal because of a disease that's ravaging her body. I believe she could also use a female friend, but it's your call. But, please, only come because you want to, not because you think there's something between us that you need to stop."

****

Dorothy Flanders and a tall, grey-haired man stood up to greet them as the restaurant hostess led Dave and Lynne to the table. The four shook hands as Mrs. Flanders made the introductions. "This is our senior attorney, Arthur Winner; thank you for coming to meet with us. May I call you David and Lynne, or would you prefer more formality?"

They had agreed Dave would do most of the talking in the car because Lynne was worried she might lose her temper. "First names are fine, Dorothy. I didn't know you would bring a lawyer with you." He took out a voice-activated recorder, switched it on, and placed it on the table. "You must have felt the need to protect yourself, so maybe we need to do the same. I hope you don't mind us recording our conversation?"

She smiled and took out a recorder from her purse. "Not if you don't mind if we have our copy too?"

Dave shrugged, and she turned it on. Silence ensued as no one seemed willing to speak first. Suddenly, they all laughed, starting with Dave because of the ridiculousness of the situation. Eventually, Dave opened his other hand and handed her a small thumb drive. "You brought a laptop with you, Mr. Winner, I see. Feel free to listen now. Lynne recorded several conversations in her attempt to get him to confess the embezzlement charge was trumped up, so the recording is quite long, even though I have edited out the sounds of them having sex. That is a copy you can keep. You will hear your husband, Dorothy, admitting during their final meeting that he fabricated evidence so he could have sex with my wife after she had earlier refused to go to Chicago for a supposed three-day conference. Your husband admits he was in love with Lynne and believed they were destined to be together. He believed once he threatened her with the police for the fictitious embezzlement and she agreed to go along with his demands, then she wouldn't want to stop. While he says he knew she loved him as much as he loved her, Lynne repeatedly tried to get him to admit what he'd done. When he did, Lynne slapped him and told him it was over and that she was going to tell me everything. That's when he forced himself on her and raped her."

Mrs. Flanders beckoned for the waitress. "Arthur will leave us to listen to your recording. I don't want to hear it myself, and I don't believe I need to. The last thing I want is to hear my husband not only betray me but force himself on you, Lynne. I have evicted Marlon from my home and business for having an affair in the first place, thanks to the pictures you sent me, Dave, so I have no reason to disbelieve your explanation. Now, I have had time to think things through; regretfully, I believe Marlon was capable of such despicable behavior. Naturally, I couldn't foresee what he would do once we put him in the management position we did. The question is, what do you want to do about it?" The waitress arrived before he could reply. "What would you like to drink? I'm having wine."

"Just a light beer for me, thank you. I'm driving." Dave turned to the waitress who had appeared over Lynne's shoulder. "And a dry Martini for my wife, thank you, with an extra olive." He watched her walk away as the lawyer picked up the device and stood to leave.

Arthur won't stay for dinner, so Dave, your fears were groundless. He came only to get the recording so he could go and assess just how bad things were. I don't need him here to listen to your demands or devise a solution. Strategic planning is what I do best, don't I, Arthur?"

He smiled and nodded. "You are your father's daughter, and that's a fact. Mr. and Mrs. Margolis, I hope to meet you again. Please don't worry; there was no intent to ambush you or play down the dreadful things that have occurred. We have conducted inquiries in the office this afternoon and have some insights into what happened. You can trust us to take care of things. Good evening."

"Before you go, Mr. Winner, may I have your business card? I'm guessing you'd like our attorney to contact you directly rather than go through Dorothy?"

Comically, he froze in place. "What for?" he asked, and Dave could tell by the tone of his voice he knew what was coming."

"To serve papers. My wife was a hardworking, diligent employee whom her predatory senior manager singled out. First, he continually tried to seduce her after giving her a promotion to be his assistant. Next, he fabricated evidence to blackmail her into having a sexual relationship and finally raped her when she ended things after he admitted it had all been lies to get her into bed. Proof of which is on that thumb drive. As the CEO of an enormous corporation with high moral and ethical standards, we will be suing and have engaged an attorney keen to take the case. No employee should be subjected to that kind of behavior. Writs are being drawn up now as we speak. Giving you a copy of the recording is a goodwill gesture to open lines of communication, as we have nothing to hide, and Lynne has done nothing to be ashamed of. I might also tell you our lawyer didn't want us to do this until pre-trial discovery."

The lawyer sat back down again, removed his spectacles, and cleaned them on his napkin. "That may not be in your best interests. A long-drawn-out trial where your actions and motivations will be aired in public would be lapped up by the press, Mrs. Margolis."

"My actions?" Lynne almost shouted, and Dave reached out and placed a calming hand on her arm.

"It's okay, Lynne; I'm sure Mr. Winner didn't mean to make that sound like a threat. But, Mrs. Flanders, sorry, Dorothy, did you honestly think we would slink away and do nothing? Your husband, Lynne's boss, behaved despicably, almost ruined our marriage, and could have left long-standing psychological effects on

Lynne's ability to work and trust an employer ever again. Lynne isn't sleeping well because of the nightmares. She has been raped and fired from her job as if she is the one to blame, and you think a pleasant dinner in a nice restaurant will buy us off? You cannot possibly think we are that naive. Regardless of what action we take against you as the employer of Marlon Flanders, we will be bringing a suit against him for *Alienation of Affection* and *Sexual Harassment.* He tried to ruin our marriage for his gratification."

Before the lawyer could speak, Mrs. Flanders held up a placating hand. "Arthur, do not say another word. Please leave us to speak as two wronged spouses, not piranhas circling a wounded animal. David is correct. Lynne, may I call you by your first name?" Lynne nodded, and she continued. "Lynne, you've been treated abysmally, and while we as a corporation have already taken steps to remove the aggressor, the magnitude of what you have been subjected to will not be taken lightly or lost in legal speak because everyone is frightened of litigation. Arthur, please go back to the office and transcribe the recording. You can email me a copy; I will read it at home later. For now, I will accept everything Dave and Lynne say is factual because I cannot see why they would lie."

Once again, the lawyer stood, cleared his throat, and held a hand toward Dave. "I apologize to you both. I meant no disrespect but was merely trying to point out how a long-drawn-out court case in the public eye would not do anyone any good. Please accept my apology. I will leave you to your dinner." Dave stood and shook, but Lynne ignored him, pretending to study the menu instead.

The drinks arrived, and Mrs. Flanders suggested they order. "The lemon sole is divine here," she mentioned, but Dave smiled when Lynne screwed up her face, seafood not being her favorite. They ordered entrées and mains, deciding to wait to order desserts if they had room later.

Dorothy Flanders leaned back in her seat, crossed her arms across her breasts to sip from her wine glass, and observed her dinner companions. "Lynne, I understand how you feel. Let's not forget the man who treated you so appallingly was my husband, so I am equally devastated. Call me stupid, but I loved him and thought he loved me, so it was a shock when I opened Dave's email. Marlon comes from a wealthy Canadian family, so I doubt he was only after my money. There is a prenup in place, which means he gets only a quarter of a million because of the adultery clause. If you are serious about going after him for *Alienation of Affection,* I can only caution you that Marlon may not take that lying down. Especially now he has lost whatever prestige and position he had by being with me and running one of my companies. Marlon is no pauper; he has his own resources and comes from an old money family. Even without his job as CEO, he has sufficient funds to drag this case out for years."

"Dorothy, why do you think he did it if he stood to lose so much?" Dave asked, ignoring her implied threat. Being a policeman, he had endured hundreds of those over the years.

"I'm not sure, but I do have an idea," she responded and turned to Lynne. "He does have his own means, though mostly in Canada, and now he can't access our corporate assistance, so he is on his own until the divorce settlement. Did he say anything that might explain why he pursued you, Lynne? Please understand I'm not blaming you; you are beautiful. I just wondered if he gave any reason why you were his target."

Deep in thought, Lynne sipped from her martini glass, then shook her head as she blushed. "Looking back, I think it must have been infatuation with me. He was debonair; he complimented me a lot, but in the early stages, it didn't seem sexual, if that makes sense. After seeing the family photos on my desk, he seemed genuinely interested in me and my children. He listened to my day-to-day woes about Ben and Molly as if they were the most wonderful things in the world. He made me feel like a twenty-year-old again, and I found that very good for my ego. He flirted, yes, but only respectfully rather than sexually. He was never crude, and I'm sorry, Dave, I reacted the way I did, possibly sending him the wrong message. I felt flattered and gave it right back, but only in an innocent way because I am a happily married woman with two small children. He often offered to take the children and me out at the zoo or Central Park for a picnic if Dave were working on a Sunday as if that would be the most normal thing two friends would do."

Dave smiled. "It's fine, hon. You're a natural-born flirt and always have been. I know it never means anything and is just who you are."

Lynne grinned back and reached for his hand to squeeze. "Mrs. Flanders, looking back now, I can see that he was slowly trying to orchestrate situations to get me to be alone with him, but he was so subtle and skilled that he completely fooled me. He always talked about Ben and Molly and how I was their perfect mother, yet still sexy and beautiful. He insisted that I attend the trip to Chicago as his assistant and that he would show me all the best places while there. I declined after I told Dave, and he became upset with me. I began to suspect your husband had ulterior motives when he changed how he spoke to me after my refusal. We have two small children, and Dave is a policeman, so for me to take off for a three-day weekend would have been a huge imposition when, after all, I was only his assistant, and I didn't believe he needed me there for business reasons. Marlon changed then. He became distant, even angry with me, and continually found fault in my work when there was nothing wrong to find."

"Please, call me Dorothy. Would you say Marlon acted like a sulking schoolboy who didn't get his own way?"

"Yes, exactly. But I'm a nobody compared to you. You're stunningly beautiful and rich, and you move in all the right circles while I'm a housewife with two kids and thankfully, a husband who loves me. My family is my life, and while my career is important to me, it's nowhere near as important as Dave and my children."

"Yes, I see. I guess your morality could have been the attraction for him." Dorothy responded, then opened her purse and took a tissue from it. She dabbed her eyes, and Dave saw she was unsuccessfully trying to hold back tears. "God, I'm a fool. I blame myself. I loved Marlon, and I still do, even after this mess. I know from his previous relationships he had a reputation for being a control freak. He wanted children, and I didn't, although let me clarify. I did, but when the time I considered was right. I wasn't ready to stop working to have kids, and because of our business strategy plans, Dad insisted I wait. He has big acquisitions for our expansion and needs me by his side for the next two years. My father put a stop to any thoughts of having a family. He never liked Marlon and told me he wouldn't trust him as far as he could spit him into a hurricane. But I now wonder if he and I didn't put too much pressure on Marlon. Maybe things could have been different if I'd agreed to bear Marlon's children when he wanted to because I can see now that he so desperately wanted to be a father. Nothing Marlon did was good enough for my dad, and I now think he set Marlon up for failure. To be fair, with the business side of things, Marlon did well, I thought, but Dad pushed and pushed, and I probably didn't help enough and give Marlon the support I should have as his wife. Marlon wanted a family because his childhood was miserable. His wealthy parents traveled a lot and hired nannies to care for him, and I suppose I snatched that dream away from him by being too wrapped up in business. In our early days, we used to make love a lot, but over the last few months, maybe I became a bit of an ice queen, and my father's incessant niggling got the better of me. Marlon never let a week pass when he didn't talk about us having children, and he believed that he would make the perfect father. He even offered to be a stay-at-home dad while I still went to work. I'm so sorry, Lynne, but I think I pushed him away, and for some reason that only he could explain, Marlon fixated on your being the perfect wife and mother he didn't have in me. I see that now, so possibly he felt that if he could win you and get you away from Dave, he could claim the two children you already have, plus have more with you. I can tell you from personal history that when he pursues something he wants, Marlon is single-minded. I fear chasing and trying to ruin him as retaliation in a legal battle may not end well."

"You do know he threatened Lynne with legal action over her exposing him for the sexual harassment and the bogus claim of embezzlement?" Dave asked quietly as he took a sip from his glass. "The senior officer from the sexual assault squad has advised him that move would not be in his best interest in a civil suit because the recording can be used as evidence. Supposedly, he agreed to back off, but for all I know, he still might. He seems to be furious at Lynne's reaction and subsequent rape allegation, plus, of course, he's also lost his wife and job as CEO."

Before Dorothy could reply, the entrees arrived. Oysters for Dave and Dorothy, though his were cooked, and pâté served with grilled sourdough bread for Lynne.

When they were alone again, Dorothy squeezed lemon over her shellfish and popped one in her mouth before leaning back in her chair. "You don't need to concern yourself too much about any of that because I think that was bullying, bluff, and bluster. Marlon is far from destitute, thanks to his family wealth, as I said, but he can't use our company attorneys because they work for my father and me, and again, he is no longer employed by us. We've had an initial audit performed, and there is no money missing that we can discover, which supposedly he attributed to you, Lynne. However, it does appear Marlon has been using company funds for his selfish pursuits, such as motel bookings. Trust me on this: the courts are the last place Marlon would want to face the mess he has created, which is why I also believe his threat of a wrongful dismissal case is a bluff."

She shrugged, and a silk strap fell from her shoulder,

momentarily exposing the merest hint of a pale lilac bra strap. She used her thumb to replace it. "Marlon is by no means dumb; quite the opposite, so he will be hoping for an out-of-court settlement to make him cease. Sadly, he doesn't know my father or me very well if he thinks we will cave into that kind of pressure. Marlon is single-minded, driven, highly intelligent, and vindictive, so he should be treated cautiously. I instantly dismissed him when I received the photos you sent me, Dave, and I told him not to come home. He knows I will divorce him, and I have sent his clothes and things to one of our corporate apartments where he can stay for one month or until he makes other arrangements."

She stopped to eat, holding a hand up to signify she hadn't finished what she intended to say but didn't want to leave her oysters any longer. Eventually, Dorothy sat back and began again. "Marlon begged and pleaded. He lied to me and blamed you, Lynne, before I threw the photos you sent me at his face. Then he cried and begged forgiveness, which, at the time, I told him I needed to think about whether we had a future together. However, I could not forgive him when I discovered it was an affair with a staff member because he had brought the company into disrepute. Then there are the other things you've since told me he did, and I cannot possibly condone blackmail and rape. Our initial investigation showed that your claims were likely true, as far as we could ascertain in our limited time. Now you've handed over a recording there is no possible way I will ever speak with him again, let alone forgive him."

Dorothy took a breath, raised her wine glass to her lips, and took a long drink. "I'd like to know, Lynne, where do we go from here, and how can I help you? Of course, I don't want this to get played out in the court of public opinion because I'd be humiliated. Plus, and I'm being sincere here, we would probably lose the case anyway, so dragging it out seems pointless, though I'm sure the lawyers and insurance company will want it to be years before it gets to court so their fees mount into the stratosphere. I do want to help you if I can. I'm a realist, and I can see you have a case that will cost us. We have insurance for such events, so it won't affect our bottom line terribly. But I don't think you are the kind of person taking this action for money alone. I believe you have more character and scruples than that. So again, please tell me what I can do to help you both *and* make this go away?"

She reached for her recorder and theatrically turned it off before dropping it back in her purse, then ate the last oyster on her plate while looking from Dave to Lynne. "This is off the record so far as I'm concerned; please speak freely."

"I'd like to work in an environment where I don't have to worry about a predator manager trying to screw me and ruin my life," Lynne said, with an angry tone of voice. Dave noticed her entree had barely been touched, proving her emotional state as he knew she loved pâté usually.

Dorothy nodded. "That's understandable, and I can help you there. I've read your personnel file, and not only do I know you are an excellent employee who worked hard and diligently, but I think you are capable of so much more than just being a personal assistant to the manager. I've asked around among your work colleagues, and they all speak very highly of you. What if I appointed you to replace Marlon as General Manager to be CEO in twelve months if you prove you're capable?"

Lynne dropped her knife, which clattered on the plate before pinwheeling off the table to land on the floor. In an instant, a waiter arrived to pick it up.

"Let me get you a fresh one, ma'am," he said before twirling away, his apron sending a puff of breeze over her. Within one minute, he returned and placed a replacement on the table by her hand.

"Thank you," Lynne murmured.

Dave considered Dorothy's offer and busied himself with his meal, which he had to admit was fantastic. The oysters had been cooked in a light tempura batter and served with Asian sauces, which complemented them superbly. However, his mind was in turmoil. *She can't be serious, can she? Is this some sort of plan to shut us up, offer Lynne a choice job, then fire her three months down the track, so we go away quietly having signed a non-disclosure agreement?*

"I know you're both thinking this is a trick to get rid of you. I understand why you would think that, but you should know I never make snap decisions or try to con people I want to employ. I have discussed this with my father by phone this afternoon, and he agrees with my judgment and assessment of you. I have an offer for you to consider, which is in writing. Would you like to read it or have me summarize it?"

"Please," Lynne said, pushing her plate away from her, seemingly not hungry. "Summarize for us. I don't know what to say because you've surprised me."

"All right." Dorothy tented her fingers. "Before I tell you, I'd like you to understand that I do not consider this to be buying your silence if that makes sense."

"How would you describe it then?" Dave asked.

"Being fair and acknowledging that your wife has suffered, Dave. Also, I'm trying to develop a plan that proves our sincerity in trying to make amends, not trick you into silence." She glanced at him, then turned her attention back to Lynne. "Okay, I think the contract terms will convince you that I mean what I say. There are three facets to our offer. One is a twelve-month contract as General Manager at one hundred and fifty thousand dollars per annum, with quarterly reviews for performance bonuses. You cannot be fired for any reason other than proof of illegality or immorality until the year ends. Hence, the reviews are for salary and bonus assessment only. If you do not perform and we choose to terminate your employment, we agree to pay you for the full year, no matter how long you have served, plus a one hundred-thousand-dollar severance payout. Full medical insurance is included for you and your children. You will not work weekends, so there will be no adverse effect on your family life. Similarly, there will be no traveling out of State for the first year of service. How does that sound so far?"

Dave glanced at Lynne, who sat open-mouthed.

Dorothy continued, "Second, I will take you under my wing and train you in the skills you need to be an effective manager. If you choose to take classes in business management, the company will pay your tuition fees, but you don't have to do that. I believe you have the necessary determination and grit so that I can help you to be the best manager you can be. I think that will be a vast improvement to the man you are replacing. Next, your children. I want to set up an endowment to provide for their college education to the value at maturity of two hundred and fifty thousand dollars each. We will also make a lump sum payment to you immediately and take care of its tax implications. Lynne, call it a bonus, if you will, for services rendered and acknowledgment of the trauma you've experienced of one hundred thousand dollars. Finally, I think you both need quality time together as a family before starting your new career. My father owns a fully staffed home in Barbados, so, Dave, if you can swing some time off from work, you can use our private jet and the house for two weeks, any time you want."

Dave felt overwhelmed, and glancing at Lynne again, told him she was also experiencing disbelief. He suddenly thought of a way of testing Dorothy Flanders. "No doubt, Dorothy, you will require Lynne to sign a confidentiality agreement?"

She smiled, took a long sip from her wine glass, and slowly licked her lips. "Dave, you misjudge me, not that I blame you; you don't know anything about me. If you ask anyone I deal with in business, they will tell you I can be ruthless but always fair. The answer to your question is no; non-disclosure is not part of this. I sincerely want to make compensation and offer you a new career, Lynne. I trust you to follow your heart and do whatever you think is the best outcome for you. If it's to litigate, so be it; I'd still like to give you a chance to come and work with me. Naturally, I prefer not to drag this through the court, but it's your call. Let's eat and enjoy the food. I know you have much to consider; we can talk more later."

Chapter 4

Obsession

"When I saw you I fell in love and you smiled because you knew."
William Shakespeare

Dave and Lynne were quiet on their way to pick up their children after the dinner with Dorothy Flanders, both deep in thought. For Dave, he wondered if there was some sort of trick that he couldn't see, like a magician with a pack of cards. He knew without asking that Lynne's thoughts were disbelief and that she could be worthy of such a career in upper management. Yes, she was usually self-assured and a good decision-maker, but that was generally when she was in her own environment. Otherwise, she held back until she found her feet. As the street lighting intermittently swept through the windshield from above, it dawned on Dave that Lynne could be a strong enough person to run a business so long as she had time to settle in and learn the ropes. She had fantastic people skills, and her actions in trying to get proof of her innocence showed a ruthless dedication regardless of the consequences. He believed Dorothy had seen a side of Lynne that was latent, maybe, but nonetheless there.

They still hadn't spoken other than to thank Lynne's

mother and father for babysitting when they approached their home. The children were asleep, strapped into their seats, and aside from being lost in their individual thoughts, Dave knew neither wanted to wake Ben and Molly.

Dave's sixth sense that something was wrong, a feeling that had saved him more than once, emerged from the depths of his subconscious as soon as he turned his car into their street. When he reached the driveway, he was on high alert, and beads of sweat broke out on his forehead, though he did not know why. He slowly and deliberately drove past their home and pulled up in front of his neighbor's house. Dave had noticed something peripherally while deep in thought, and he wracked his mind to work out what it was, but nothing came.

"What's wrong, Dave?" Lynne asked with a worried tone.

He switched off the lights but left the motor running. "I don't know, maybe nothing. Get in the driver's seat while I check out the house. I have a bad feeling. Have your cell phone ready to call emergency if I don't come out in three minutes. Tell them an officer needs assistance because an armed intruder is on the premises. And Lynne, be ready to drive off if there is any sign of trouble. I want you and the kids safe."

Dave didn't give her any time to argue as he eased out of the door and she slid across into his seat, reaching down to move it forward. "Dave," she said urgently, and he looked at her before closing the door. "I love you, please, be careful."

At that moment, Dave realized something that eased some of his recent worries about her. She loved him, and because she did, she had done as he asked without question. Dave knew that she trusted him. They were a *team,* as they had always been. Maybe she had lost her way for a while because she felt threatened, but whatever had transpired, she was with him now. Dave felt Lynne had lifted a burden from his shoulders without trying and that their future together was far more important than the past. "I will, hon. I love you, too. Be ready to leave here if things turn nasty because my instincts are on high alert. The most important people in the world to me are you and the kids, and if I'm right, we've had, or still have, a visitor or visitors."

Dave closed the driver's door quietly and sprinted to the majestic oak tree adorning their front garden. He saw the screen door hanging askew from the bottom hinge and realized that he must have subconsciously picked up on that and caused his anxiety. He automatically reached for his hip, where his gun would usually reside in its holster, but it wasn't there. It was in the gun safe bolted to the floor under their bed.

The house seemed quiet, with the only light coming from the porch, which they had left on before leaving for the restaurant. Ready to turn and run at any time, Dave left the cover of the tree and jogged to the house, weaving from side to side in case someone was waiting to shoot him. Although Dave knew they'd had an intruder, he didn't believe he was facing imminent danger, but his instincts screamed at him to be cautious. Dave made it safely to the porch and breathed a silent sigh of relief. He stepped up the three stairs, avoiding the creak the second one always made using the extreme right-hand edge. He pressed his body against the wall at the side of the door, using the wall to shield him from being shot by a gunman inside, as per his police training.

He glanced back to the car that housed Lynne and the children, gave a wave, and then slowly pushed open the damaged fly screen. Dave saw the tongue of the deadlock of the heavy wooden front door had smashed away the striker plate, yanking it out of the frame, and it lay on the floor with two screws protruding from it.

Dave stepped inside, careful not to make any noise, and opened the closet. He fumbled with his right hand while watching for a potential attacker and found the aluminum softball bat he was searching for. Feeling comforted by having a means to protect himself, Dave raised the bat like a Samurai sword and stepped inside the hall, ready to confront the intruder. As his eyes adjusted to the dim interior, Dave sensed he was alone, at least so far at this end of the house. It took four steps, and then Dave entered their living room and stopped. His heart pounded, and rage threatened to engulf him as Dave saw the devastation illuminated by the light from outside coming through what remained of the net curtain across the bay window.

It looked like a hurricane had moved through the room, leaving a trail of mess in its wake. Furniture was upturned; the flat-screen TV lay broken on the floor, and the drinks cabinet was pushed over, causing the broken bottled contents to seep into the carpeted floor. The once comfortable room now smelt like a Friday night brewery during a stag party.

Dave hoped that whoever caused the damage was still in his home because if so, that man would be leaving in an ambulance. Scanning the devastation, Dave noticed the framed family portrait, which hung above the gas fireplace, was not only hanging askew but slashed with a knife. *Marlon Flanders has done this,* Dave thought, sensing that such damage was more personal than a burglary. "You better be armed if you're still here, Flanders," Dave called out, no longer interested in stealth. "If you're not, I hope your medical insurance is current."

One minute later, Dave knew the house was empty. There was a trail of vandalism everywhere but the children's rooms. The main bedroom was the worst, not for the destruction, but because it was their private and personal space—a place where they had made love and conceived their children. Dave felt violated, like he assumed a woman would feel after a rape, which reinforced in Dave's mind that his wife's ex-paramour was seeking revenge. He needed to do an inventory check, but his first impression was that nothing appeared missing, just damaged and the home ransacked.

Lynne's clothes lay forlornly strewn across the queen-sized bed, with her underwear drawer emptied on the pile. Sitting on top was Lynne's vibrator, her most private possession, and it seemed to Dave the person who left it there was making a statement, a disturbed sexual one. There was only one person he could think of who would do that: Marlon Flanders.

Dave lifted the edge of the bedspread and saw the unopened safe, which meant their passports, cash, and jewelry were safe inside, along with his pistol, though he couldn't confirm that for fear of spoiling any fingerprints there might be. He sighed, knowing he had to report the break-in and explain why he suspected Flanders, which meant more embarrassment for them from his colleagues. *When will this nightmare end?*

****

Dave returned to Lynne in the car, and she put the

window down as he approached. "What's wrong?" she asked, glancing between him and their home.

"We've had a break-in, hon. By the looks of the damage and vandalism, I guess it's your ex-boss making a statement. When he said he would come after us, he meant it." She made to open the door and get out, a fiercely angry expression on her face. "No, babe, don't go in. It will only upset you, which is obviously what he intended. It's also a crime scene. I want you to take the kids to your mother's, spend the night there, and come back in the morning. I'll wait for the cops to come and check it out to see if he has left any fingerprints, though I don't guess he would be that stupid. If he has, we can nail him. I also need to make some repairs to our front door and try to tidy up a bit. There is also a chance he may come back."

Dave could tell Lynne wanted to say something, but he spoke first. "I hope Flanders does come back later because I will be waiting for him. I think it is time I had a quiet word with him."

"Oh, Dave, I'm so sorry I've brought this mess into our lives. If only I hadn't been such an idiot. Please promise me that if he does come back, you won't do anything stupid which will mean you get arrested. I couldn't bear it if anything happened to you because of my stupidity."

Dave didn't reply immediately. How could he? Lynne *had* been an idiot. But she was remorseful, so there was no need to beat her up over it continually. Dave acknowledged she could never have imagined the fallout from her actions, but he still harbored anger for her not speaking to him before having sex with the man who had extorted her. Eventually, he whispered, "What's done is done, Lynne. We can't go back in time, and I promise I won't be risking my future freedom by killing him, though, of course, I'm entitled to protect my home and family from an intruder, especially if he is armed."

She gazed into his eyes, and he stared back, unwavering. He knew what she was thinking. She remembered the small .32 automatic pistol he had given her for home protection and that it could end up in Flanders' hand if Dave shot him to make it appear it had been self-defense. He saw her shudder, and then she softly said, "I love you, and I'm going to spend the rest of my life making this up to you. Thank you for believing in me." Lynne turned away, started the engine, and slowly pulled the car away from the curb. Dave watched her disappear at the end of the road, knowing she had given her tacit approval for him to face Flanders and do whatever was necessary to ensure his family's safety.

****

Dave greeted the first responders, two fresh-faced patrolmen, who checked the home out and radioed in their findings after a short talk with Dave when he told them he was a cop. Fifteen minutes later, a detective he knew, Dan Conroy, from the precinct arrived with his partner, Matt Smith, whom Dave had also met before but had never socialized with. Dave stood aside to let them in. "Just follow the trail of destruction," he murmured, then added, "I've checked and can't find anything missing, and I'm pretty sure I know who's done this. When you've looked through the place, I will be on the back porch."

It didn't take long. The two detectives sat at the picnic table opposite Dave only ten minutes later. "Okay," Dan began, "tell us who you think has done this and why. We can see no signs of fingerprints, so it is pointless to get forensics out, especially as nothing appears to have been stolen. You're a detective yourself, so I know you know I could never get permission for a full forensic sweep of a burglary scene where nothing has been stolen. You're primarily a negotiator these days, we know, so do you believe this is because of your work, or is it more personal than that? I gotta say this looks to me to be extremely personal."

"It is personal." Dave agreed as the bug zapper pinged the death of a mosquito. "Two nights ago, my wife was raped by her boss, one Marlon Flanders, after a series of sexual liaisons he had extorted her into having. She reported the attack to the rape squad, who ran all the usual tests. Detectives questioned him, and it was his word against hers, even though there was a recording of him doing it and admitting the extortion. Unfortunately, Lynne made the recording without his knowledge or consent because of the blackmail forcing her into having sex. The public prosecutor said the tape can't be used as evidence, and even if it could, he would claim entrapment and have it thrown out at trial. Flanders said when interviewed that he and Lynne were having an ongoing consensual affair, which I had suspected myself and had hired a PI to get proof." Dave sighed deeply. "I confronted Lynne before she told me of the rape and the blackmail. Tonight, we met with Flanders' wife, the company's owner who employed him. She told us she had kicked him out of the house and fired him from his job earlier today because I sent her proof of the affair I had suspected. While Lynne and I met with her over dinner to discuss and inform her that we have hired a lawyer to sue her company, Flanders came here and did this to take revenge against Lynne."

Both detectives took several minutes to digest Dave's explanation. Neither looked shocked, but he could also sense some disbelief. Eventually, Dan asked if Dave had any proof that it had been Flanders or if it might have been local youths who had discovered Dave was a cop. Had Lynne possibly picked up a stalker, or was there any other reason Dave could see for the break-in?

Dave slowly shook his head. "No, I don't have any proof, and he is intelligent; I'm not surprised he wore gloves and didn't leave obvious DNA traces. We've lived in this house for years, know all the neighbors, and never had any trouble. I also realize there is very little point in you guys talking to Flanders because he will deny it. Even if he doesn't have an alibi, the CPS won't charge him without evidence, and he's far too smart to admit coming here. He would be laughing at us for even trying. I want to get our story on record with you because things could escalate and worsen. His wife told us Flanders is single-minded and is likely not to give up easily now he has set his sights on taking my wife and children from me. I believe he is either obsessed with Lynne and could stop at nothing to be with her, or he is psychotic and wants to punish her for refusing to leave me for him. With losing his career and wife, I guess he has nothing left, which can make him dangerous."

"Start at the beginning and tell us everything. As you know, sometimes obsession cases can end badly."

****

Just after one a.m., the cops left, and Dave went to the safe under the bed and removed his gun and holster. He couldn't imagine a scenario where Flanders was stupid enough to return, but Dave didn't want to take a chance. He clipped the gun to his hip and immediately felt better for doing so. He also removed Lynne's Baretta and tucked it into his pocket, which barely made a bulge, being so small compared to his Glock. He intended to insist that Lynne always carry the small but deadly pistol when Dave wasn't with her because he couldn't protect her twenty-four-seven; after all, he had to work for a living.

Dave decided to tidy the bedroom first and put away his wife's clothes and underwear. Lynne had been through an emotional roller coaster of betrayal and abuse, and Dave didn't want her to see what Flanders had done to their sanctum, especially since he had touched her clothes and undergarments. Dave felt sure that if Lynne saw the room how it was, it would seem as if she had been raped all over again.

As he worked, he thought about his earlier conversation with the detectives and agreed with the futility of questioning Flanders. There wasn't any tangible proof it was him, and yes, it was clear to not only Dave but the cops too the man had a motive in his warped mind. But there was only so much the police could do without evidence.

As a courtesy to Dave, being a fellow cop, the detectives offered to have an *off-the-record* chat with Flanders and warn what would happen if he didn't desist from harassing the Margolis family. Dave appreciated the sentiment but thought that such a move could do more harm than good if Flanders was fixated on Lynne and wanted her and her children, as Dorothy Flanders had suggested. Dave knew an extremely obsessive mentality could be fatally dangerous, as numerous cases had proved. Flanders was enraged by Lynne's rejection. He'd lost his career and wife over the affair and had been questioned about the subsequent rape. Dave saw it could be enough to bring the man to the brink. A further police interview could tip him over the edge and make him do something unthinkable. During his years of being a cop, Dave had seen many examples of mentally unstable people causing violence and even murder to innocent victims. Dave's priority must be the safety of his wife and children, but he wondered what more he could do unless he, too, resorted to violence. To do nothing was unthinkable when his family was threatened, but there was no escaping the fact that inaction could achieve the safest result. If Flanders felt Dave was backing him into a corner…well, Dave knew and believed the old saying that a cornered rat would always attack.

As painful and distasteful as it was, Dave saw that ignoring Flanders could be the safest option. Make the man lose interest and hopefully realize he could not take Lynne and her children away from her husband. Dave would act decisively if doing nothing to antagonize Flanders didn't work, and there were further attempts to disrupt his family. Dave had no fears for his safety when protecting his wife and children. Quite simply, Dave would do anything to make sure they were safe, up to and including shooting Marlon Flanders dead. Dave was not usually violent but had been a marine and seen action in a foreign land. He had killed several times and hadn't lost sleep doing so because he knew, in those circumstances, *it had been the right thing to do.* Protecting his family was not only the right thing to do, but his entire world revolved around them, and he would rather die than run away from his responsibility to shield them from a maniac, which was how he was beginning to view Flanders.

Dave considered tracking Flanders down and confronting him, but the problem with that plan was it wouldn't take too many smart-ass comments from Flanders, and Dave wouldn't be able to keep his temper and hands off the rapist. If Dave were then imprisoned for assault, that would leave Lynne alone and vulnerable, with Flanders being seen by everyone as the victim. At the very least, Dave would lose his job, and he didn't want that. For all he knew, that may be Flanders' intention, to break into their home and provoke Dave into acting so that he would be imprisoned. Dave sighed as he realized the full extent of the mess Lynne had created by not coming to him at the first instant. Events seemed to be spiraling out of his control, and Dave didn't like that.

Chapter 5

Understanding

"The noblest pleasure is the joy of understanding."
Leonardo Da Vinci

"You do not understand even life. How can you understand death?"
Confucius

Friday

Dave made a temporary repair on the damaged striker plate of the front door and hinges of the screen as his last task after he cleaned the worst of the mess up and straightened the fallen furniture. He then went to the back door and called for *Bubbles,* their children's cat, but she didn't appear, which wasn't entirely unusual but made Dave feel uneasy. He waited five minutes, calling, but she didn't come, and he thought that possibly the trauma of the earlier intruder may have scared her off. Dave shrugged, locked the back door, tucked his gun under the pillow, and collapsed into bed. He was asleep within minutes.

He had been careful to take pictures of the damage for the insurance claim he intended to lodge, though money could not replace what he knew had been taken from him by Marlon Flanders. While cleaning up, he occasionally daydreamed of their life before Flanders' intervention. Then, with a start, he remembered Lynne's face as she cried tears of anger and frustration at the memory of what he'd done to her, and Dave trembled with barely controlled rage.

Dave awoke lying on his left side, facing the roller blind-covered window, to the sound of chirping birds in the trees. While stuck between oblivion and complete wakefulness, he was momentarily happy with the world. Then, he realized Lynne wasn't beside him, and the reason she was absent came flooding back, making him feel nauseous.

He groaned as he swung his legs out from under the covers and sat on the edge of the bed. He rubbed his face, feeling the stubble on his cheeks, and wondered what he had done to deserve the last few days' events. Then he stopped feeling sorry for himself as he recalled the photographs of Susan's disease-ravaged back and sighed. *Who the hell am I to complain about the shitty stick life has handed me? Everything that's gone wrong in my orbit is rectifiable. Susan can recover, but maybe she can't and is living on borrowed time. I've got to stop feeling sorry for myself and worry about more important things.*

He crossed the floor to the bathroom while stripping off his boxer shorts. While Lynne usually slept nude, Dave never felt comfortable in bed, not wearing anything unless he and Lynne were making love. Perhaps because Dave was a cop, he knew the accuracy of statistics in New York and suburbs for break-ins and home invasions, and he couldn't imagine facing an armed intruder naked. For some reason, Dave thought the feeling of being so nakedly vulnerable might make him less able to defend his home and family, though he knew if push came to shove, he would willingly die for them.

Dave shaved languidly, brushed his teeth, and took a hot shower. By the time he finished, he felt better about himself and their situation. When he returned to the bedroom, he stopped mid-stride when he saw the blind still down, which darkened the room to a golden glow with the rising sun behind it. Dave smiled as he realized he was acting on autopilot. Usually, while Dave was in the shower, Lynne tidied the bed, opened the curtains, and began breakfast for the family. Of course, she and the kids were at her mother's that day. He quickly dressed in faded jeans and a white T-shirt, a look he knew Lynne liked, pulled the bedclothes into approximate place, then crossed to the window.

Dave slid the roller blind up and froze in place at what he saw. An icy finger of sheer horror slowly ran down his spine. *"Oh no,"* he said out loud in a despairing voice. He was looking at the family cat. Its battered and bleeding body was hanging from the roof of the rear verandah by the neck; a rope, tied in a hangman's noose, held it in place, and it swung gently in the morning breeze.

Hang on, just a freakin minute. Dave thought in a slowly rising tide of panic. *Last night, I sat out the back with the cops, and Bubbles wasn't there. That can only mean...Jesus wept. He came back later; while I was asleep, the bastard came back.*

****

Dave initially thought to take their poor, unfortunate cat down and bury it in a hole in the back garden. He reasoned that Ben and Molly would be less traumatized if he did that, but his police training urged him not to take that step. The murder of the family pet and the display of its body showed an escalation from last night's break-in and, in his mind, proved the perpetrator was deranged. *Is it Flanders?* he asked himself, *or is it someone else with a motive for hurting Lynne or me? Surely, Flanders can't be that obsessed, can he? But if not him, who?*

He sighed and realized he had no choice and went to find his cell phone.

"Dan Conroy," a groggy-sounding voice said, and Dave realized he had worked late last night, so he was entitled to be still asleep.

"Dave Margolis," he said, trying to sound apologetic. "Sorry to wake you, but there's been a development you should know about. He returned sometime after I finished cleaning up and waking up this morning."

"What's happened?"

He doesn't sound so sleepy now, Dave thought. "Our cat. She looks like she's been kicked to death, then left as a present hanging by the neck outside our bedroom window. I guess the intent was that Lynne would see it and be scared enough to run away to be with Marlon Flanders."

Dan paused, and Dave knew what his fellow detective was thinking. Eventually, he said, "Is there any evidence, anything at all, that suggests it was him?"

"Nope, that's the cunning of it; he's smart, sick, mentally deranged, and obsessed but intelligent enough not to leave obvious evidence."

"Don't touch anything, and I'll be there soon; I think it's time to let forensics look around. Oh, you need to report this to your captain. This is getting serious, Dave."

"Yeah, that's an understatement."

****

His next call wasn't to his captain but to Lynne. He had to tell her about the gruesome discovery, no matter how upsetting he knew it would be for her.

"Hi, hon," she answered a little quietly. "We're just having breakfast; then I was calling straight after. Do you want to talk to the kids?"

"Maybe later, babe. There's been a development. Can you go outside so you're not overheard?"

"Okay."

Dave waited patiently, though he felt his anxiety raising a few notches as he worried how Lynne would react.

"I'm outside, what's happened?"

Dave paused. He thought he'd worked out what to say, but now it came to it, he stumbled. "Lynne, umm, oh heck, there's no easy way to say this, Bubbles is dead."

"What? Why, how?"

Dave sighed, knowing this would hurt, but she had to know. "The cops are on their way back now. Last night's break-in seemed as if it *could* be just wanton vandalism. We couldn't find fingerprints, obvious evidence to indicate who broke in, or anything I could see missing. So, it seemed to me, and the attending detectives agree, while it might be a personal attack to send a message to us, it might have easily not been that."

"You believe it was Marlon, though, don't you? I was hoping it might turn out that it wasn't. The thought of him trying to terrorize our family is too scary to contemplate. I've seen him get aggressive with staff and suppliers he thought weren't doing the right thing, and he's a force to be reckoned with. What else has happened, Dave? I can tell you're holding back."

"When I put the roller blind up this morning in our bedroom, after barely two hours of sleep, I found Bubbles. She had been killed and strung up by a hangman's noose." Lynne gave an audible gasp. "The thing is," Dave continued, "I sat on the back deck with the cops making the report, and Bubbles wasn't there then, so…"

"So whoever it was came back after you went to sleep? He could have killed you. Oh my God, what have I done?"

"You haven't *done* anything, Lynne. *If* it's Flanders, and it seems too much of a coincidence not to be him, I don't believe he had any intention of killing me. I think he still wants you back, and he's trying to scare you enough to leave me. Maybe in his warped brain, he believes his actions show you how much he wants you. Sometimes, stalkers genuinely believe their victim does love them. *If* it is him, I must keep saying if because there's no proof whatsoever."

"He must be sick if for one minute he thinks he could scare me into leaving you for him, especially after I accused him of rape. So what do we do?"

That's my Lynne. "*We* don't do anything. I want you and the kids safe, so you stay with your mother. I will pack enough things for you all and drop them off later. *If* it is Flanders, there's no way he can know where they live or where Molly and Ben go to school. Sooner or later, he will realize he can't have you, and then he may try to hurt you. When that happens, I will be waiting for him, alone."

"No, Dave, not going to happen. Ben and Molly can stay with Mom and Dad; I agree with keeping them out of this, but I will be with you. I started this mess, and I will be there when it ends. Don't even think about stopping me from coming home. I will carry that little gun you gave me when you're not there for protection, but I will not give up my house through fear."

Dave smiled. When Lynne made her mind up, she was like an immovable object, a trait he loved about her. Dave knew that her self-determination would be why Lynne had sex with her boss in the first place. She would have been stubbornly sure she could solve their problems alone. It was a reminder she did not have an affair; she allowed herself to be abused to clear her name. "Lynne? I love you. Please stay there because I will worry too much if you come back here."

"My place is with you. I made a stupid mistake, but I'm not making any more. I'm taking the kids to school, and then I'm coming home. I've told Mom and Dad everything, and they offered to help however they could. Ben and Molly will be safe here with them for now. How long they stay with them, we will decide later. We can come and visit, have dinner with them, stay till bedtime, and then go home together. Dave, it's non-negotiable."

****

Dave's next call was to his boss, which he had been dreading. The rules said that if he were a target because of his work as a police officer, the Internal Affairs department would investigate him. Those investigations rarely ended well, and at the very least, Flanders' actions could tarnish Dave's reputation. Dave hoped Lynne's reported accusation of rape and the break-in, and now the mutilation of the family pet could convince his captain, Mark Brennan, that he hadn't been doing anything wrong and that he was a victim.

"Boss," Dave began, "sorry to call you so early, but

I have a situation and need some personal time to deal with it."

"Go on; I assume it has someting to do with your wife's rape allegation? De report crossed my desk last night, as it must when an officer's family member is a victim of crime," he replied in his gruff Bronx accent.

Dave sighed at the knowledge word was spreading through the precinct about his marital woes. "Yeah, her boss blackmailed her into having an affair, and she tried to get a recording of him admitting it. When he did, she ended things, and he forced himself on her, without violence, thank God. There is insufficient evidence to support a charge as the recording is inadmissible, so it was all for nothing. She's been through the wringer, but it hasn't ended there. You should get a second report today because last night, while we were meeting with the guy's wife, who has kicked him out of their home and business, we had a break-in at home. Nothing appears missing, but there was a lot of damage and vandalism to our furniture and belongings."

"You tink it's him?"

Dave sighed loudly. "Yeah, I do. The perp destroyed our wedding photo and messed with Lynne's clothes, including her underwear, making it look personal rather than random vandalism. This morning, I found our pet cat strangled and hanging from the patio roof. It wasn't there last night when Dan Conroy and Matt Smith filled out the report. Someone has it in for us, so what I think, but can't prove, is that Lynne's former boss is obsessed with her and is trying to frighten her enough to make her leave me. If it's not that, then I can assume he wants to punish her, and us, for the rape allegation and loss of his wife and management position with the family-owned business. According to his wife, he was desperate to have children, but she didn't want any because she was too focused on the business, and he thought that meant forever. He showed a lot of interest in Molly and Ben, and of course, Lynne herself."

There was a long pause, and Dave knew his boss was contemplating the ramifications of his situation and whether it warranted an *Internal Affairs* investigation. "Do I need to oida you not to go afta him? I always tought you was smarter than that, and I don't wanna have to take your badge and gun off you," he said.

"Captain, I have no intention of going after the man, but I will protect my wife and family. We're parking Molly and Ben with Lynne's parents, and with your permission, will spend a week together, getting the house back in order. I figure we give Flanders some space and time to either shit or get off the pot. I will be ready if he comes for me, but I won't look for him. I'm hoping he gets bored and gives up, and so long as he leaves Lynne and me alone, I intend to leave him alone."

"All right, you got a week. But Dave? I hear you've gone within a hundred feet of dis guy, and Internal Affairs are gonna chew you a new ass. Are we clear?"

"We're clear, Boss."

"One more ting," he said before Dave could hang up. "Can you think of anyone from your past arrest records who could have done this?"

Dave expelled air suddenly, so his lips vibrated in a sibilant raspberry sound. He seriously had not considered that. Sure, Dave had given it a glancing thought between bouts of obscenely cursing Marlon Flanders, but he hadn't considered it a definite possibility. But then, he realized that was why his captain was a captain. "No one comes to mind who hated me this much. And Jesus, it would be some coincidence, don't you think?"

"Well, *dats* as may be, but I'm gonna have Mallory and Smith look into your previous cases, see if *anyting* sticks its head up."

"Couldn't hurt, Boss. Thanks for taking the initiative."

****

Lynne arrived at the same time as the two returning detectives and introduced herself to them as the forensics vehicle came to a juddering halt on the lawn. A man and woman climbed out, wearing white uniforms and rubber boots. "Mrs. Margolis, this is Chad and Laura. They will check for fingerprints and swab your deceased pet for extraneous DNA samples that hopefully might lead us to find who committed this act of cruelty."

Dave arrived through the repaired front door to join them, and wordlessly, Lynne nodded to Dan Conroy before turning to her husband and hugging him. "Hi, she whispered, I missed you."

"Missed you too," he replied, holding her tightly while the others looked around, embarrassed at their intimacy. Dave knew this was because they all knew of her history with Marlon Flanders, and with a sinking feeling, realized people's nervousness around them would continue for some time. "I don't want you to see Bubbles like this," he said gruffly, angry at Lynne and himself for letting their awkwardness affect him, then turned to the others. "Dan, feel free to take the others through the house to see the body; we will wait in the kitchen. You know the way."

****

"What do you think?" Dave asked the two cops as Lynne made coffee. After taking their samples, the forensic officers had left, no doubt, to go to the next job.

"No rest for the wicked," Chad exclaimed glumly as he and his partner loaded their cases into the van.

"This is one sick son of a bitch, that's what I think," Matt Smith said.

"Thanks for that," Dave said, trying his best not to laugh or scream; he couldn't decide.

"Forgive *Captain Obvious;* he's not known for his tact," Dan said, "though he does have a point." He paused, then shrugged. "You wanna know what I think? I think forensics will turn up Jack because this perp is sick, but sick like a fox. Yeah, I think it's the guy who forced himself on you, Mrs. Margolis, but can we prove it? No way. We have to wait at least a week to get the DNA result because, well, sorry, but that's how it works. It will be deemed a low priority. But even if we get a half-decent sample, it means squat if he isn't in the system already, which he isn't likely to be by the sounds of things. So, what do I do? I got no evidence. He's an obvious suspect, but I'm worried that if I push him too hard without due cause, he might make things worse."

"Worse?" Lynne screamed suddenly, making everyone jump. *"You think things can get worse?"*

"Yes, Mrs. Margolis, I think your situation could get a lot worse; it could escalate, which it does sometimes with obsessed stalkers," he replied to her retreating body as she ran crying to the bedroom. "You know what I mean, don't you, Dave?" He nodded and hurried to the bedroom.

"Are you okay, Lynne?" Dave asked quietly.

She was perched, sitting on the edge of their bed,

wringing her hands, and Dave breathed a sigh of relief when he noticed Lynne wasn't crying because she was upset; it was more like she seemed furious.

"Oh, yeah, I'm fine, Dave. I'm just angry. I'm mad at him for targeting me and at the system that will let him get away with it, but mostly mad at myself for letting it happen. On top of all that," she nodded toward the kitchen, "he says it could get worse. God, I'm just so dumb; look at the havoc I've caused to our life and family. I don't deserve you, Dave; I just don't; you'd be far better off without me."

"Wait here one second, okay?" Without waiting for an answer, Dave went to his study, grabbed his laptop, and entered his password as he walked back and sat beside Lynne. "When I woke up alone this morning, I felt depressed at what's happened to me. I thought of it as life handing me a shitty stick. I want to show you something."

Holding the base of the computer on the flat of his hand, he turned it so Lynne could see the screen. She gasped and then recoiled. "That's Susan Bodinsky's back," he said quietly. "She has a terminal bacterial disease eating her skin, and I think I've got problems? Kinda puts things into perspective, don't you think?"

She nodded as she rocked back and forth. "I want to kill him, Dave."

"I know, so do I, but then there's this old saying I read somewhere that goes something like if you're going to seek revenge, better dig two graves. Our strength is our marriage and love for each other. He can't take that from us unless we let him."

Lynne turned her head to stare at him. "What did I ever do to deserve you? Someone up there must *really* like me to have sent me you." She grabbed his hands in hers. "I *promise* with all I hold dear; I will never betray your love again."

Dave gazed into Lynne's eyes and saw her sincerity. He wanted to believe her, but deep down, in a place he didn't want to visit, for the first time in his marriage, he didn't think she would, or possibly could, keep her word.

Chapter 6

Compassion

"You have not lived today until you have done something
for someone who can never repay you."
John Bunyan

Susan Bodinsky tried to work on the manuscript by a new writer she'd been hired to edit but failed. Her mind alternated between getting distractedly lost in the story on her computer screen rather than editing and worrying about what would happen when she met Dave's specialist friend later that evening. She found the plotline of the book interesting enough. Still, it was almost *too interesting in parts,* which caused her to read rather than edit objectively and discover the myriad of faults in the manuscript. The author, Seymour Styles, indeed needed the help of an editor, far more so than her usual stable of writers who had learned with experience what an acceptable standard with each successive submitted manuscript was.

Wildgate Publishing had contracted Susan to try to *knock it into shape,* and boy, it required a lot of that. Susan knew well enough how hard it was for a new writer to get a foothold into the cutthroat world of publishing, and she wanted to help but felt so lost in her life issues that she couldn't think straight.

Luckily for Mr. Styles, Wildgate's senior editor, Shannon Brookes, had fallen in love with the story the author was trying to tell, even though he had presented it poorly. When Shannon phoned her, she said, "Sue, this guy can tell a brilliant story, but his tenses are all over the place, he has no idea about point of view, and don't get me started on his overuse of comma splicing. Would you be a dear and turn his MS into something I can contract? I think he's got that mystical *something* that can make him a best-selling author. Happy to pay you the usual rate, naturally."

Susan knew the never-ending stream of unsolicited manuscripts that crossed Shannon's desk created a pile an athlete would have trouble leaping over. *The Slush Pile, senior* editors called it, and they rarely read more than a few paragraphs if the story, or quality of the writing, didn't grab their attention quickly. Once the publisher contracted the work, their in-house editorial staff would take over, working with the author to produce the finished story. Susan's job was more developmental and getting the rough first draft readable, so Wildgate's staff didn't run for cover.

The story on her computer screen revolved around a protagonist suffering a series of nightly recurring nightmares, spaced one minute apart, beginning at midnight. Susan had read it to the end to understand the plot and agreed with her friend Shannon that the story moved along rapidly, reached a thrilling conclusion, and was unlike anything she had read before. Still, the grammar was schoolboyish, making it unpublishable in its preset state. Hence, here she was with a deadline looming ever closer, and Susan couldn't think straight for long enough to finish the job.

Shannon's call for Susan's services had come a few days before Mark left her to fight her skin disease alone, and she had cleared her schedule to begin work the very day he walked out. Mark's abandonment caused Susan's world to fall apart and her subsequent suicide attempt. Sadly, she realized that no matter how good Seymour Styles' plot was, it could not mask the pain of her separation from Mark and Susan's descent into depression.

Susan sighed, stood suddenly, and went to her coffee machine to pour her fourth cup for the day. She'd skipped breakfast because her appetite had been at an all-time low since Mark had left. Susan briefly considered a taco lunch from a local Mexican food van but dismissed it, though she had not eaten since the night before when her new flatmate, forced upon her by her guardian angel, Dave, made her eat some eggs on toast.

Remembering her last meal brought her thoughts to the man himself. Dave. Now, there was a mystery wrapped in an enigma. *Why does he bother with me?* she wondered. Sure, it was his job to stop suicide victims; that was a given, and Susan was sure he would be very good at it because of his warm and caring nature. To Susan's mind, though, after Mark walked out of her office, leaving Susan distraught, no amount of any man's nature was going to keep her from ending her miserable life, yet she was still here. To Susan's surprise, Dave had been able to talk her out of jumping off the ledge when he told her about his marital woes, and something *clicked* like a light switch in her heart. Somehow, in a way that Susan couldn't fathom, the acknowledgment of his evident abject misery usurped her suffering, and Susan wanted, no, that was wrong, *needed* to try to help him, as he was intent on doing the same for her. *Like a yin-yang kind of thing, maybe?*

Perhaps they had just been kindred spirits drawn together for a moment in time, or possibly her subconscious reasoning was because Dave's problems could be repairable, and she was in the right place and time to help. At the same time, Susan was aware hers could only ever end in pain, suffering, and ungodly ugliness before a lonely, untimely, and early death from a ravenous skin disease.

Susan understood why she was fascinated with Dave's marriage; it was like being a part of a soap opera rather than watching one on TV. He had distracted her temporarily from ending her miserable life like a magician, making a red handkerchief disappear with one hand. At the same time, the other caught your attention, using his cheating wife's story. Not that she believed he'd done it deliberately or even intentionally; he had just seemed lost, which had drawn Susan to his plight. Susan sighed; *maybe that's my latent mothering nature, though I've never wanted to bear children since I was told I couldn't.*

Susan couldn't see why Dave cared more for her struggle with her disease than her husband had. *He can't possibly be attracted to me; he's too in love with his wife despite her momentary lapse of good sense.* But something had, she believed, drawn him to her, as she had been drawn to him.

Susan going out on the ledge to end her life hadn't been a cry for help or sympathy. It was a clear intention to finish things before her world became shrouded in pain and her skin disease worsened until she became a human serpent, or perhaps a walking fish might be a more accurate description of her future looks. Mark hadn't been able to touch her for weeks, and he hadn't made love with her in months. He'd said it was out of concern for her wellbeing and hadn't wanted to hurt her. Still, Susan thought the truth was that the transformation of her skin into scale-like leather sickened him so much that he had stopped massaging the salve into her back that her doctor had suggested because doing so made him gag.

Mark had always been squeamish, so much so that he couldn't kill spiders or cockroaches, which had been part of Susan's attraction to him when they first met. He was a gentle and kind man who initially seemed to care more for her than his wants and needs. But when the chips were down, and Susan started her transformation into what she sometimes thought of as her version of the Loch Ness Monster, he showed his true colors and ran away because it was too hard for him. Too hard for him? What about her? After Mark abandoned her, when Susan was at her lowest possible ebb, ready to jump into oblivion, Dave climbed out on the ledge with her and told her of his wife's affair. Susan wondered later why she had even listened, let alone gave a damn. *One last sunset, then plunge to sudden and blessed death*, Susan remembered thinking just before Dave climbed out after her. Death would release her from the pain and suffering, and if Mark felt any guilt for abandoning her when he heard of her death, that would be a bonus.

Susan realized that caring whether Dave and his wife reconciled or not provided a distraction from her problems, a deferral, but nothing more. She loved romantic stories and happy-ever-after endings but knew she couldn't be that lucky with her life's direction. That realization brought her back to Dave's skin specialist friend and his offer to examine her for free. Now, that was a coincidence, or was it more? *Kismet, maybe, fate?* Would he be able to help her? Could he save her from her fate worse than death? *I don't think so; I've never been that lucky.*

Susan glanced toward her window, saw the approaching rain, and thought about climbing back outside again, and this time, ending it before the cavalry arrived. *I can't; I gave Dave my word.* She sighed and glanced up at the clock on the wall, then groaned as she saw how the day dragged. The window softly called her: *come outside; the weather is perfect for jumping. It's so peaceful down here; there is no more pain or suffering, just peace.*

She stood, trancelike, wanting to walk to the window. *Yes, I can do this; Dave can't help me, nobody can,* Susan thought, then stopped. She knew she needed to speak with Dave and hear his calming voice. *Will he mind if I phone? He told me to call him if I felt the urge to go back out on the ledge, and boy, do I ever want to go back out there now.*

****

"Hi Susan, are you okay?" Dave answered the call on the third ring.

Susan realized she had been holding her breath and released it in a long, drawn-out gasp. "Yeah, I think I am now. I'm so sorry to intrude, Dave; I was so tempted to resume what I started the other night, and I just needed to hear your voice. I'm so sorry; you must think I'm a dummy."

"You're not a dummy, Susan. I admire you. I think

you're an extraordinary person who is going through hell. I'm at home with Lynne. We've had some problems overnight, and if you don't mind, I will put you on hands-free so Lynne can say hello to you. Is that okay?"

Susan froze, regretting the call and realizing she did not want to speak with his wife. *What if she thinks I'm trying to seduce him? I'm not. I do not have designs on him, but Lynne won't know that. I have no choice. I can't hang up, not now; Dave will send a patrol car to check on me. Damn, I shouldn't have phoned him; what was I thinking?*

"Hello, Susan." a softly sweet and gentle woman's voice said. "Dave has told me all about you, and I told him I'd like to meet you and thank you for helping him when he needed a friend. I hope you don't mind, but I'm coming with him when you see Bart tonight and then to that amazing restaurant that he's told me about afterward, though trust me, I will find something different on the menu than what you both will order. Please don't feel bad about calling him. Dave is one of those special men who genuinely cares for people, and we both want to help you."

Susan couldn't breathe. She felt like the walls were closing in on her while a heavy stone had been placed on her chest. She felt shame, embarrassment, and fear and wanted to end the call and get out on the ledge as fast as possible. Suddenly, Susan blurted out the only thing she could think to say: "I'm sorry, I have to go. Someone just turned up. Bye, Dave, bye, Lynne."

"Marlon Flanders broke into our home last night and vandalized the place. He then came back after I'd gone to bed and murdered our cat," Dave said suddenly, which stopped Susan from ending the call.

"Oh my God, are you both okay? I'm so sorry; you've got so much on your plates that you don't need me complicating your lives further." Susan replied, knowing she should not have phoned. She cursed her selfishness.

"*Susan,*" Dave shouted, then immediately softened his tone. "Stop it this minute. I told you to call me any time, night or day if you wanted to go and finish the job you had started. We've had a hell of a time here, and I know you want to hear about it, right? So calm down, and don't feel embarrassed. Lynne knows everything and is on your side as well as me, so you have two friends who care for you. Would you like to hear what's happened here since we last spoke? I promise you; it rivals something you could read in one of those thrillers you edit."

Dave and Lynne took turns relating the previous night's events, how the dinner had gone with Dorothy Flanders, the job offer, the trauma of their home being broken into, and a description of the damage the intruder left.

"Are you sure it was him?" Susan asked. All thoughts of going out on the ledge were gone once more. She realized she had found her mojo. Again, Susan realized she cared more for Dave's problems than hers.

"Good question, Susan," Dave answered. I believe it was him; though it's true, there is always a possibility it could have been a coincidence. Whoever it was didn't steal anything, so it seemed more of a personal attack, but there is no proof it was Flanders."

"But when Dave woke up and opened the bedroom window blind, he found our family cat murdered and left hanging," Lynne added. "That made it obvious, though there is still no evidence, and of course, Marlon would deny it, and no doubt have an alibi. For sure, he is smart enough to cover his tracks."

"What will you do now?"

"Probably bury him under a peach tree in the garden," Dave replied.

"Flanders?" Susan gasped.

He laughed. "No, silly, Bubbles. We'll bury him in the garden and will break it to the kids when it's safe for them to come home. Flanders, well, what do we do about him? I could shoot him, and believe me, I considered that, but the more practical side of me says to just…ignore him."

"What?"

"You heard me; ignore him. Suppose I take any physical action against him. In that case, he wins because, being a police officer, the courts will punish me more than a member of the public who takes retribution because I'm supposed to know better and be superhuman. So, with me locked up, Lynne would be vulnerable. If I try to warn him off or beat him up, he gets me fired or arrested for harassment or assault. If I'm locked up, I can't protect Lynne. I want to think of him like a spoilt child stamping his foot and holding his breath, trying to get his way. And what do we do with naughty children?"

"Spank them, send them to their room, punish them somehow, and make them see the consequences of their actions, a deterrent if you will. You can't just do nothing. What if that makes Flanders violent, makes him try to hurt you, or worse?"

Dave exhaled loudly as Lynne gasped. "I'm sorry," Susan said. "I should learn to shut my big mouth. I didn't mean to scare you, Dave. I'm sure you know what you're doing."

"It's okay, Susan; it's not like we haven't considered all the options, and yes, there is a risk that ignoring him may make him more irrational. Possibly, he will come after me to clear the field so he can have what he sees as a clear run at Lynne. If he does, I will be ready for him. I am armed and entitled to protect myself, my home, and my loved ones. But that's *if* he comes after me. With what he's lost: his wife, career, standing in the community, and the rest, he's just as likely to give up and go somewhere else."

Susan sighed and didn't reply. Dave could read her like a book as he knew; she thought, *Yeah, but what if ignoring him only makes him worse?*

After more small talk, Susan said she did have to go, knowing Dave and Lynne had a lot on their plate. Again, Lynne thanked her for helping Dave. After she hung up the phone, Susan stood at the window, staring at the New York skyline without thinking of opening it and crawling out on the ledge. She felt so engrossed, so *damned* interested in Dave and Lynne's marital woes, that for the moment, she was no longer worried about her skin disorder. At least until the blues hit her next time, she acknowledged, but what was happening in Dave's life was far more interesting for now.

Like a bolt from the blue, Susan suddenly realized that she liked Lynne as much as Dave. Susan admired who and what kind of woman Susan thought Lynne was: strong-willed, loving, and kind. Her strong and independent will got her into trouble, but Susan still admired her. With a slightly lopsided grin, which she noticed in her reflection in the window, Susan knew she idolized Dave in ways she had never experienced with another man. She could have loved him in another life with a passion that perhaps eclipsed her feelings for Mark; now, he had deserted her. Or maybe not, Susan sighed. Dave clearly adored his wife. And his love for Lynne, unlike Mark's for her, was something Susan could only dream of. *Lynne is one lucky woman.* She sighed again and went to pour another coffee before taking one more look at Seymour Styles' manuscript.

****

Susan noticed Dave standing with a woman who must be Lynne on the sidewalk outside the Towers block as she exited through the revolving glass door at the end of her working day. Susan took a deep breath, feeling nervous about meeting Dave's wife and her deep-seated fear that Lynne thought she had designs on her husband.

Susan had tried to analyze why she was almost to the point of running away while waiting for the elevator and on its downward journey and had concluded it wasn't just nerves about meeting the skin specialist; it was because she was about to meet Lynne. Lynne knew Susan was suicidal and why, so Susan felt embarrassed and ashamed, though not in the slightest bit guilty for wanting to end her miserable life, which to Susan still felt inevitable. On the other hand, Susan knew all about Lynne's infidelity and realized that that would be as embarrassing for Lynne as Susan's suicide was for her. It was nerve-wracking to come face to face with someone she knew so many intimate details about yet had never met. She felt sure it would be the same but reversed for Lynne.

Then there was Dave. Susan's feelings for him had grown exponentially since he crawled out on the ledge to save her, though she didn't want them to. Susan didn't need more complications; she was already overflowing with more than anyone should have been burdened. It was like an internal out-of-control bushfire or swarms of butterflies had taken up residence in her tummy. It reminded Susan of when she was at school with her first crush. Dave seemed like one of those dreams where you reached for something or someone, but the harder you tried, the further away they became. Dave was unattainable even if Susan wanted to pursue him, which she didn't, or did she? Was she like that Shakespeare quote about protesting too much? The sad and unavoidable fact was that Susan had decided to end her life, not complicate it further and extend it. But she felt trapped, a prisoner of her own making, forced to see their three-way relationship to its conclusion and postpone her date with death.

So far as Susan was concerned unless Dave's friend could offer a miracle, she had no will to live any longer. Mark had left her; she suffered nagging and itching pain like insects were constantly crawling on her skin and biting her open sores. Without Mark, she couldn't even dress her wounds effectively, so she had to wear white cotton tank tops, change them three times a day, and wash them in the hottest water her laundry machine would allow. Susan was sick of fighting any longer because there was no hope. Yes, she would meet this doctor friend of Dave's because he had gone to so much trouble on her behalf, but Susan knew it was just a waste of time. Even if there were a cure, she could never afford it without insurance to cover the lion's share.

The waiting couple on the sidewalk stood straight and warmly smiled as she approached. "Hi," Susan said quietly, her terrified gaze locking on Dave's.

"Hi, yourself," Dave replied. "Susan, this is Lynne, Lynne, Susan Bodinski."

Susan turned to face Lynne and forced a smile but was shocked when Lynne flung her arms around Susan's neck and hugged her tightly. Susan blinked back tears at the warmth of the greeting but felt even more surprised when Lynne burst into tears against her shoulder.

"Thank you so much for talking Dave into listening to me. Thank you for supporting me and helping Dave forgive my stupidity," Lynne whispered between muffled sobs. "I can never repay your kindness to us and for helping me keep my husband."

Susan didn't know what to say in response, so instead put her hands around Lynne and hugged her back. She looked at Dave over Lynne's shoulder and noticed he stood smiling, almost smugly. "I didn't do that much. I could tell he loved you so incredibly much, and I knew he was looking for reasons to forgive, not leave. I envy your marriage." She shrugged while still squeezing Lynne.

Lynne moved her head back and looked Susan in the eye. "I am lucky to have him and am fortunate he met you. I want to be your friend, Susan, not because I feel sorry for or pity you, but because I admire you." She grinned. "Dave would be the first person to tell you I've never had too many girlfriends; I seem to do much better with males." Lynne shrugged. "I'm not an outrageous flirt or anything; I just seem to relate better to men. But you're different; you're someone who took time out to help us despite your severe problems. You put your plans on hold to help me, a woman you've never met, keep her husband even though I did the stupidest things by forgetting I should have trusted him."

People milled around them, hurrying to go home at the end of their workday while Dave watched the two women's faces, not entirely surprised at Lynne's words, though he had no idea she'd intended to say anything remotely as sincere as she had. He agreed with Lynne's statement that she had hardly any serious women friends other than the female partners of couples they knew through the children's school, the neighborhood, and Dave's married work colleagues. He'd always thought Lynne would have enjoyed having a close confidante, though he never thought it would happen, and now that it had, it was with someone intent on killing herself. The irony was palpable.

Dave hailed a cab, which swerved to the curb almost immediately. He climbed into the front, leaving the rear for the women, and gave the address to the driver. Dave turned slightly in the seat to see Susan and Lynne and marveled at how they talked incessantly about trivial things as if they had known each other for their entire lives.

Women, he thought with a smile until he realized most of the small talk revolved around him. "I am sitting here listening, you know," he said when he heard Lynne tell Susan about an embarrassing story from their past. He had made love with Lynne in a restaurant restroom before they married and had walked back into the dining room with his zipper down, glistening manhood still on display.

Susan covered her mouth while giggling and then blurted out, "Did it make someone order the Italian sausage pizza?" Both women subsided in hysterical laughter.

"More like the Danish Salami," Dave murmured as they stopped, setting them off again.

Susan wiped tears from her eyes, then looked from Lynne to Dave. "You're such good people," she said softly. "I wish I'd met you both under different circumstances."

"Can I call you Sue?" Lynne asked, and Susan nodded. "Good, Susan is too formal. I know we only just met, but I feel like I've known you for years. Will you promise me something, Sue?"

"If I can, yes, because I feel the connection, too."

"Promise me you won't go back out on the ledge until we have exhausted all possibilities of curing your skin disorder." Susan gasped, and Lynne grasped Susan's hand and squeezed. "I promise you, Sue, that if there is no way of helping you, I will respect your wishes and not try to talk you out of it later. I cannot even begin to understand how horrible this must be for you, and I accept it is your right to end things the way you choose. But having just met you, I don't know if I can explain it, but it feels like this is just the beginning of our friendship, not the end. So, I need you to promise to give us some time."

Susan nodded. "Seems like time is all I have left; it's just about the quality of it. Yes, I promise. I don't believe Dave's friend can help." She shrugged. "I've been there, done that, and bought the T-shirt with other doctors. No one can help me, and I don't have the money to pay for the treatment even if they could. I give you my word not to do anything for two weeks; how's that?"

"Okay, good enough. Will you come and stay with us?"

"What?" Dave and Susan asked at the same time.

"Oh, come on, it will be fun. Dave doesn't mind; he has a study with a good computer where you can work from home and do your editing, and I can keep you awake with coffee. I'm out of a job for a while. So I will be there during the day, and we can have some girl fun for two weeks. Then, if you still decide to end it, we can say goodbye, then you can go back to work, and I promise I won't stop you."

The three made the rest of the journey in silence. Dave didn't want to be the first to speak because while he didn't mind if Susan came to stay with them, it hadn't been his idea, so consequently, he had been as shocked as Susan had been by Lynne's suggestion. He thought he knew Lynne well enough to know she had made the offer with sincerity, and Dave thought it was a good idea because sooner or later, he would have to go back to work, and there was the problem of Marlon Flanders and what he might do then. Then, of course, there was Susan and what she thought of such an idea. Would she want to move in with them for two weeks? Dave thought she would consider herself a burden and would not want her problems to be a possible issue with Dave and Susan's fragile relationship. He decided he needed to add his opinion into the mix and did so as the cab pulled up in front of their destination.

"Susan," he began as he removed his wallet to pay the cabbie. "I didn't know Lynne would suggest you move in with us, but I want you to know that I think it's a great idea. You would also be doing me a huge favor. I must return to work soon and don't want Lynne left alone, so I am one hundred percent for it." He took a twenty before Susan could answer and handed it to the driver. "Keep the change." He stepped out and opened the rear door for the women, determined that Susan would decide without undue pressure from him or Lynne.

Susan stepped out, followed by Lynne, and stood before the nondescript concrete and glass office block. "Bart's suite is on the second floor," Dave said as he turned toward the front entrance, but Susan grabbed his arm and stopped him.

"Look, you two. Your kindness has taken my breath away, and the friendship you have offered me leaves me speechless. I can't just move in with you for two weeks, then run off and kill myself, and please, make no mistake, you've conspired to defer my ending, that's all. I have no future other than pain, loneliness, and ugliness, and I will not hang around to wither away and die in agony. I'm sorry. Please don't think I don't appreciate what you're trying to do, but I must say no."

Dave nodded slowly; he expected such a response, but Lynne had other ideas. She tucked her left arm through Susan's right. "Now you listen to me, my girl, hang on to that thought. Firstly, the loneliness, that's why we want you to move in so that you won't feel it. You will be so busy you won't have time to feel lonely; you'll be aunty to two boisterous kids. As for the pain and ugliness, Bart will work on that. All I want is for you to give it a chance. If it doesn't work," She shrugged. "I will get over your death knowing I did all I could, and I will miss you. I will respect that it is your choice, not mine. Come and stay and have fun with me while Doctor Bart does his thing; what do you have to lose?"

Chapter 7

Generosity

"You cannot do a kindness too soon because you never know how soon it will be too late."
Ralph Waldo Emerson.

Dave smiled as he watched Lynne not wait for an answer but instead grip Susan's arm in hers and guide her inside the building to the bank of elevators. He tagged along and reached in front of them to press the button for the second floor.

"I feel as if I'm being press-ganged," Susan whispered.

"Oh, you are, make no mistake, Lynne generally gets what she wants," Dave said with a grin.

The doors hissed open, and they stood to one side while an older man in a wheelchair pushed by an equally older woman exited. They entered the lift, with Lynne still holding Susan's arm tightly as if she would never let it go. "I'm not going to run away, Lynne, I promise. You can let go of my arm now."

Lynne smiled and tilted her head to one side, the way Dave always found so alluring. "You silly woman," Lynne whispered as if others were crammed in with them. "I'm holding your arm to give you support and strength, not force you to stay. Whatever you decide, I will be here for you no matter what happens. That's why I want you to stay with us, so I can help you, not because of any responsibility I have to you, but because I want to. I want us to be friends, and support in tough times is what a true friend does."

Dave saw tears form in Susan's eyes and held off pressing the second-floor button. "Why would you do this? Why would you be so kind to me? I don't understand?" She asked, seemingly fighting back her need to cry.

"Why would you help Dave to help me? Why postpone ending your life to help two total strangers repair their marriage?" Lynne paused and glanced at Dave, and he imperceptibly nodded, knowing what Lynne was trying to say, and agreed with her feelings. "We have something, we three, some bond that can't easily be explained away with cliches or glib comments. You are going through hell, and we are going with you because we want to. So get used to it. Don't question or fight it; accept it. Now, let's go meet Doctor Bart."

****

When they entered, Dave noticed the reception area had been decorated in a pale lilac color that looked calming and warm. Next, he saw Ilene Whittaker standing on her side of the welcome desk, smiling broadly. In her mid-forties, she was an attractive middle-aged African American with short curly hair and a touch over her best weight.

"Mr. Margolis, I am so happy to see you so I can thank you face to face for saving my life. If allowed, I'd run around to that side of the desk and give you the biggest hug I've ever given anyone except my husband."

"Ilene, you're very welcome, but no need to thank

me. I just did my job. I am very pleased to see you fully recovered, though, and please save all your hugs for your husband. This is my wife, Lynne, and the patient we've brought to meet Bart, Susan Bodinski."

"Mrs. Margolis, I am so thrilled to meet you. I guess you, of all people, know how brave your husband is?"

"Oh yes," Lynne beamed, "he is one in a thousand."

"More like one in a million, I think. Mrs. Bodinski, welcome. Would you please fill out this form with your details? Doctor Chisholm has said there is no charge for today's consult, but we will require your insurance details if there is any follow-up treatment or blood work." She handed over a clipboard and pen."

Susan smiled and took the paperwork. "I feel duty-bound to tell you that my complaint has already been declined coverage by my insurance company, and my funds are limited."

Ilene leaned closer conspiratorially and winked. "I know, but we do need to know who we are treating, even if there isn't a bill for services rendered. It's a formality but a necessary one, I'm afraid. You can sit over there to fill out the paperwork." She pointed to the waiting area. "Doctor Chisholm is just finishing up with his last patient for the day and will be with you shortly. Mrs. Margolis, may I ask you the biggest favor? Would you permit me to hug your husband? I owe him my life but never got a chance to thank him face to face because they whipped me off to the hospital, and he never visited."

"You certainly may, though you may need to lasso him; he gets embarrassed when people want to thank him for doing his job." Lynne grinned at Dave.

Dave held both hands up as if warding off an attacker as Ilene hurried around her desk, and her gaze never left Dave's face. "Ilene, honestly, it's okay. I was doing my job, and you are very welcome. I didn't do anything special…ouff," he exclaimed as the receptionist barreled into him like a linebacker hitting a quarterback.

"Thank you, thank you, thank you. My mother said to thank you, my husband, too, and my kids wanted me to give you a medal when I told them all I would see you." She squeezed Dave tightly, and he made a pained expression to Lynne over Ilene's shoulder but hugged her back.

"You're welcome. I'm glad I could help and that you recovered fully. But, as Lynne said, I was doing my job," he said eventually when he realized she would not let go any time soon.

"He does do it well, though," Susan said while filling out the paperwork. "I'm living proof of that. I wouldn't be alive today if he hadn't climbed out on a forty-story high ledge."

Lynne seemed to be trying to stop having a fit of the giggles at Dave's discomfort by holding her hand over her mouth while her shoulders shook.

Dave backed away, his face blushing bright red, but Lynne shushed him. "Dave," she said softly, "you go from job to job, too busy to look back, and everyone knows you do it amazingly well. But do you ever stop to think of the effect you have on the lives of the people you save? I am so unbelievably proud and in love with you; please accept that what you do makes a difference in people's lives. Don't shy away from it; embrace it. *You are a good man by anyone's definition, but especially mine*."

Dave suddenly felt choked with emotion because he

hadn't ever thought of the after-effects of his negotiations; he had always shied away from the limelight. Still, for the first time in his career, Dave realized he was in the same room as two people, and soon to be three, when Bart finished with his patient, whose lives he had saved because of his negotiating skills. He felt humbled, and at the same time, grateful that he had been there and been able to make a difference.

"Ilene," Dave said when he thought he had successfully halted the quiver in his voice. "I am so glad I could help, but Lynne is right." He shrugged. "I do my job going from job to job because if I stopped to think of the individual innocent victims I tried to save, I would be less effective. Especially if I focus on the times I fail. That's why I don't dwell on it; it would make me depressed if I thought too much about my failures, of which I've had a few."

Ilene Whittaker nodded and then smiled. "I understand, Dave. I work with doctors who are built the same way. They must separate their feelings into compartments. Otherwise, they, too, would go mad thinking about the times they couldn't save their patients. Oh, sorry, Mrs. Bodinski, I am sure Doctor Chisholm will be able to save you."

Susan looked up from the clipboard and smiled but with a melancholy air. "Well, that's the thing; I don't believe he will be able to save me, so it's okay. I figure I can't be disappointed if I have no expectations." She lowered her head and resumed filling out the form.

****

Doctor Bart Chisholm was a large man in every sense of the word. Standing over six foot five and built like an athlete, with crew-cut blond hair, Dave had always thought his old friend resembled a Viking who was about to rape and pillage. But, if ever there was a suitable definition of a gentle giant, Bart was it.

His final patient, a young man in his twenties, left the inner office and spoke quietly with Ilene while the three waited on the seats scattered in the waiting area. Bart approached, smiling broadly, and Dave stood and shook hands. "Good to see you, Bart," he said. Let me introduce you to my wife, Lynne. This is the dear friend I've brought to see you, Susan Bodinski. I would love for you to be able to help her if you can."

"Well, Dave, you can rely on me to do my best. Lynne, I'm delighted to meet you and would love for you and Dave to come to my home soon for dinner. My wife, Darlene, is dying to meet you and has been on my case ever since the incident to get you guys to come. I'm unsure if he told you, but we were close back in school and drifted by going to two different colleges. Ms. Bodinski, please don't feel I'm ignoring you, but I owe this man my life, and he has been hard to pin down to say thank you."

Susan smiled the ghost of a smile. "I understand; he saved me, too, so we all have much in common. I'm considering starting the David Margolis Appreciation Foundation, but we'd need a function center to hold meetings."

"Okay, everyone, calm down; this is not why we are here. Please chill out; otherwise, I'm out of here. I did my job and was successful, but I'm no Superman or Demi-God; I'm just a man who pulls up his pants and goes to work like every other guy. Bart, we'd love to catch up for dinner, but only if you stop thanking me, okay?"

Bart smiled and shook his head. "Whatever you say, Dave. Now, Ms. Bodinski, I hope I can call you Susan?" She nodded shyly and held out the clipboard that he had taken. "Please come through, and let's look at your back. Ilene, please make these lovely people a coffee while they wait out here. Dave, we're probably going to be an hour or so. I know you brought her in, but Susan will be my patient, so it's up to her how much or how little she tells you." He held his arm out to guide Susan toward his room, leaving Dave and Lynne alone with his receptionist.

****

Ilene fussed over them, serving coffee with cookies she said her mother had baked. Afterward, she left them alone on one of the leather couches in the waiting area.

"So," Lynne quietly asked when they were alone, "Are we going to meet Bart and his wife for dinner, or will you keep hiding from them just because you saved his life? I must say he seems nice."

Dave could tell she was teasing and not being malicious, so he ignored her jibe. "Well, in his younger days, he could pull the girls, and I always did well as his wingman, so I can see why you'd think he was *nice*. I bet his wife is an ex-model, actress, or something similar, so yes, we should socialize with them." He grinned to show Lynne he, too, was only teasing.

She squeezed his thigh, dangerously close to his groin. "I've made one terrible mistake, Dave; there will never be another. He could be Mr. Universe, and I would never fall under his spell; that's a promise you can take to the bank. To change the subject, we haven't had a chance to speak about Dorothy Flanders' offer last night. What should I do, take the job or take them to court for the money? Was she being sincere, do you think?"

He shrugged. "She certainly seemed genuine, and let's not forget she, too, has been hurt by her husband's antics. I don't know what to suggest, Lynne, and it's not my decision; it's yours. I will support whatever you feel is best for you emotionally and your future. But I will say, I always thought you could do far more than administrative work or being someone else's PA."

"Thanks for the vote of confidence. What do you think of the offer of using their home in Barbados for that holiday?"

"Hmm, let me think about that for a minute. Luxury home with staff for free with flights for a two-week luxury getaway in the sun or stay here in the gloom. Tough call that one, Lynne." He grinned again. "If you want to learn to be a CEO, then two weeks for us to reconnect would be a fantastic way to start a new adventure. The kids would love it, too. It would be a blessing in disguise to get away from Marlon Flanders, let him cool down for a while, and lose interest in you. Still, there is a complication now that you've offered Susan to be a houseguest for a time. And, knowing you, if Bart can't help Susan and she goes back out on the ledge, the last thing you will want to do is go away and have a vacation to end all vacations."

Lynne sat pensively for a while, deep in thought. Eventually, she turned to Dave. "You're right, of course. But I meant what I said to Susan; I feel a connection as if she is the best friend I never had. I honestly like her and want to help. I'm so glad you saved her and brought us together. At first, I was jealous, but I know you, David Margolis. You are a kind and gentle man who only intended to help her. Well, I feel the same, so I'm happy to miss out on going to Barbados to have two weeks in her company. And if it ends, that is her choice, but I'd be lying if I didn't admit wanting to talk her out of doing that and having her in my life as a friend forever."

"Why don't we let Mrs. Flanders sweat for a few days? There's no rush, so far as I can see. Let's see what develops with Susan, Bart, and your manic ex-boss. We could take Susan with us if she needs some recovery, don't you think?"

"Oh, my good God, that is a brilliant idea. Let us take her away from all this for a couple of weeks. I'm sure we can get Dorothy to pay for Susan's flights, too, though didn't she say it was their own jet? If she wants me badly enough and wants us to go quietly, what's an extra person?"

Dave shook his head while smiling as he stared adoringly at his wife. "Now just hang on, Lynne. Should we ask Susan if she wants to go to Barbados for two weeks or just kidnap her? She's got a lot on her plate right now like her ex-husband leaving her. She might be hoping he comes to his senses, and he can hardly beg her forgiveness if she is a couple of thousand miles away. Plus, we assume Bart can treat her, which is far from a given. So calm down, take a deep breath, and stop trying to organize everyone's lives. By the way, I love you for your enthusiasm. Your taking charge of this situation is precisely why I think Dorothy can see you as capable of running her multi-million-dollar enterprise."

"I can't help it, love; this feels so right. I know you like her and feel connected to her as I do. We *must* help her, Dave; we just must."

****

They heard Bart's door open fifty minutes later, and

he stepped through. They looked up expectantly, and he beckoned them over. "Would you both come in, please? Susan has permitted me to share my thoughts with you." He held the door open and waited until they entered. "Please take a seat by the desk, and let's have a chat."

Susan sat in the middle of three seats in front of a colossal mahogany desk, the biggest Dave had ever seen. Susan appeared sad, and Lynne dashed to be with her new friend, stooping to hug her shoulders. "Are you okay, babe?" Lynne asked, but Susan only nodded silently.

Bart sat down, leaned back in his black leather swivel chair, and waited until Dave and Lynne sat. Lynne held Susan's hand as if she would never let it go and looked imploringly at the specialist. "I know we only just met, but Bart, if you can help Susan, you will have my eternal friendship for life."

He smiled but seemed to have a melancholy air. "Mrs. Margolis, Lynne, I consider that a precious gift, but we have many rivers to cross and a long way to go. It won't be easy, and finding a cure may be impossible. Today, I thoroughly examined Susan, took some blood samples, and did a biopsy of the infected areas. It is unlike anything I've ever seen, and that is a worry because I thought I'd come across every skin disorder known to man. However, there are similarities to other necrotic skin disorders I have come across, though true to say, I have never seen anything this aggressive. I will speak with Susan's insurance company tomorrow to see if I can get them to relax their stringent rules on humanitarian grounds. If that won't work, I will try to get a research grant, though that could take time, time Susan may not have. I will consult with other specialists in the field to see if I can get them to donate their time and expertise to help me help her. The lure for them will be that this could be a new disease, the kind of thing that, if we can halt its progress, papers can be written and careers made. But, even if I get them to help, without the insurance company on board, the treatment I believe Susan needs will be beyond her means to pay for."

"No," Lynne burst into tears and threw her arms around Susan, hugging her tightly.

Dave felt a lump in his throat, and his eyes turned misty. He thought *this couldn't be. It just can't; we must find a way. We have some savings; we can help,* he realized. "Best guess, Bart, what will it cost?"

He shrugged and shook his head. "It would be a guess, Dave, and I don't want to do that until I've checked the samples and made those calls. The cost may be irrelevant if there is no way to halt its progress."

"Lynne and I are going to help, so give us the worst-case scenario; we have savings and want to donate to her cause."

"*No, you will absolutely not donate your life savings to help me,*" Susan yelled. "I'm a lost cause. Dave and you, Lynne, thank you both. You are wonderful to offer, but I will not allow your children's future education and your life savings in some forlorn hope to save me. I have other options, and I have made my peace," Susan said in a frantic but determined voice.

"Please," Bart thundered. "Everyone, calm down. I've got tests to run and people to speak with, but know this: I will not charge a single cent for my time, and I will call in every favor owed me by others to try to help. So, please, Susan, stay calm and give me some time to do what I can. Let's meet on Monday night at the same time, and then I can give you a better idea of what we can do. I will say this, though I cannot be specific: I think there is an underlying factor that is making your condition worse, and one of the tests I'm running will confirm or deny. If my gut feeling is correct, then there may be hope."

"Bart," Dave said quietly but with a tone of voice that inferred he would not take no for an answer. "Tell us what the worst-case dollar-wise will be, then anything better will be a pleasant surprise."

"I just don't know, Dave. But if you want an educated guess, let me think. I'd need an operating theater; we must excise the infected areas and perform skin grafts over several appointments. Radiation therapy would halt the bacteria from spreading and further mutation. Then, of course, drugs; Susan will need some expensive antibiotics. Even If I could plead a good enough case and get specialists, nurses, and anesthetists to donate their time and use hospital theaters after hours to not interfere with emergency surgery, we would be talking forty to fifty thousand dollars."

Susan sobbed. "I knew this would happen. I don't have that sort of money, and I will not accept your savings. It's over, it's over."

****

Dinner at Romero's was a sad affair. Dave picked at his scaloppine, saddened knowing that their savings would not stretch to anywhere near fifty thousand even if Lynne and Susan agreed with him to use them. And the problems didn't end there because if Lynne decided and they had enough money, Susan would kill herself before she would let them give it to her. Dave realized that he loved Susan in some way he couldn't define.

Sure, not in the same way he loved Lynne, but a profound love nonetheless, and Dave knew that he would be devastated if Susan died. He just felt so sad.

Lynne didn't seem interested in her Arrabbiata pasta either, even though she had admitted it was sensational. She suddenly pushed it away and looked at Susan. "Sue, let's not pussy foot around this. I promised I wouldn't interfere in your decision to live or end your life as you please, and I am guessing you are planning when you are going to back out on the ledge, right?"

"I plead the fifth," Susan replied, trying to smile but failing as she, too, only played with her food. Dave suspected that while Susan had expected what Bart would say, it still felt like a kick in the stomach because no matter how much Susan tried to ignore it, she had some hope, which in her mind was now dashed.

"Well," Lynne sounded excited to Dave, enthusiastic even. "I've decided to accept the new position that Dorothy Flanders offered. The package includes a free two-week vacation at her luxury home in Barbados, including using their private jet. Please come with us. Let's make it memorable if it's your last two weeks. Will you go with us?"

Susan looked from Lynne to Dave. Tears sprang to her eyes, and she stood suddenly, almost knocking her chair over, and ran toward the ladies' restroom, much to the interest of the other diners.

Lynne stood as if to follow her, but Dave grabbed her arm. "No, Lynne, give her a few minutes. This news from Bart must be overwhelming for her; let her get her mind around it. Her husband has left her, and she had a plan, but now, she has two friends who care and have thrown a spanner in the works. Let her get used to that;

give her time." He smiled and reached across the table to grip her hand in his.

"Lynne, I have an idea about getting the money, but I'm unsure if it will work. Please don't let Susan know about it until I try. That way, if I fail, it won't devastate her further. Don't let her out of your sight until I check it out, just in case she takes matters into her own hands before I can raise the funds to save her."

"Okay, I can do that, but what's your idea? Maybe I can help?"

"Well, if you're sure you want the new job?"

"Oh, you sneak," Lynne interrupted with a bright smile that eclipsed the candle on the table. "You're going to ask Dorothy for a fifty-thousand dollar starting fee and for us to drop the lawsuit, right? That's a fantastic idea; she promised me a sign-up bonus; we could use that."

"I thought I would, but not quite as you've put it," he answered softly so as not to be overhead. "Dorothy can afford it, and I will tell her why we want the money so she doesn't get the idea we are mercenary or taking advantage of the situation. It will still cost her a lot less than litigation, though I don't want to blackmail her; I want her to donate willingly, not compromise your chance of being a CEO. Call me a dummy, but I think Dorothy Flanders is an honorable woman. Yes, she is a ruthless businesswoman, but I believe her to be honest and ethical. If I can present this in the right way, she may *want* to help, especially if I tell her you decided to take her up on her offer but that Susan is your best friend and is going through hell. As you said, she already offered you a one-off payment of one hundred thousand dollars after tax, so even if Dorothy says she won't help, we could use that if you wanted to. The problem with that is

Susan's pride. She knows you deserve that bonus for what you went through, so she may refuse to take it. But if it's an *additional* payment from Dorothy, that might just be the answer."

Lynne's smile was all the confirmation Dave needed to know she would gladly donate the money if required. "Lynne," he continued, "when we tell Susan of the plan, it's probably best not to mention we will use your bonus payment if Dorothy refuses to help. Her pride will not allow us to donate our own money. So, my suggestion is even if Dorothy refuses, we tell Susan she agreed."

"God, I love you, Dave Margolis."

****

Susan appeared from the bathroom with her makeup touched up, and they finished their meal, though no one had a clean plate when the waitress came to clean up.

Eventually, Susan looked from one to the other. "Lynne, Dave," she began hesitatingly, "I think you are two of the most amazing people in the world, and I love you both for your kindness and friendship. I cannot accept your offer; I'm sorry, I just can't. I came with you to see your friend, Dave, and he was just like you, a fantastic person who tried his best, but let's face it, I'm a lost cause. The best thing I can do is just…fade away and let everyone get on with their lives."

"*No, not yet,*" Lynne pleaded. "You have to give us some more time. Seriously, what are a few more days? Maybe Bart can get some sense from your insurance company. Perhaps the test results will offer a different solution, and even if they don't, Dave and I have a backup plan that does not involve our savings, but he needs some time to make it happen. So this is what we will do, and we will not take no for an answer. You are coming to stay with us. There are no arguments now; that's how it will be. We won't even talk about this; we will ignore you if you disagree. I will be there to help with your back in whatever way you need. Monday, we go back to see Bart and get his opinion, and depending on what he comes up with, then you can decide whether you want to end your life or not."

"Why? Why are you doing this? Why delay the inevitable? I don't have the money and refuse to let you go into debt to help me, so what's the point?"

"Because," Dave joined in to show he and Lynne were a united front, "we want to. Please don't give up hope, not yet. Us meeting, me knowing Bart, it all has to mean something, Susan. It can't be for nothing. Please give us a few days. Then, come to Barbados for a holiday, and when we return, if there is no hope, do whatever you feel you need to do. I promise we will not argue, but please give us a chance to help you. I promise I do have a plan."

Susan sighed, and Dave knew they had broken through, and she had resigned to her fate. "Okay," she whispered, I'll do it; let's go to Barbados, but only if I have your word that you will not stop me when we get back."

Chapter 8

Acceptance

"Accept the things to which fate binds you and love the people with whom fate brings you together, but do so with all your heart."
Marcus Aurelius

A tall, dark shadow crept across the lawn until the man casting it stood behind the majestic oak tree that dominated the front garden. Besides the porch light, which glowed, the house was in darkness, but the stranger watched for a few minutes to ensure no one was home. Once satisfied that no nosy neighbors were watching or anyone was inside the house, he crossed to the front door.

The man smiled at how the fly screen hung askew and no longer latched. His gloved right hand pulled it open and propped it behind his back while his other removed a cylindrical container from his overcoat pocket. He unscrewed the lid, opened the old-fashioned brass letter slot he had noticed on his last visit, and upended the tube so the contents spewed inside the door and pooled on the carpeted entrance hall.

Smoke rose from the carpet. The man grinned at the crackling, angry, hissing sound. He screwed the lid back on when the bottle was empty and returned it to his pocket. Next, he took a folded sheet of paper from the inside pocket and a thumbtack from between his teeth. He pinned the note to the door. Quietly, he closed the screen and slinked back into the night, looking around to make sure no one watched him leave.

****

Dave suggested dessert, but the two women weren't interested and simultaneously shook their heads in the negative. Lynne attempted to cheer up her new friend, and Dave tried his best by talking about how wonderful the trip to Barbados would be, but he feared Susan had all but given up hope. Dave realized that what she was going through would be enough to drive even the sanest person into depression, and he worried she would kill herself the first chance she got despite her assurance that she wouldn't. Deep down, Dave thought he could convince Dorothy Margolis to help, and he asked himself again if he should take a chance and tell Susan his plan rather than wait any longer. He decided and looked at Lynne, trying to convey what he was about to do through his eyes.

"Susan, Lord knows you have every reason to be down, and I know you have resigned yourself to your fate. We also respect you do not want us to give up our life savings for you, though I think you can see that we would willingly do that if it would save you." Susan shook her head and made to interrupt, but Dave gripped her arm to silence her. "It's okay; I will not talk you into doing anything you don't want to, but remember earlier, we said we had a plan?"

Susan nodded, and Lynne took her other hand while nodding at Dave to continue. "Lynne has decided to accept Dorothy Flanders' offer, and we will drop the lawsuit because we believe Dorothy is honorable and her offer is fair and generous. However, no matter how genuine it is, Lynne's acceptance will still save the company a small fortune and reputation. So, my idea was to ask her for a donation to a charitable cause—your charity, The Save Susan Bodinski Foundation.

Susan looked shocked and jerked her hands out of their grips. "No. You, you can't blackmail them on my account." She shook her head emphatically. "I won't have that; I've got to sleep at night and will not permit you to do anything underhanded on my behalf."

Dave grinned. "You know I'm a cop, don't you, and that blackmail is a crime? I wouldn't extort money for you or anyone. No, I plan to tell Dorothy that Lynne has decided to accept the offer, thank her, and tell her we will not seek compensation. I will then *ask* if she wants to donate to a worthwhile cause to save our dear friend. If she says no, she does. But I'm hopeful that Mrs. Flanders will want to say yes to show us how appreciative she is that the legal action will go away. I also think she is a good and decent person who will see the big picture and want to help." He shrugged. "Don't worry, Susan; it will still be much less than the two to three million dollars our attorney suggests we could win. What do you say? Do you feel like dessert now?"

Susan sat open-mouthed and looked from one to the other. Her eyes misted, and it seemed to Dave that she swallowed and took a deep breath to avoid bursting into tears. He smiled at her and winked. "I have a good feeling about this, so for the moment, just go with the flow and trust that somehow things will work out." He shrugged. "What do you have to lose?"

She nodded, blinking rapidly. "Thank you both; I

promise to give it my best shot."

****

Dave, Lynne, and Susan picked up Dave's car and drove to Susan's apartment so she could pack a suitcase. Susan seemed happier, even cheerful, during the cab ride, then the drive, and she admitted her hopes that her husband Mark would either be there, left a note, or at least a message on the answering machine, but he hadn't. Lynne accompanied a further saddened Susan to help pack while Dave admired the fifty or so framed pictures from the ill-fated African safari. The action shots of the wildlife were nothing short of spectacular and made Dave want to jump on an airplane and do it himself. He knew his children would be in awe of the larger animals because they loved it on the three or four occasions when the family had gone to the zoo. *What would they think of seeing these majestic beasts in the wild?* he wondered.

As he moved from left to right, he stopped and laughed aloud at a candid shot of Susan holding a small monkey who seemed to be playing with her hair, making her laugh. *My god, she is gorgeous when she smiles,* he thought.

Dave realized that while Lynne was the love of his life and certainly was no slouch in the looks department and was beautiful in her own right, the picture of Susan showed him that she eclipsed his wife and could easily have been a model or an actress. He realized how wonderful he felt being in the company of two such women. Life would be fantastic if we could cure her skin disorder and Susan could become friends with Lynne. *Maybe Susan can reconcile with Mark, and we all become pals.* He daydreamed about the couple visiting them for a barbeque and nodded. *Yes, that would be good.* But then, out of nowhere, Dave felt a pang of jealousy hit him in the chest, and he realized a part of him selfishly hoped, just for a moment, that Susan wouldn't make up with her estranged husband. The thought troubled him deeply as he had always considered himself to be an honorable man.

****

"What's that smell?" Lynne asked as Dave inserted his key into the front door lock.

He took two steps back, leaving his keyring hanging, and slipped his gun out of its holster at his hip, where his jacket had hidden it from view. "Girls, get back in the car. Lynne, start the engine and be ready to get out of here pronto if there is any trouble."

Lynne grabbed Susan's arm, causing her new friend to drop her suitcase. Before she could complain, Lynne hurried them back to Dave's car. Five seconds later, the motor roared to life, and Dave heard the clunk as Lynne selected reverse gear. Once again, he silently applauded Lynne for doing as he asked immediately without complaining or asking for an explanation.

Dave ignored the pinned note, unlocked the door, turned the handle, and pushed it wide, gun at the ready to shoot if needed. The burning smell was overpowering with the door open, and he saw what had caused it.

Their entrance hall floor was Dave's pride and joy. He had re-tiled it two years before in Italian slate, predominately white with blue and grey hues. To help protect it, Lynne had insisted on a rug by the door so wet or muddy shoes, especially if worn by their children, could be wiped off on that and not the white tiles. Dave could see that someone had poured something through the letterbox, possibly acid, he thought, and it had eaten through the rug leaving a large gaping hole.

No one was waiting inside to attack him that he could see, so Dave reached in and gripped the mat by a corner, pulled it up, and dropped it on the path outside. Sadly, he noted the acid had seemed to have stained the slate, but he hoped it wasn't terminal.

Dave felt his temper rising. The vandalism was sheer bloody-mindedness so far as he was concerned and meant to upset or annoy them rather than cause any real damage. *Of course, this must be more of Marlon Flanders' handiwork.* Dave couldn't think of anyone else who would do such a thing. He stepped over the darkened stain and into the hall and called out in a loud voice, "I am a police officer and am armed; if you are inside, lay down on the floor with your arms outstretched, or I will shoot." There was no answer.

As Dave had trained numerous times during his career, he entered, using the gun to cover a wide arc, safety off, finger poised over the trigger, turning lights on as he moved from room to room. Dave knew he would shoot if he had to, not that Dave had ever killed anyone before or even fired his pistol at another person as a cop. But, with what Flanders had done to Lynne, his marriage, their cat, and the turmoil caused to their lives, Dave felt no hesitancy in shooting to kill if he had to.

The house was empty. There was no sign of a break-in or any other vandalism, and Dave wondered what possible motive Flanders would have to drop acid in their entrance hall. He shook his head in disbelief, holstered his gun, and returned to the front door. Using a latex glove from his jacket pocket to avoid smudging any fingerprints, Dave tugged the note from the pin and opened it.

This is only the beginning.
****

"It's all clear, girls," Dave said to the anxious-looking women when he strode back to the car. Lynne switched off the ignition as Susan got out and ran around to the driver's side, and Lynne stepped out, too. "We can go inside; there's no major damage, just some corrosive liquid like acid poured inside, which has melted the rug by the door. Oh, and he has left us a note saying this is only the beginning." He glanced at Lynne, who glared back, her rage bubbling to the surface. He imperceptibly shook his head and darted his eyes toward Susan, trying to convey there was nothing to be gained by upsetting her.

"I have an idea," Susan said as she saw the interplay, and they both looked at her. "Why not come and stay with me rather than me with you? You think this is Marlon Flanders' handiwork?" Dave nodded; he could see no reason to hide his suspicions. "Well, he doesn't know where I live, and I have enough room in my condo for you. Maybe if we stay there until we go to Barbados, he will get bored, give up, and slink away."

Before Dave could reply, Lynne hugged Susan and said sadly, "That's a wonderful idea, but Dave won't want to leave the house in case the nut job comes back and vandalizes it further. Plus, knowing Dave, he wants to meet with Marlon, and I wouldn't want to be in his shoes if he did. I want to get a slap or two in for what he's done to me, too. But, Susan, we don't want to put you in danger. I didn't think there would be any risk when we invited you to stay with us. Sorry about that."

Susan grinned conspiratorially. "No, you just wanted to ensure I didn't give up and finish what I started the other night. Look, I'm past caring about myself, so I'm game to stay if you are. This is just about the most exciting thing that's ever happened to me. So bring it on, I say, if you still want me."

Dave saw that decisions were being made that were beyond his control and felt he had to put his point of view across, though he suspected how successful he would be. "I'd feel much happier if you both stayed away and let me deal with him if he returns, but I can see I'd be wasting my time trying to get you two to leave me alone. Come on, let's get inside." He picked up Susan's bag, stepped over the smoldering rug, and walked inside the house.

Dave called Matt Smith, the police officer from the previous visit, and reported the latest incident. He mentioned the note and that the thumb tack securing it to the front door may have a print on it, as well as the paper Flanders used.

A long silence followed, and Dave could almost hear the cogs inside his fellow officer's mind turn over. Eventually, he said, "Marlon Flanders flew out to Vancouver earlier today."

Dave felt as if someone had slapped him. "How do you know that?" he asked as his skin crawled like a hundred spiders crawled over him.

"Because he called me from the airport and asked permission to leave. Of course, I had no grounds to force him to stay, so I agreed he could. Flanders said that he felt he had to get away with his wife leaving him, the loss of his job, and false accusations by your wife. So, he decided to return to his family home in Canada."

"But how do you know he left as opposed to saying he just left?" Dave pleaded.

"Because, Dave, I'm not a rookie and checked with the airline. He flew out at ten fifteen this morning."

Chapter 9

Togetherness

"Unity to be real must stand the severest strain without breaking."
Mahatma Gandhi

Saturday
Dave barely slept, except for perhaps two or three hours, but that wasn't until after two a.m., the last time he'd looked at the clock. He'd tried everything, including snuggling into Lynne and spooning her from behind as she made the cute noises she always made when deeply asleep. But doing so only made him desire her, and that feeling caused a conflicting state of mind.

Dave realized, as he inhaled Lynne's scent from her shampoo, body spray applied after her shower, and just the essence of her, that while he adored and wanted to make love with her, he couldn't shake off the mental image of her being with Marlon Flanders. That bothered him, and he felt he was trapped in a mental maze with no correct turns he could make to get out. Yes, he chose to believe what Lynne had told him, but he still harbored the nagging doubt that maybe she hadn't been entirely truthful. Sure, she sounded convincing; deep down, he knew her to be honest. Right up to her sleeping with Flanders, he had always believed in her truthfulness. But what if she had enjoyed the sex? Perhaps Flanders had been a more fulfilling lover than him or better endowed. Possibly, the thing that had appealed to Lynne had been raw sex with a powerful man rather than the loving, gentle lovemaking he had always provided for his wife.

The erection he had when he first spooned with Lynne vanished, and for a moment, he worried if it would ever return. Would he ever be able to get those unwanted images that flickered like an old-time sepia movie out of his head? Then, Dave realized his suppressed feelings for Susan complicated his troubled mind, and she was asleep only a few yards away in the spare bedroom. Susan was many things Lynne wasn't, and Dave knew that, but that didn't make him love Lynne less, though it did make him desire Susan in a way he never had before. Susan was, without a doubt, stunningly beautiful, incredibly sexy, and vulnerable. *What red-blooded male wouldn't be attracted to her?* he mused. But then Dave saw that musing was all it was. Sure, he was attracted to Susan and desired her, but did he want her more than any of the famous movie actresses he also liked? Dave felt comfort in that while it was acceptable for anyone, male or female, married or single, to have a secret wish to make love with someone, it was fine so long as it stopped at desire and did not cross the border from wanting to doing.

Dave and Lynne often joked when watching a movie together that each would allow the other to have a one-night hall pass for someone utterly unattainable. Dave considered that fantasy normal because he knew he would never meet a sexy movie starlet in his everyday world, just as Lynne would never meet a hunk of a leading man. He saw it as harmless fun that helped spice up their lovemaking as they each encouraged the fantasy of enjoying the other's dream lover.

The difference between such role-play and the reality of Lynne having sex with Flanders was obvious, no matter how genuine her motivations were. That deeply bothered him, as simultaneously, he berated himself for feeling that way. Lynne had been coerced and even raped. He sighed silently so as not to wake Lynne and turned over to face away from her, feeling depressed, angry, and sad. As she often did, she followed his movement and spooned into him, her arm across his hip and warm, gentle breath on his neck. He smiled. Could there be better proof of her love for him than her subconscious decision to be as close to him as she could while she slept? Maybe Susan had nailed it when she pointed out his male pride had been wounded.

Then, like a bolt of lightning streaking down from a darkened, stormy sky, overriding everything about Lynne's affair, even if it hadn't been an affair, came a stark realization. It now appeared it hadn't been Flanders who had broken into their home, killed their cat, and poured acid through the front door. So, if that were true, who the hell had? Dave knew further sleep would probably elude him as he wracked his brain for possible suspects. One by one, like hotel guests arriving through a revolving door, he recalled the people he had been responsible for locking away during his police career. There wasn't a single person that stood out as a likely candidate, and eventually, the parade of criminals became like counting sheep, and Dave fell asleep.

Dave woke, facing the window, and heard the patter of raindrops hitting that side of the house. He glanced at the green electronic digits of the alarm clock and saw it was two minutes before the scheduled time for the alarm to switch to the local FM station as a gentle way of waking him for work. Dave reached out and turned the alarm off, not wanting to wake Lynne; then, as quietly as possible, he swung his legs out and slipped them into the sheepskin loafers he wore around the house. Dave stood and grabbed his robe in one fluid movement. He put it on, reached under his pillow, grabbed the Glock pistol, and slipped it into his pocket, *just in case*, he told himself; then, *better safe than sorry*.

Dave flicked the bedclothes back in place, so Lynne wouldn't get cold and softly walked out of the bedroom, gently closing the door behind him. He intended to get the coffee machine going and take a mug full out onto the back deck, where he always did his best thinking. Even in the gentle rain, without a driving wind, it was his favorite place to sit and think. The fact was that Dave could not come up with a possible contender for anyone mad enough to terrorize him and his family other than Marlon Flanders, and that deeply troubled him.

"Good morning, Dave," Susan said as he entered the kitchen, making him jump in shock. She sat in a dining chair, wearing a fluffy white bathrobe, staring out the window to their back garden.

"Jesus, Susan, you frightened the crap out of me," he replied, suddenly realizing his hand was halfway to his robe pocket that held the gun. "What are you doing up this early?"

She smiled grimly. "Oh, I don't sleep much these days. There are too many raging thoughts, worries, and fears. Plus, I miss Mark, and I worry about him."

Dave noticed tears forming in her eyes and wanted more than anything to cuddle her and reassure Susan she was loved and cared for, even if it wasn't by her husband. But he knew that no matter how much he would like to, he could never offer the love, devotion, and physical contact her husband could. Right then, Dave decided to track down Mark and try to talk some sense into him, and if that failed, slap him. Her worry about Mark only reinforced to Dave that Susan's limitless ability to love others more than herself made her one incredible human being. With all the pain and suffering she was going through, she worried about the well-being of the man who had chosen to abandon her. *If Lynne loved me half as much, would she have let Marlon Flanders screw her?* Dave sighed, realizing he would never know the answer to that question.

"Good morning to you too, Susan; how about a coffee?" he replied, hoping she didn't notice he had almost drawn a gun.

She smiled. "I'd love one, thanks. I'd have made one myself, but I didn't want the noise to wake you both."

He shrugged. "Susan, while you are with us, I want you to feel like family, not a guest, so do whatever you wish to, eat or drink whatever takes your fancy, and if you accidentally wake us, don't worry about it.

She gazed at him, and he back at her, and the silence built. "Dave, Lynne is so lucky to have you." Susan eventually murmured so quietly that he barely heard.

"Maybe tell her that, not me." He smiled.

"She knows, Dave. I see it in her eyes. The way she looks at you and hangs on your every word. She feels the need to touch you every chance she gets. You, sir, are one very loved man." She smiled faintly, then continued, "My point is, I wish Mark loved me one-tenth the way you love Lynne, then he would still be with me."

Dave didn't know what to say; that wouldn't sound like a useless platitude. "He'll be back, Susan; he would be mad not to. One hour without you must feel like a year. I bet he's as worried about you as you are about him. I think he just needs some time to accept what you are going through. You know what they say? 'You never know what you've got till it's gone.' Now, how about that coffee?"

The rain had gathered in intensity, and the wind suddenly picked up, so Dave didn't go out to the back deck but sat with Susan at the table instead. He slid her coffee toward her.

"Thanks." She smiled. "You know I was sitting here, watching the sun trying to break through the clouds, and wondered what the hell has happened to me in the last couple of days?"

He grinned over the top of his mug as he took a sip.

"I mean that when Mark walked out on me, I had a simple plan to end my suffering. But here we are three days later, and wow, just wow. I'm going to Barbados with two amazing people who have welcomed me into their lives. There is a chance, albeit a tiny one, that there may be a cure for my condition because those same two wonderful people have been to hell and back themselves but still care enough about me to help. Even more incredible is that they can raise the money, maybe to pay for my treatment. I mean, my God, what are the odds?"

"Buy a lottery ticket kind of odds, I'd say."

"But how can I ever thank you both enough?"

"Well, firstly, you don't need to, and secondly, you already have by offering me help in my time of need and instantly bonding with Lynne. Honestly, you don't know what a difference you've made to her life. When Lynne told you she had never had a real girlfriend, one she could confide in and be close to in ways only two women friends can be, she wasn't lying. I've never seen her so happy as when she is talking to you. She's like a mother hen, friend, confidant, and fashion advisor rolled into one. Honestly, I've never seen her like this, so trust me, that is thanks enough. I've always thought she would be a better person, more complete, with an actual girlfriend, and then you came along. So yeah, what are the odds?"

Susan leaned forward in her chair and lowered her voice to just above a whisper. "Do you honestly think Dorothy Flanders will give you fifty thousand dollars to help me?"

Dave nodded while holding her gaze. "What makes you so sure?" she asked earnestly.

Dave paused to think. He knew he couldn't admit they would use Lynne's redundancy payment if Dorothy refused, so he had to make his reasoning plausible. "Dorothy Flanders strikes me as being not only a very astute businesswoman but also a decent human being. She has not demanded a non-disclosure agreement in her offer to Lynne, which speaks volumes because she wants to promote Lynne and make her successful in the business world, thus keeping the scandal secret. Fifty or sixty thousand is nothing compared to what we would win in litigation if the judge decided in Lynne's favor. So, I believe she will see it as an investment and a way to build our obligation to keep this mess out of the press. I won't blackmail her. I wouldn't do that anyway, but I don't think I will need to. She will help, I'm sure. I'm good at reading people due to my job and psychology training."

"So now we wait for Monday and Doctor

Chisholm's results." She sighed deeply.

"You guys know it's a Saturday, no work to get to? A sleep-in wouldn't have gone astray," Lynne said from the doorway.

Dave jumped up, heading for the coffee machine, but detoured toward his wife and hugged her. "Morning, beautiful, coffee?"

She nodded. "I didn't sleep too well; my mind was racing all night, so I got up and found Susan had the same problem. We've just been chatting."

Dave smiled as Lynne moved to the table and sat on a chair alongside Susan. "Are you okay?" she asked her new friend and immediately reached out her left hand to squeeze Susan's right.

"For the first time in a very long time, I'm better than okay; I now have hope and two of the best friends a woman could ever have."

"Well, just so you know, I feel the same about you. Dave, what's the plan for today?"

"Breakfast at Cha Cha's, then I have some stuff to do. I need to go to work, look at some of my old case files, chat with the boss, and let him know what's happening. I need to confirm or deny that Marlon Flanders is in Canada, or did he sneak back into the country? So, I will see Dorothy Flanders and enlist her help by getting her to contact his family there. The problem is, if it isn't him who killed Bubbles and damaged the house, someone else has it in for me. That could mean an Internal Affairs investigation because they will want to see if I am involved in some criminal activity that's caused someone to target us. It's a mess, and I need to sort it out quickly. Whoever is playing cat and mouse with us is holding all the cards right now, and

I don't want to sit back and wait for him to come to us."

"What do you want us to do?" Lynne asked, and once again, Dave realized how in tune they were. She would do whatever he told her without question.

He exhaled slowly and took a moment to think about that. Eventually, he spoke. "On the one hand, I want you to be safe; that is my main concern. Secondary to that, I don't want us to live in fear because that's no life. I don't want whoever does this to dictate how we spend our lives, so we must act prudently. Susan, with your permission, I'd like you to be armed, as Lynne will be with her Baretta. We've dragged you into our mess, and I want you to be safe and defend yourself and Lynne while you are together. I will arrange a weapon for you today if you're okay with that, and this morning, I'd like Susan to take you to the gun club so she can teach you how to shoot."

Susan shook her head. "I am a pacifist and prefer to photograph animals rather than kill them. I don't believe in guns and doubt I could kill anyone; I'm sorry."

Dave smiled. "I knew you'd say that, but please consider this. You don't have to kill anyone, but if you are armed and learn how to use it, and something happens while I am not here, you can choose to shoot or not. If this maniac is threatening your or Lynne's life, the sight of you waving a gun may be enough to make him stop. Susan, I can assure you that I've come across many victims of violent assaults who were pacifists, too, but they would have given anything to have been armed and able to stop an attacker from hurting them."

Lynne stayed silent, but the look on her face showed she agreed with Dave. Susan glanced from one to the other, then sighed once more. "All right, you make a powerful argument. I agree you can teach me to shoot at paper targets and become another Annie Oakley. But please understand, I can't see a scenario where I will knowingly be able to take another human life, ever."

"Not even Mark?" He replied with a smile to try to lighten the mood, but he failed.

"Especially Mark."

Dave changed the subject, knowing he had said the wrong thing. "So, after breakfast, you girls go to the gun club with the Baretta and practice. Then, Lynne, how about introducing Susan to Molly and Ben? Take them to the park or Staten Island, and I will meet you there later. We will be in two cars, but after dinner at Chuckie Joe's, we can drop the kids back at your parents, then come home and watch a movie."

At that moment, Susan's cell phone buzzed and vibrated, and her screen lit up, showing a picture of a man's face and the name Mark. "Oh, my God, oh my God, it's Mark. What do I do?"

"Answer it, honey," Lynne urged as she placed a hand on Susan's shoulder and squeezed.

Dave watched Susan pick up the phone with a hand that shook. She stopped to take a deep breath, then touched the screen and raised the phone to her ear. "Hello, Mark."

Dave and Lynne stood to leave her in private, but Susan shook her head frantically and motioned for them to sit down.

"No, I'm not at home. I'm staying with friends. What do you want?"

She listened as Dave tried to make out what Susan's husband was saying from her facial expressions.

"I see," she responded. "Well, thanks for your

concern. Please don't call again if it's only to satisfy your conscience." Another lengthy pause followed. "What do I mean by that? Well, let me tell you. I stupidly thought that when we married, it was for life. Remember our vows: for better or worse, in sickness and health? Do those words ring any bells with you?"

She paused again and listened. Dave noticed tears forming in the corners of Susan's eyes. "Mark, I will hang up now; thanks for calling to check on me. Before I do, you should know this. I am with two of the most wonderful people in the world who, four days ago, coincidentally, the day you walked out on me, I'd never met before. These two wonderful people care more for me after four days than you did after all our shared years. They saved my life, invited me to stay with them, are taking me to Barbados for two weeks, and will stand by my side no matter what happens to me. They even offered their life savings to try to cure me. They don't want or expect anything from me in return; they…just…care. Here's the thing, Mark. If you were one-tenth the kind of man these people I'm sitting with right now are, I'd have never met them. So thank you for your lack of love and compassion, which allowed that to happen. Oh, and one last thing: have a nice life."

Calmly, Susan ended the call, turned her phone off by its power switch, and tossed it gently on the table.

"Good for you, babe," Lynne exclaimed as she threw her arms around Susan's neck. Dave slowly shook his head in wonder as both women burst into tears and rocked from side to side, hugging each other in the way only two women could.

****

Across the street from Cha Cha's Café sat a

nondescript tan-colored Chevrolet with a man in the driver's seat wearing a baseball cap pulled low to hide his hair and eyes. He held small binoculars, the kind someone might use at the opera or the racetrack, to his eyes and watched the table containing a man and two women eating. Realizing he had sufficient time, he slowly exited the car, adjusted his faded designer denim jeans and matching jacket, and casually walked to the car park a few yards past the café.

He spotted the car he was looking for, a compact blue hatchback, and as he drew close to its rear, he squatted down and re-tied the lace of his right trainer. He glanced around to ensure he wasn't being observed and removed a small round object from his jacket pocket. He reached up under the rear bumper and held the metallic disc close to the underside of the trunk. Being magnetic, it almost jumped from his palm and stuck to the steel as if with glue. The man stood and walked on.

Several minutes later, when he was around the corner and out of sight of the café, he ducked into a doorway of a lawyer's office and took his cell phone from the inside jacket pocket. He hit the home key and searched for the locator app. Once opened, it showed a map of the area, and there, flashing once a second, was a tiny light that was the signal from the small device he'd attached to the car.

Smiling, he tucked the phone back into his pocket. He knew that he could track where Mrs. Margolis was for at least a week, which was the battery life expectancy of the bug. He would take action soon; he had everything in place. He would teach them a lesson they would never forget, and he would have Lynne crawling to be with him.

****

"Mrs. Flanders, sorry, Dorothy," Dave began the phone call from his work desk an hour after a beautiful breakfast at the café that had become his and Lynne's favorite, family-friendly place to eat. "It's Dave Margolis. I hope you don't mind the call."

"No, not at all; I'm glad you did because I've been thinking of your wife non-stop since our dinner and hoping she would decide to come and work for me. How can I help you?"

"Well, I'm unsure where to start, but significant developments have occurred since we met. Firstly, though. Lynne has decided to accept your offer, and I support her decision completely. In keeping with that, we have instructed our attorney to cease all litigation. We have a request; however, your compliance or refusal will not affect her decision to join you as your General Manager. She looks forward to working with you and sees it as a great challenge. What I mean is, you can say no to our request, and it will in no way influence her decision."

"I am delighted, Dave. Honestly, I am excited about this, though you would have had some influence over her, too, so thank you both. I think it's the right call for everyone concerned. I do believe this will be a fantastic career move for Lynne. Now, you have me intrigued as to the nature of your request. What is it?"

"If you don't mind, Dorothy, I'd like to talk face-to-face about that and some other matters that have come up. I'm at work for a couple of hours or so. Would it be convenient if we could meet up after that?"

"I can make that work. I was going to spend the weekend at my father's place in The Hamptons, but I can put off leaving until this afternoon. I will SMS you the address of my condo in Manhattan."

"That works, thank you. In the interim, can I ask a small favor?"

"You can always ask; it doesn't mean I will agree. Shoot."

"My information is that your husband…"

"Ex-husband."

"Sorry, your ex-husband has returned to his family in Vancouver, Canada. I need to know if he did and is still there."

He heard her intake of breath before she asked, "Is he making a nuisance of himself?"

"Not if he is in Canada, but that is why I need to know if he is here or there."

"Are you asking as a policeman or Lynne's naturally outraged husband?"

"Both."

"I'll do what I can. I will see you here later."

****

Dave put the phone back in its cradle on his desk and then turned on his computer to begin his search. Lynne had said something about a lake house Flanders owned upstate. Maybe it was nothing, just Flanders big-noting himself, or perhaps it did exist. If Dave could locate it and Flanders was there, he would visit him—maybe not now, but one day.

****

"Enter." The muffled roar of Dave's boss came when he knocked. Dave opened the door, stepped through, and stopped when he saw Detective Matt Smith sitting in front of the captain's desk. Both rose to their feet to greet him. "Come in, Dave, sit. Matt has been bringing me up to speed with what's been happening at your house. Any concrete thoughts on who is responsible?"

Dave sat and exhaled a breath he didn't realize he'd been holding. "No idea whatsoever if it isn't Marlon Flanders. He is the only person I can imagine capable of this mentality."

"Tell me why you tink that, Dave."

"According to his ex-wife, he is self-absorbed and goal-focused. She had denied him children, and he not only became obsessed with Lynne but somehow thought if he could steal her away from me, she would come with two ready-made kids. Lynne not only spurned him but then brought the rape allegation, so she thinks he may well want to punish her for denying him. Meanwhile, when I thought they were having an affair, I sent his wife evidence of them having sex in a motel. She has kicked him out of the home and the marriage and fired him from her and Daddy's business. He has every reason in his sick, twisted mind to do this. He still wants to take Lynne and my kids from me, and in my opinion, he is off the rails and will stop at nothing."

"All makes a weird kind of sense, Dave," Matt said as he leaned forward in his chair. "But we know he left the US after the first break-in and murder of your family cat, so he couldn't have come and dropped the acid in your hall."

"Sure, but what if Flanders convinced a friend to drop the acid through the letter slot as a threat or practical joke? Whoever did it may have no part in the affair but could have been convinced it was a prank. He may not have even known it was acid. Or what if Flanders did fly to Vancouver but immediately caught another flight back?"

"Dave," the captain drawled. "I agree that's plausible and may well be the most likely scenario, but you gotta understand I have to take the broader view that this may be connected to someone you put away or may be otherwise unrelated to your wife's blackmailer. I've had Smith here looking at your previous cases without success so far, so I'm gonna hafta notify IA."

"And ruin my reputation? They will think and act like I'm corrupt and keep digging, trying to prove it. Everyone will believe: *'There's no smoke without fire,' so I will be guilty until proven* innocent. I've been a negotiator for the last five years and haven't put anyone away who would want to make my life hell. Yeah, a few bank robbers and hostage takers, but seriously, none of them would threaten my home and kill my kid's cat. This vendetta is way too personal for that. I don't mess with underworld figures or do drugs, and if I did, do you think I would have called in cops with the first break-in? I've done nothing wrong here, but I'm being treated like a criminal when I and my wife are the victims."

The captain raised his arms as if preaching from a pulpit. "Calm down, Dave. No one is treating you like a criminal, but dere is protocols here, things I gotta do. Even as a negotiator, you've been responsible for putting people away. You convinced those bank robbers to give up the siege at the First National Bank in Manhattan last August. Maybe one of them feels aggrieved because you stopped them from killing those nine hostages. Personally? I believe you, 'course I do, and I'm sure IA will draw a blank because we all know you're one of the most honest cops in the department. But if I don't notify them, it's my ass in a sling. I tell you what. Mat here has volunteered to give up his weekend. I will get him to keep digging into your old cases and check airline records to see if this Flanders guy has returned. Maybe you're right, and he only left so he could build an alibi, and if that's the case…"

"He may be planning something much worse if he needs an alibi to hide it," Dave muttered.

"Yeah. Stick close to your wife and kids over the weekend and keep 'em safe. If Mat here finds something all well and good, if not, I will get IA involved Monday at noon. Best I can do, Dave, sorry."

****

"Yes, who is it?" A woman's voice echoed from the tiny speaker.

"It's Dave Margolis, Mrs. Flanders."

"Come on up. It's the twenty-third floor."

Dave entered the elevator when the doors swished open. Inside, the walls were light purple, with a white marble floor. He pressed the correct button, and just as silently, the doors closed. With minimal inertia, the elevator climbed to the twenty-third floor. When the doors opened again, he was face to face with Dorothy Flanders. She wore a white jumpsuit in a material Dave couldn't identify, but he realized the outfit probably cost more than a week's salary. Come in, Dave. I'm having a gin and tonic on the balcony because the sun is well and truly over the yardarm. Would you care for one?"

"I won't, thank you, but a light beer would be nice if you have one."

Dorothy nodded. "I think I can find one." She turned, and he followed at a discreet distance trying not to look at her ass as it jiggled. Not for the first time, Dave wondered why her husband threw Dorothy away to steal

Lynne from him when he had such a woman at home. He decided that the man was stark raving mad, but that didn't bring him comfort, just the opposite. The realization that someone so mentally deranged he would give up his life with Dorothy wouldn't give up trying to get Lynne away from him quickly, if ever.

She led him through a living room with immaculate décor, the size of which he saw was nearing the floor plan of his entire home. A wall of glass sliding doors led out to a huge balcony, and she pointed to a wicker chair, part of a lounge setting that surrounded a glass and chrome coffee table. Instead, he crossed the patio, stood at the glass fence, and admired the view. The East River meandered below him, and off to his left, he could see Rikers Island in the distance above the Robert F Kennedy Bridge, which connected Randall's Island to Astoria.

Dorothy joined him and held out a bottle of ice-cold beer. "Thanks," he muttered, then turned to her. "You live here?"

"Mostly, why?"

He took a long, slow draught from the bottle before answering. "I don't get it. This makes no sense at all, Dorothy."

"What doesn't?"

"Why would your ex throw all this and you away for my wife? You have beauty, position, and more wealth than I could poke a stick at. If you sold this place, you could buy a hundred houses like mine, well, fifty at least. Any man would kill to be with you, even if you weren't rich, but the fact that you are completes the package. Why would he do that? Throw all of this and you away for my wife, who is beautiful to me, but I mean, come on, she isn't in your league."

"Why, Dave Margolis, are you trying to woo me? That sounds very much like you're trying to make a pass." She smirked and took a sip from her glass.

"With respect, no, I am not making a pass. I'm a one-woman man. But surely, you can see what I mean. Why would he do it?"

She sighed deeply, and her smile disappeared. "I've asked myself that many times since you sent me that email. With Marlon, everything is about him. I'm not saying he is a narcissist, but I guess, considering recent events, perhaps he is. The problem is that I am, too, to a certain extent. I'm ruthless in business. Ethical and truthful, yes, but relentless. Building our family business and growing our portfolio is intoxicating and addictive to me, and I take after my father, being an only child. Marlon is all these things, too, but he isn't honest. He will bend and even break the rules to get his way. And the more I think about Marlon, the more I realize he was always at his best when we were with other people's children. Marlon would be the life and soul of any party if kids were present. If, for example, we went to a friend's house for a pool party or cookout, he would be happiest playing with any children there rather than drinking with the adults. Nothing inappropriate," she hastened to add. "I'm not inferring he was a pedophile, but he loved kids. I realize now that when I kept putting off having a baby with him, I was pushing him further away from me, and I suppose in the end, he saw he was playing second fiddle to my company and business interests, and he gave up waiting for me to relent and get pregnant. You are right; Lynne is a beautiful woman, and while she doesn't have the money and power I have, she has two wonderful, loving children, and so far as Marlon is concerned, they trump my money. For Marlon, a sexy new wife and two kids he could control would complete his life, and on that basis, in his mind, Lynne beats me hands down. Marlon didn't marry me for my money; he has enough of his own because his family, too, is wealthy. I'm sure he loved me once, but he wanted a family, and I refused him."

Dave considered Dorothy's explanation, and it dawned on him that her keyword was *control*. Marlon Flanders had shown he was a control freak by using blackmail to get Lynne to have sex. In a warped way, it made sense. Dave knew of the children's photographs and crayon-drawn pictures Lynne proudly displayed on her desk at work. He supposed the lure of bedding Lynne and getting her to leave her husband to move in with him and bring Molly and Ben with her would have been an uncontrollable urge for Flanders. *How far will he go now that it has all blown up in his face?* Dave wondered.

"What are you thinking, Dave?"

Dave paused while looking into her eyes. "While Lynne and I were dining with you the other night, someone broke into our home and wrecked it. Later, after the cops had left and I was asleep, that same person returned and killed our family cat. They left it hanging from the rear patio, so when I opened the blinds in the morning, it was the first thing I saw. Thankfully, Lynne and the kids were at her mother's. It was something like a scene from a horror movie." Dorothy raised her hand to cover her mouth as he spoke, which gaped open in shock. "The same person returned while we took a good friend to a doctor's appointment and poured acid into our entrance hall, ruining a doormat and the Italian marble flooring underneath. Does that sound like something your ex-husband would do to get his way?"

Still, with mouth agape behind her palm, Dorothy's eyes clouded with tears, and she nodded in assent slowly.

"And do you think he might do something worse if he thinks it will mean Lynne and our children leave me to be with him, even if it's through fear and intimidation?"

She nodded again and whispered, "I don't think he is in Vancouver. I've spoken to as many members of his family and friends as possible, and no one will give me any specifics. They've closed ranks because they blame me for the breakup. I don't know what he has told them, but they would barely give me the time of day. I'm not saying he isn't there, but I fear he turned around and came straight back. He doesn't like losing, Dave."

"Nor do I, Dorothy."

Chapter 10

Normality

"The only normal people are the ones you don't know very well."
Alfred Adler

"Normality is a fine ideal for those who have no imagination."
Carl Jung

While driving, Dave phoned Matt Smith and reported the conversation with Dorothy Flanders. He included her thoughts that her husband may have returned to the US. Matt remained silent for so long that Dave thought the call had dropped out. "Are you there, Matt?" he asked.

"Yeah, I'm here, just thinking it all through. Dave, I agree it all makes sense chronologically, and possibly we are dealing with a devious nutcase. But there is no evidence it's him. The wife is biased when all is said and done, so her statement, while possibly true, could also be seen as unsubstantiated vitriol from a bitter, scorned wife. I've requested all airlines that fly out of Vancouver to La Guardia, which is a long list, to see if he has returned to the States on a direct flight. It is a weekend. Unfortunately, most administration staff can only get to it on Monday, and a few have requested a warrant to release passenger information, which we can't get without any evidence. If Flanders flew back here on a standby ticket, it would be even more difficult, and if he flew indirectly, it could take weeks to get information from immigration and would most likely require a warrant. It will be tough to prove he is in New York without corroboration, especially quickly. So, if he is back and intent on doing something untoward to you or your family, there is no way to prove it before the fact. We need more evidence to put out a BOLO on him, though it has been requested and is in progress. The other aspect is that without anything concrete, the powers that be will still consider it's not Flanders but someone from your past. After you left the meeting, the captain impressed upon me that he wanted me to investigate the whereabouts of the men you've arrested over the last five years as a priority. He thinks maybe someone has been released and has it in for you."

"Yeah, I get it. I like the idea of a *Be On The Lookout* sent out to the patrol guys, but I'm stuck between a rock and a hard place with a maniac closing in who wants to steal my wife and children." Dave sighed deeply and rubbed his right eye with his index finger, realizing how tired he felt.

"What can I do to help?" Matt asked. "Do you want me to park outside your parent's house to ensure the kids are safe tonight?"

Dave felt shocked and overwhelmed at his colleague's kindness. "Wow, you'd do that; give up a Saturday night to sit in a car?"

"Sure, my wife Darlene is away helping her sister, who is having their first child, so I'm free over the weekend. That's why I volunteered to help out; nothing better to do except drink beer and watch baseball."

Dave flicked the indicator to turn left as he approached Central Park. "Well, thank you, Matt. I want you to know I appreciate it, but I can't see any way Flanders will know where the kids are staying. Lynne was cautious that she wasn't followed when she dropped them off, so they should be safe. What you can do for me is stick close to your cell phone, and if I call or text, come running."

"Gotcha."

****

Ben spotted him first as Dave walked across the grass toward the makeshift picnic area Lynne and Susan had set up. "Daddeeeee," he screamed in delight, jumped up to his feet, and was off running before the women could stop him. Molly followed him at a gallop, and Dave swung them up into his willing arms to rest one on each hip.

He kissed each in turn and listened as each excitedly regaled him with what they had been up to with Mummy and *Auntie Susan.* Dave smiled at how quickly Susan had become part of their family; *Aunty,* he mused, *that didn't take long.* He was not surprised; he had known that his children would instantly like Susan. She was one of those special people with magnetism and loving nature; no one would be immune to her charms.

"Ouch, Daddy. Your gun is digging into me; put me down, please," Molly wriggled around, and he gently bent to put her on the grass.

"Sorry, baby girl," he replied.

"S'okay." She reached up, and they held hands as they crossed the distance to where Lynne and Susan sprawled on the rug.

"What do you both think of Susan?" he asked casually as they walked toward the women.

"She's nice," Ben nodded, which was high praise for him as he usually understated his feelings.

"She took us on the roundabout and the carousel; we had so much fun, Daddy. I like her a reeaaallllll lot," Molly said with much more enthusiasm than her brother. Can you take us on there, too, after lunch?"

"Yep, we can arrange that. Have you both been good for your mom?"

"Yes, Daddy," Ben replied.

"Of course we have," Molly responded. "Ben dropped his ice cream, but I shared mine with him because he was crying."

"Good for you, Molly Polly," she giggled when he used the pet name he had for her.

"Here we are, back with the two most beautiful women in New York. Hi, girls," he said to Lynne and Susan.

Susan peered over the top of her sunglasses. "Hi, Dave. Is that just New York City, or are we talking New York State?"

"Well, I would have said state, obviously, but there is that one woman in Albany who does the news broadcasting; she is simply stunning."

"As soon as you put Ben down, I will throw this can of soda at your head if you don't recant," Lynne said with a radiant smile.

"Okay, okay, okay, you win. How about we say the two most beautiful women this side of the Mississippi?"

"Hmmm, better. How about I pour the contents over you rather than throw the whole thing?"

"The planet then, if not the entire universe, how's

that?"

"Good enough, nice recovery. You may now join us for lunch."

Dave put Ben down on the rug, bent and kissed Lynne gently on the lips, and then, without thinking, he turned and kissed Susan's cheek. She beamed in response.

"Dave," Susan said, "I've had such a good time. I adore your children; thank you so much for welcoming me into your family. I don't remember having such a fun day for years."

"That's fantastic. Well, I can make it even better; here, a present for you." He took a folded slip of paper from his jacket pocket and handed it to her.

"*Oh my God.* Is this what I think it is?" Dave nodded, and tears sprung to her eyes as she opened it up and saw it was a check for $50,000 made out to Susan Bodinski from the personal account of Dorothy Flanders

Susan's shoulders shook as she wept, clinging the check to her breasts.

Lynne shifted onto her knees, wrapped her arms around Susan's shoulders, and cooed in her ear as she, too, burst into tears. "See? I told you he could do it. I'm so happy for you, Sue."

Dave was struck with the emotion of the moment and almost cried himself. He cleared his throat. "Dorothy says if it costs any more, she will top it up; we just need to let her know how much. She also said you can come with us to Barbados before or after treatment. The plane is an eight-seater, and the house has twelve bedrooms."

Susan shrugged off Lynne's arms." Sorry, Lynne, I have to do this." She jumped up, threw both arms around Dave, and hugged him tightly. Dave placed his hands on her hips, knowing she didn't have a skin condition there, so he wouldn't hurt her. "Thank you, thank you, thank you, you wonderful man," she whispered.

Dave glanced at Lynne over Susan's shoulder and saw her smiling as she wiped away tears with her fingertips.

"You are welcome, kiddo." Dave realized how lame that sounded, but he couldn't think of anything else he could say that would sound better. "You're worth it." As much as he loved the feeling of Susan's incredible body pressed against his, he gently pushed her away. He was only human, and he didn't want any evidence of his arousal to be evident. "I'm starving; what's for lunch?"

She stepped away, grinning, and waved the check in the air. "Seriously, thank you, Dave, you have no idea what this means to me. Thank you. You and your beautiful wife have gifted me hope after all this time.

"Feed me, and we'll call it quits."

"I told you before, Sue," Lynne smirked, "he hates it when people thank him; he gets all embarrassed. It can be annoying, but it's also one of the things I love about him; he is the least egotistical and humble man I've ever known." Lynne grinned. "Sit you down, Dave; we stopped off at Max's Deli and got sandwiches. I got you pastrami and cheese on rye with extra pickles, just as you like. I also grabbed you one beer from home and kept it cold. Here." She passed him a bottle with beads of condensation on it.

He glanced at her sternly. "You went home?"

Lynne nodded, then raised her eyes. "Yes, we went to get the picnic hamper. Don't stress; I made sure it was safe, and no one followed us when we left; plus, I am armed, remember?"

"Okay then." He twisted off the cap, sipped, and looked forward to his sandwich.

****

They shared a wonderful day as a family, and Dave marveled that Susan wore a radiant smile every time he looked at her. It had only been five days since he had been with her on a forty-story ledge, talking her out of jumping, and the change in her was remarkable. She radiated beauty and happiness as she ran and played with Ben and Molly.

They had burgers with fries followed by soft-serve ice cream sundaes at Chucky Joe's, which, because of its amazingly intricate playground, was the kids' favorite place to eat. They took two exhausted children back to their grandparents, where Lynne, aided by her new *best friend,* Susan, bathed them before bed. Dave smiled as he chatted with Beryl and Simon, Lynne's mother and father, and could hear his children's constant giggling.

During a lull in the laughing from the bathroom, he spoke to the couple to thank them. "I know Lynne has explained what has been going on, and I want to thank you for looking after the children as you have. Knowing they are safe here with you while we wait for this maniac's next move is a huge weight off our minds."

"Oh, you're welcome, and we love having them, don't we, Simon?"

"We do that. Dave, Beryl and I have always thought the world of you, but I must ask, is our daughter safe with you from this man if he comes back again?"

Dave did not want them to worry, but he did not want to mislead them; he knew they were too intelligent to spot a lie. If they caught him understating the danger, they might worry even more. "I don't know how dangerous he is, and we have no proof it is Marlon Flanders, so it's all up in the air. For sure, it made sense to keep the children away from any harm, and I wanted Lynne to stay here too, but we both know how headstrong your daughter is; she refused. We are both armed; as of tomorrow, Susan will be too. If he breaks into the house while we are there, we can arrest him, or if he threatens Lynne in any way, I won't hesitate to shoot him. We refuse to live the rest of our lives in terror of what might happen, so I hope he does come after us, and this nightmare can end, one way or another."

"I still have my shotgun in the wardrobe; do you want it?"

Dave smiled at the mental image of the gun-toting grandfather. "Best you hang onto it, Simon. There is no way Marlon Flanders knows where you live, but we can't be positive. We do know part of his fascination for trying to take Lynne away from me is the kids, so keep the gun close, just to be sure."

****

Dave left a few minutes before the others, so he had time to check they hadn't had another break-in while enjoying their family time. He parked in the street behind, snuck along the neighbor's driveway, and climbed on a garbage bin to help vault a side fence. Dave used a tree from their garden to climb over the boundary fence and dropped down onto the flower bed that ran the perimeter of their rear yard. Dave smiled as he realized he looked comical if anyone was watching as he tried his best to dodge Lynne's flowering shrubs in the dark.

The house looked as silent as the grave, so Dave crossed to the deck, avoiding the boards he knew creaked. He tiptoed to the glass sliding door and shifted the Glock from his right hand so he could slide the key into the lock, then said a prayer as disengaging the latch made a loud *click.*

Hurriedly, Dave slid the door open, gripped the gun back in his dominant hand, and charged into the room. Silence greeted him, and in his heart, Dave knew there wasn't an intruder but had to check to be sure. Within minutes, Dave called Lynne's cell phone, reported it was "all clear," and waited for them to arrive before retrieving his car.

Dave poured two glasses of wine and grabbed a beer for himself, and then they sat around the dining table and laughed about what a wonderful day they had with the children. Lynne suggested they adjourn to watch a downloaded movie, and Dave knew it would have to be a rom-com chick flick, not that he minded. Suddenly, Lynne's cell phone chirped that she had received a text message, and she gleefully stood to get her phone. "Hmm, a blocked number; it's probably Dorothy checking in. I wish I'd thought to call her myself earlier, but we had such a wonderful day I didn't think to."

She picked up her phone and opened the message. Dave watched her face change from blissfully happy to an angry scowl. She looked up from the screen to Dave. "It's from Marlon. You need to read this. He is stark raving mad."

She handed the phone to Dave while Susan leaped to her feet to comfort her friend.

—*Dear Lynne*

I've returned to Vancouver, but I want you to know I understand why you did what you did and lied about your love for me. I forgive you. Once your husband discovered our desire for each other, you panicked and made the rape allegation to cover your tracks. Leaving him to be with me is a big step for you and our children, though I know you know I will love them far better than their current father. I understand your fears and will wait for you. In preparation for our life together, I have left Dorothy as it would be unfair to both of you if I stayed with her.

I am making plans for us, dear Lynne. I've secured a house for you and our children that you will love — I can't wait for you all to see it after I carry you over the threshold.

I count the days until we can be together permanently in our hacienda. You don't need to worry; I will take care of the details, including ensuring your ex knows to leave us alone. He won't come between us; I will make sure of that. I love you, Lynne, and know you love me, as you told me many times when we made love. We will be together soon, my dear; be patient.

Yours forever
Marlon—

"Dave, none of this is true; I swear, he is delusional; please believe me," Lynne cried frantically.

Dave stared back, conflicted as always. *Of course, it's all untrue; his words are the desperate ramblings of an unhinged mind...aren't they? Yes, they are. Don't be an idiot. Dorothy kicked him out, not the other way around, so if he is lying about that, it stands to reason he is lying about everything else. There's no way Lynne told him she loved him. He forced her into an affair, and Lynne was never a willing participant. Ergo, he is delusional.*

As these thoughts raced through Dave's mind, he suddenly realized he was taking too long to answer, and

Lynne was looking at him, horrified that he believed Flanders' claims in the text message. Dave tossed the phone back on the table, took two steps to Lynne, and wrapped his arms around her. "Of course, I don't believe a single word of it. He is unhinged. Mind you, I do admire his taste in women. I love you, Lynne Margolis." They hugged while Susan watched.

When they broke, Dave said. "Please forward me that message. I will send it to my boss and Matt Smith, who is making inquiries on my behalf. He may be able to tell where it originated from. That could tell us if he is in New York or Vancouver. After we've sent it on, we will work out a reply to send, but I need to think how to word it so we can try to outsmart him."

Dave called his captain and explained the content of the message and that he would forward it to him and Matt Smith directly. Dave explained that while Flanders said he was in Vancouver in the SMS, Dave believed it was nothing more than a smokescreen. Dave thought Flanders' motive for sending it was to reinforce his alibi and, secondly, to terrorize Lynne into leaving Dave to save him from Flanders' veiled threat to "take care of him."

After a long pause, his boss said, "Dave, I've been on the job for nigh on thirty years, and I gotta tell you, this is the screwiest case I've ever heard. In my experience, the simplest explanation is usually the correct one. Are you sure you can't think of anyone from your past who broke into your home, and this Flanders guy is just a wife stealing good-for-nothing who got mesmerized by your beautiful wife?"

Dave sighed. He could hear his boss's skepticism loud and clear, and the problem was that if his boss didn't believe him, how could Internal Affairs? "I've wracked my brain, and no one from my previous cases would do this. It wasn't a robbery; it was sheer bloody-mindedness, more like psychological warfare. So, if that's the case, read the SMS from Flanders, then listen to the recording Lynne made just before he raped her, and you will agree; this guy is mad enough for this kind of shit. I spoke with Matt Smith a while ago, and he can't find a likely candidate from my case files so far, so this isn't just me being paranoid. Matt was so concerned he offered to park outside my in-law's home, where our kids are, to ensure Flanders doesn't try to take them."

"I can't authorize that kind of overtime."

"Don't worry; he offered to do it in his own time, but I told him I couldn't see any way Flanders knows where our children are, so I said thanks, but no thanks."

"Okay. Tomorrow is Sunday, and we cannot do much more until Monday. Come and see me first ting, and we will go over everything from the top, including anything Matt can bring to the party."

****

Dave looked up from his notebook. He had been composing what he thought would be the correct response to send to Flanders. The women had alternated between chatting about Susan's upcoming appointment with Bart and Molly and Ben's schooling while he scribbled. "Okay, here are my thoughts. Susan, you're an editor, so I'd like your input on this, and Lynne, if you agree with the content, I'd like you to repeat this, but using your words, not mine. We need him to believe you sent this message, not me, if that makes sense."

Lynne and Susan nodded together. "I'm all ears, Lynne said, a serious look on her face, while Susan didn't say a word."

"Here goes:

Marlon, I don't know what planet you are from, but here on ours, people who love each other do not blackmail to have sex and then commit rape when they don't get their way. I hate you for what you tried to do to my family. I have never said I loved you and never will. I will never leave Dave for any reason, and certainly not to be with a low-life rapist like you. I have met your lovely wife and am sickened by how you could disrespect Dorothy. I would never be with you if you were the last man on Earth. You may have more money than my husband, but Dave is ten times the man you are, a hundred times the lover, and a million times the father that you could ever hope to be. Lastly, you have threatened Dave. If you are brave enough, come back to New York and face him, man to man. That is if you are a man. You won't, though, will you? You will scurry away and try to steal someone else's wife. Don't ever message or try to see me again.

"Oh my God, Dave. Are you trying to make him angry? This will be like waving a red rag to a bull."

"If he wants to try to take you, yes, I want him irate because angry men make mistakes. I don't want to do nothing, sit back, and wait for him to make a move, maybe years from now, while we live in fear until he does. This message will either make him desist or bring him to us so we can resolve this situation one way or the other. Susan, what are your thoughts?"

"Hmm, well, it's hard for me to think like a man, especially a crazy, obsessed one. I see your point, but this might make a bad situation worse. You know what they say: *'Don't poke a sleeping bear.'*"

Dave nodded; she made good sense. "Lynne, what do you think?"

Lynne glanced from Susan to Dave and then back again. "Sue, you're right; this could be a dangerous move. But I am beyond furious with this man for trying to wreck my life, and like Dave, I don't want to be looking over my shoulder every time I go to the market or pick the children up from school, waiting for him to make a move. If this flushes him out, I have faith in Dave's ability to stop him. So I think, send it, and be damned. Pass me the notepad, Dave; let's finish this."

An hour later, they watched a movie when Lynne's phone chirped again. She picked it up, read the message, and passed it to Dave.

—Nice try. He is there with you and made you say those things. It's okay, baby. I know you love me and can't wait to be with me. I'm counting the hours until I can hold you again. Trust me, we will be a couple, and your soon-to-be ex-husband won't see me coming to get you. Please stay safe and think of me before you go to sleep. I love you.—

Dave looked at his wife. "Marlon Flanders is one fucked up guy. He is coming, and we must be on our guard."

****

Sunday

Dave woke to a wonderfully warm feeling from his groin area. As he slowly came awake, he realized Lynne had burrowed under the bedclothes, and the warm feeling he was enjoying was from her lips and tongue. Dave reached for her, firmly but gently raised her until her head lay on the pillow beside him. He kissed her, long and deep, and noted she was breathless and naked;

she must have removed her nightdress and underwear as he slept. He maneuvered his body on top of hers, and slowly, almost as if he was scared to hurt her, Dave made love to Lynne.

Afterward, she clung to him, crying softly, her face buried in the cleft between head and shoulder. "I love you so much, Dave; thank you for forgiving me," she whispered between heart-wrenching sobs. "You're my rock, world, and everything, and I would die without you."

Dave held her, knowing for him to say he loved her too would be a platitude Lynne didn't want to hear. He knew her well enough to know her thanking him and acknowledging her love was something she needed to say, and he squeezed her tightly in response and kissed her softly again.

They showered together, taking their time, living in the moment while laughing and joking. As they toweled dry, Lynne stopped and said, "What's that smell?"

Dave stopped, too, and smiled. "I think our houseguest is cooking breakfast. If I'm not mistaken, I think that's the smell of cooking bacon."

She held the towel over her breasts and smiled. "Dave," she whispered, "do you think it's weird for me to feel so close to Susan?"

"Not really, no. I feel close to Susan because we supported each other during a highly emotional time. Then, when I introduced her to you, I think you bonded because of the continuation of those same feelings."

Lynne shook her head slowly. "It's more than that, Dave. Don't ask me why, but…no, you will think I'm losing my mind." She began to cry softly.

Dave suddenly realized what she meant and hugged

his wife. "Is it Sarah?"

She nodded her head against his chest, and Dave understood as a veil lifted from his eyes. "Baby, I don't think you're crazy; far from it. Losing your twin to meningitis when you were nine years old was traumatic and left deep scars. Maybe that's why you've never made close friends with other women. I don't know; I'm not a psychologist. But along comes Susan, dreadfully sick, terminal even, and she goes out of her way to help our marriage, and you want to save her because there was nothing anyone could do to save Sarah."

She looked up at Dave as tears streamed down her cheeks. "I want, no, it's more than that; I *need* Susan to live. I am so close to her that I can feel what she feels, just like I used to with Sarah. I know Susan senses that closeness, too. Dave, sometimes, the skin on my back itches in the same spots as the sores on her back. When that happens, in my mind, I can even see her depression. Susan is the sister I lost as a child to me, and the feeling is wonderful. Does any of that make sense?"

Dave smiled and squeezed her tighter. "Don't ask me how, but yeah, it makes sense. I couldn't possibly understand why, but when I look at you two together, I can see you are inseparable, and it's more than an instant friendship. You both have a connection, and yeah, it is like you are sisters. Because you lost Sarah when and how you did, I think, makes it more understandable, not insane. What makes it even more fascinating is that I can see the same affection Susan has for you that you have for her. It's like you are two peas in a pod, yet so far as I know, she didn't lose a twin."

"Spooky, huh? But she did have her husband walk out on her, and she is invested in us. I don't know; it's like it's fate or destiny." Lynne shook her head. "But what is the spookiest is that you picked it, Dave. How could you know I see some part of Sarah in Susan?"

Dave shrugged. "No idea unless it is that empathetic part of me my instructors saw when I was training to be a negotiator. Let's go eat."

****

Susan had most things prepared when Dave and Lynne walked into the kitchen. Dave saw the table had three roses in a vase taking center spot, which she must have picked from the rear garden. "Sit down, sleepyheads." Susan smiled at them. "I was just about to come and wake you."

Lynne crossed the room and hugged Susan as Dave sat at his usual head of the table, knowing anything he offered to do to help would be refused. "Good morning, Sue," Lynne whispered. "You shouldn't have gone to all this trouble, but thank you for doing so. We've been up for a while, chatting. We've showered and are ready to face the day and whatever it throws at us."

"Pish, it's the least I can do. If you want to help, make the coffee while I serve. Hungry, Dave?"

"You bet. Thanks, from me too, for doing this, Susan; it smells amazing."

She smiled over her shoulder at him, then bent to take things out of the oven where they had been warming."

****

Dave pushed his plate away. "Susan, you have my permission to cook breakfast any time you like," he said contentedly.

"Happy to do that," she smiled. "What's on the agenda for today?"

"Yard work first, then I have to fix the screen door and a few other jobs around the house, thanks to our intruder. If our visitor returns, I will install some hidden cameras and link them to my phone so we know who he is. Lynne wants to visit the kids and take them more clothes and toys as their stay with their grandparents will extend. Then we need to go to the gun club this afternoon. I got your permit yesterday; my boss helped push it through, so we need to pick something out for you and get you to get some practice in. Was there anything you wanted to do?"

"I was hoping you'd forgotten about getting me a gun, though Lynne and I had fun at the club yesterday. I should do some work. My deadline for a book I'm working on for Wildgate is approaching rapidly, and if I need to take time off for treatment, I need to finish it."

"Do you need to go to your office for that, Sue?" Lynne asked.

"No, I have it on a thumb drive if the offer to use your computer is still open?"

Dave nodded enthusiastically. "Sure, go ahead. My computer is your computer. Lynne, are you okay to stay here with Susan while I go to the hardware store to get what I need?"

"We'll be fine, Dave. Don't worry, I will keep my Baretta handy, though I don't believe he will return here now, do you?"

Dave shrugged. "I don't think he has any intention to harm you. Me, yes, but not you. Still, keep the door locked and stay in the house with your gun close to your hand. Let's not take any chances, hey?"

****

Dave raced around and got his jobs done before one

p.m. He replaced the hinges on the screen door, installed two small cameras under the roof guttering, one at the front corner of the house looking diagonally across the lawn to the driveway, and covering the front door. The second camera had a similar viewing angle, scanning the rear deck, glass sliding door, and garden. *It may be too little, too late, he* considered as he viewed the images on his phone, *but better late than never.* He set up motion detection areas so that he would receive an alert should an intruder cross the field of view.

Next, he mowed the front and rear lawn, stopping only when Lynne brought him an iced tea and cookies. He switched off the mower and asked how Susan was.

Lynne's face lit up as she smiled. "She's doing great, Dave. I know there is no guarantee Bart can help her, but she is acting as if he can. Sue has hope, something she hasn't had for a while, and it's wondrous to see. Her enthusiasm and thirst for life blows my mind."

"Well, let's keep our fingers crossed for tomorrow." He finished the tea and handed Lynne the glass. "Thanks for the drink. Oh, by the way?"

"Hmmm?"

"I love you."

****

"How're ya doin' folks?" the small, rotund man behind the counter of the gun club asked. "How can I help you today?"

Dave tilted his toward Susan, who blushed. "Lady needs a handgun, and we're looking for advice."

He smiled broadly. "Well, you've come to the right place. My name's Bernard, and what did you have in mind? Revolver or automatic. Are you looking to shoot competitively or for personal protection?"

"I guess personal protection, though I hope I never have to use it," Susan replied.

"I'm pleased to hear you say that, ma'am. No one ever wants to shoot another human being. But, when it comes right down to it, it sure beats the hell out of being shot or getting hurt yourself, now, doesn't it?"

Susan nodded.

"So, I can show you some weapons, see what fits your hand right, and let you fire off a few rounds, but then you're going to have to run off and get a permit, though I can help with the paperwork."

Dave took the folded paper from his inside jacket pocket and slid it across the counter. "Already done. All we need is the make and serial number, and we're good to go."

"Well, come and step into my office. I have three nice guns to suggest, and I know you'll like one of them." He led them to another glass-topped counter containing fifty or sixty different pistols. He unrolled a felt mat, unlocked the cabinet, and took out a small automatic. Gently laying it on the green cloth, he began: "First up, a little beauty, the Sig Sauer P365. It takes a 9mm shell, weighs only eighteen ounces, and has a double stack ten-shot mag." He then laid a second gun alongside. "Now, if you want to stay with American-owned, we have the Smith and Wesson CSX. It's slightly longer and heavier, but we can interchange the backstraps so they can fit in your hand better. Same caliber and capacity as the Sig and a real nice piece; we sell a lot of these to women."

Susan looked from one to the other guns, seemingly unwilling to pick either, so to give her more time, Dave asked, "You mentioned three recommendations?"

"Yep, sure did. This one is slightly bigger and heavier again, though only 21 ounces and it's my favorite, and coincidentally the biggest selling handgun in the US." He laid the third gun down. "Glock 19. Used by armed forces, police, and the FBI in different formats and barrel sizes. It's hammerless, and it's the safest to use. For example, if it's dropped on the floor with a round in the chamber, it can't fire accidentally. Sure, it's a little bulkier and heavier in a purse, but it's reliable and will stop someone intent on harming you."

"Well, I am clumsy, so dropping it is always possible. May I?" Susan reached out, and Bernard nodded and placed the Glock in her hand. "Oh my, it is heavier than your gun, Lynne."

"What do you carry, ma'am?" Bernard asked.

"Baretta .32," Dave replied for her.

The salesman nodded and smiled. "Yep, that's a lot smaller and lighter, for sure. I guess you load it with FMJ rounds?" Dave nodded. "Look, the Baretta is a nice gun that is easy to conceal and can do the job with the Full Metal Jacket bullet. But, these days, most experts argue that the minimum caliber should be 9mm for personal protection. There is also accuracy to consider. In the right hands, the Glock would have close to double the effective range of the Baretta. Ma'am, to give you an idea, if you were under stress and aimed at a man your husband's size with the .32 coming through that door, which is around thirty feet away, you'd likely miss four out of five shots. Now that assumes you're firing from the hip, not in a shooter's stance, and breathing normally. I'm talking about a real-life situation where a guy is coming at you to do you harm. In such a case, trust me, you'd want a 9mm, and either of these three weapons will stop a man in his tracks, whereas the .32 he'd barely feel unless you hit a vital organ."

Lynne looked at Dave. "Maybe we should trade my peashooter in and buy two of the same. I bet Bernard can do us a deal?"

After trying the three guns Bernard proposed on the range behind the shop, they agreed, left with two Smith and Wesson CSX, leaving Lynne's Baretta behind as a trade. Lynne and Susan found the size and weight of the Glock just too big and felt more confident and comfortable with the smaller weapons.

As they drove away to visit the children, Dave cautioned the women that carrying a pistol in a purse outside the home was illegal without a carry permit, which they did not have. Sure, lots of people did it in New York, and he wanted them to have their pistols with them, just in case Marlon Flanders did try to abduct Lynne, but they needed to make sure no one saw they had a gun on their person. "Don't worry. With all that's happened, if Flanders does try, and you use a weapon, I think it would be considered self-defense. Still, let's make sure you are discreet, okay?" He noticed Susan squirming in the back seat, and she cleared her throat.

"Look, I love you both to bits, and I'd sooner die than see anything terrible happen to you. I don't like guns, and I don't believe I'd ever be able to shoot anyone, yet I've gone along with your ideas, bought a pistol, learned how to fire it, and hit what I'm aiming for. But, Dave? That's it. I will not carry it when we go out and about and risk an arrest. I'm sorry, but my mind is made up. I will keep my gun in the bedside drawer, and if this Marlon Flanders tries anything, well, I will get it, wave it around, and see what happens."

Dave grinned. He understood her love of life and animals was such that she was anti-gun ownership, and he would not try to turn her into someone she wasn't. "Sounds fair to me, Susan."

****

Dave, Lynne, and Susan spent the afternoon with Molly, Ben, and Lynne's parents. Dave offered to cook hamburgers on the outdoor grille, which everyone agreed was a great idea. Beryl made salads, and they ate as the evening sun sank behind the houses to the West.

Dave didn't bother checking the house as he had the previous night when they went home because he had not received any notifications from the cameras. However, he carefully studied the parked cars in the street for anything suspicious.

The night passed in normality, except Lynne offered to help Susan by massaging the salve into the weeping sores before bed. Susan burst into tears of gratitude that her new friend would willingly do what her husband couldn't.

Chapter 11

Hope

"I am prepared for the worst but hope for the best."
Benjamin Disraeli

"Hope in reality is the worst of all evils because it prolongs the torments of man."
Friedrich Nietzsche

"We have always held to the hope, the belief, the conviction that there is a better life, a better world, beyond the horizon."
Franklin D. Roosevelt

Monday
Dave woke with a start around midnight as a thunderclap rolled across the sky, booming and rattling the windows. His hand snaked under the pillow to grab his gun before he realized it wasn't an intruder banging through the front door, and he dropped back against the mattress in relief.

He turned his head to see Lynne staring at him, her eyes misty as if she was sad. "Hi, beautiful, what's up?"

"I've been awake for a while, listening to the rain and thinking about things," she whispered."

"What sort of things?" Though he believed he knew by her demeanor what she had been thinking. Dave realized he needed to listen and understand her feelings to reassure her of his love and commitment.

"Why do you put up with me? How could you still love me after I've been so stupid and done what I've done?"

"How could I not? You know Lynne, I remember vividly the day we married. I remember turning to watch you walking toward me down the aisle, your father guiding you. I saw your face, and it took my breath away so much that I thought I would pass out. He handed your arm to me, and he gave me a look that I've never forgotten. He was passing the responsibility he had borne since your birth to love and care for you to me and, Lynne, that feeling rocked me to my core. One day, I will hand Molly over to someone on her wedding day, and I will know then how your dad felt. When I repeated my vows to you before all our family and friends, I meant every word: *in sickness and in health, for better or worse, and forsaking all others.* Lynne, I still feel for you today, the same as I did then. Nothing has changed, and it never will. Yes, when I thought you were having an affair, I contemplated divorce, but you didn't have an affair; you were blackmailed. You and me? We're a team, *till death us do part.*"

Silently, Lynne moved into his arms, and he held her as her body shuddered as she cried. "It's okay, baby, we're in this together."

Lynne lifted her head, so she stared into his eyes. "You'd be better off with Susan."

"No, Lynne. I wouldn't," he said emphatically.

"Why not?"

"Because I care for Susan, but I love you. With all the trouble so far from Flanders and whatever may still be to come, you're my wife, and I love you. It's just that simple. Susan or anyone could never replace you in my heart."

"God. I so don't deserve you."

Lynne again sunk into his shoulder, crying, and Dave stroked her back until she stopped. Together, they drifted asleep again.

****

The rain suddenly hammered the Margolis home and woke the three occupants simultaneously at seven seventeen.

Susan smiled, glad to be awake, hoping Doctor Bart Chisholm would grant her the gift of quality and continued life later in the day. And suddenly, after meeting Dave and Lynne, she realized her life had been fantastic. She smiled as an old saying came to mind and seemed appropriate. *Today is the first day of the rest of your life, Susan Bodinski.*

She rose, pulled on her robe, and skipped to the family bathroom to prepare for the day ahead. In the shower, Susan wondered if she should return to her office and try to finish the Wildgate project, but then realized she could just as efficiently work using Dave's computer, save herself the travel into the city, and have more time to spend with Lynne. *You mean Dave and Lynne,* she admonished herself and suddenly stopped washing her body. *Oh my goodness, I adore Dave and all he has done for me, but Lynne, it's as if we are a matched pair. How did this happen? Why do I feel so close to her?*

Susan shrugged and began using the soap-filled loofa again. She had no idea how or why she had her emotions, but Susan realized she was glad she had them.

An only child who grew up on a farm in Wisconsin, Susan recalled how she yearned for a playmate during the long school holidays as a child. Then, because Susan was a good student, she went to NY State University on a scholarship, where she received her degrees. By then, she had met Mark, and other than vacations, had yet to return to live in her home state.

Like the thunderclap that seemed to roll across the house, Susan realized that other than her roommate in college, she had never had a serious *girlfriend, confidante,* or *sister. That may be why we are so close.*

Susan smiled warmly; she felt a genuine affection for Lynne and a bond like, well, she didn't know what as she had never experienced one with another woman before, but it was intense, deep, and caring. Her new friend was going through seven pints of hell, and Susan knew she wanted to help in any way she could. *Yeah, but could I shoot this guy Flanders?* She paused again and thought of the man; Susan imagined him to be big, tall, and broad, and in her imagination, he threatened to hurt Lynne. Susan saw Flanders standing over Lynne, his back to Susan as if she were inconsequential, as he attempted to strangle Lynne. Susan imagined her new Smith and Wesson in her hand, aiming it, shouting for him to leave her friend alone, and when he didn't, Susan pulled the trigger. A bullet hit his back, and blood squirted out, but Flanders did not stop strangling Lynne. Susan fired again, then repeatedly, each time hitting the target, and then she suddenly woke from her trance.

Oh my God, that was intense, so freakin' real. But could I shoot Flanders even if he was attacking Susan? I hope I never have to find out.

****

Work-wise, Dave could do nothing for the day except go into the office to be interviewed by Internal Affairs detectives. He was serving his suspension as Internal Affairs tried to find evidence that he was corrupt, while Matt Smith wanted to prove he wasn't. The situation sucked, but he knew it was what it was. While he showered, his mind wandered to Lynne and her relationship with Marlon Flanders as it inevitably did occasionally. The front part of his brain was committed to believing Lynne had been used and abused by Flanders, but despite his best efforts, some things nagged at the back of his mind. Was it how she said it had happened, a crazed man obsessed with her, or was there more truth to Flanders text messages than Lynne would admit to? He didn't want to disbelieve Lynne; he did not, yet…his trust in her had undoubtedly been damaged. If only she had come to him the moment things started, none of the things, including the rape, would have happened. Yet there, too, was a problem. He knew Lynne had an independent streak in her a mile wide, and he could understand her need to fight her own battles at her place of work, as Dave would himself if a situation arose. But to have sex with another man, pretending to enjoy it while trying to gain evidence he was lying to her? Wasn't that stretching things too far for someone supposedly in love with her husband?

Dave sighed as the hot water streamed down his face, washing the shampoo away. He realized he would never know for sure. Lynne was either being truthful, or she wasn't, and if she wasn't, how much was she hiding, a little or a lot? Maybe it had started as a mutual infatuation. Lynne did enjoy the clandestine meetings and illicit sex and then perhaps changed her mind. But if that were the case, why the recording where Flanders all but admitted he had fabricated the fraud so she would sleep with him?

Dave knew from his years as a negotiator that the truth usually lay somewhere between the two versions when two people had conflicting stories. Neither was one hundred percent correct; there were always shades of gray. He also knew from his studies in psychology that memory could be faulty. Often, the human brain gets things wrong in recollections to protect the person. Therefore, when someone swore that another person had said something to them, that was the truth as far as they were concerned. Of course, the other person strenuously denied it, and possibly they had not said it, or maybe they had, and their brain deliberately hid the memory to protect that person. The point was that memory could be faulty and often was. Lynne could well be telling the truth from her perspective, but then what about Flanders' perspective? Had he believed she was available by her flirtatious nature? And if he did believe he was in with a chance, he probably felt justified in taking the action he did. So that left Dave with an uncomfortable feeling that Lynne somehow led Flanders on, possibly unwittingly, and if she now realized that she had, that would explain her tears earlier; she felt unbelievably guilty.

Shutting the taps off, Dave determined to force the negative thoughts to the back of his mind for the twentieth time and appear to be cheerful with Lynne every moment of every day as they fought Marlon Flanders together. Whatever had happened in the past could not be changed; there was only the future and what, if anything, Flanders would do to carry out his threat. He refused to believe that Lynne was complicit in attempting to break up her marriage to be with Flanders; therefore, no matter what led her to sleep with another man, she had chosen him, Dave, and he was determined to fight to the death to not only protect her but keep her, and Ben and Molly, as his family.

****

Breakfast was a happy time. The three shared optimism for what Bart would tell them later, and it was as if the result was a given. There wasn't any negativity from Susan, and her excitement was infectious.

They discussed their plans for the day. Susan wanted to finish the Wildgate project and get it sent off. Dave had to go to work to face his boss and have his interview with Internal Affairs. Lynne wanted time to call Dorothy Flanders to discuss the new job, formally accept and thank her, and discuss possible start dates. She acknowledged that might be difficult with the potential threat of Marlon Flanders but felt it was something they had to face. After all, they needed to begin communicating for when Lynne started to work again, and Dave readily agreed. Lynne also had housework and laundry chores to do and had to go to the supermarket for her weekly shopping, which she would usually have done the day before, but they had been too busy.

Dave felt nervous at the thought of Lynne leaving the house but realized they could not spend the rest of their lives fearing what Flanders might do. He knew he couldn't be with her twenty-four hours a day; sooner or later, he had to return to work, just like their children had to return home; they couldn't stay with their grandparents forever. *I wish Flanders would make his move, just waiting for him to act is killing me.*

"Lynne, if you leave the run to the market until later,

I should be home and can come with you."

She nodded but looked pensive. "Dave, I'd love you to come shopping with me, but I know you hate doing it. So that tells me you're worried about Marlon stalking me. I promise I will take my gun in my purse and will not allow myself to be kidnapped, so you can stop worrying about me."

I can go with you, Lynne," Susan volunteered. "I won't carry a weapon outside the house, but let me tell you; it would be a brave man indeed who decides to attack you if I'm with you."

Lynne laughed. "See, Dave? I have my bodyguard. He won't mess with us. Go to work, do your thing, we girls will be okay."

Reluctantly, Dave agreed. He wondered at Lynne's demeanor. She still seemed distracted and moody, but he couldn't think why she had a different attitude. *What's changed since last night?* He worried. The sullenness was unlike her; Lynne was the type of woman to tackle a problem head-on, which, he reminded himself, was why they were in the mess they were. Then it hit him like a tornado about why she was so withdrawn. Dave knew he had to stop her train of thought, even use Susan to help if he had to.

"Lynne, what's wrong? Something is on your mind," he asked.

She looked up from stirring the muesli around in her bowl. She gave the ghost of a smile far from one of her best. "Nothing, hon, just worried, is all."

Dave reached across the table, took her hand in his, and noted Susan was also looking questioningly at Lynne. "Specifically, what is worrying you?"

She let out a long, sad-sounding breath. "Dave, I

don't want to talk about it now if that's okay. Later, we will find out if Bart can help Sue, and I hope he can. I feel like I've just found the sister I never had, and I'm scared I will lose her if Bart can't help her." Lynne glanced at Susan, who rapidly blinked back her tears and reached across to grab Lynne's other hand."

Dave wasn't convinced. Yes, there was no doubt Lynne was concerned about Susan's welfare. But she was usually the optimistic one in the relationship, so there was something else, something more serious going on in Lynne's mind, and he thought he knew what it was. "Babe, we're all worried, but I know you better than that. If that were all there was, you would be the life and soul of the party, trying to cheer everyone else up. It's those text messages from Flanders, isn't it?"

She wrenched her hands away and buried her head in them, sobbing loudly. "Yes," she ripped her hands away, unable to stop the tears streaming down her face. "If you must know, that's what it is that's worrying me! Dave, Flanders is saying he will get you out of the way to have a clear run at me. I think he means to kill you, and it's all my fault. Not only have I royally ruined your trust in me, but if he kills you, I could never live with the guilt." She buried her head again, crying with anguish at what Dave knew she blamed herself for causing.

Dave nodded. He had to be careful. He couldn't just shrug off the threat like it never happened, yet he had to ensure they faced Flanders together as a couple. He feared Lynne might well run away, find Flanders, and be with him rather than risk the maniac murdering her husband. "Lynne, look at me," he said a little more firmly than he intended, but at the same time, he knew he had one chance to stop her from sacrificing herself to save him. Slowly, she lowered her hands again. "I want you to listen to me, and while I'm talking, don't take your eyes off mine. I need you to see their sincerity and my love for you, okay?"

She nodded once more.

"Okay. I've been a cop for fourteen years. Every day I go to work, a small part of me knows that I might not come home to you because of doing my job. Do you know how many cops are killed in the line of duty in the state of New York every year? More than I want to admit. The point is that I face death every single day, and I do so because this is who I am. I'm a cop and cannot let fear rule my life. Some fear is good; it gives me an edge, makes me wary, and look for trouble before it finds me. I have lost count of the number of times someone has threatened me while making an arrest, yet I keep going to work, and so far, so good. I come home every night to the world's most wonderful wife, lover, and mother. But, in the deepest recesses of my mind, I know that one day," he shrugged, "I may not make it back. But hear me on this. I will not, *absolutely will not* give in to fear. I wouldn't be the man you fell in love with if I did. So far as I am concerned, Marlon Flanders is just one more criminal making threats. Might he try to kill me? Yep, he might. Will he succeed? No, he won't. Do you know why?"

Lynne stared wide-eyed because Dave had never once spoken to her about threats made in the line of duty. "Why," she asked quietly.

"Because you, Molly, and Ben are why I keep going to work. You are my reason for living. We are a team; what happens to you affects me, and now someone wants to steal you away? No way, Jose, no way will I let him do that. He can take a run at me; I hope he does. Lynne, if he does start something with me, I will be the one to end it. He's a businessman; I'm a cop. I'm trained in firearms and self-defense, and more than that…I'm angry. How dare he treat my wife like a possession, manipulate her, and rape her? Trust me on this: I'm angry enough to take him out. I will not hesitate, and I will not seek violence with him, but I do hope he comes after me because it will not be me who does not go home to his family. You can take that to the bank, hon."

Dave calmly and slowly sipped from his coffee mug, grimacing when he realized how cold it had become, and put it down. "Lynne, please, I beg you, do not entertain the idea that you can somehow save me by running away with him. I swear to you, if you did that, I would spend every single waking moment of my life going forward hunting him down. I would gladly go to the electric chair for his cold-blooded murder, and I probably would because it would be pre-meditated. There isn't a force on earth strong enough to stop me. You and me, together, we can outsmart him. Let him try his worst and see you are by my side. Please don't give up on us to save me; it won't work."

"Oh, my good God, Lynne, he is serious. Dave would gladly die for you." Susan whispered. "I wish Mark cared for me as much as Dave cares for you. Please don't give up on him. Dave would rather die trying to keep you than let you run off to be with a monster to save him."

Lynne got up and ran from the room, sobbing. Dave began to rise and follow her, but Susan grabbed his hand. "Don't, Dave, leave her be. Give her some time to digest what you just told her. If you go now, it will just dilute the message you're trying to send her. She is full of guilt for bringing all this down on you and the children. It is almost unbearable for her, and I understand the part of her that would give herself to him if it kept you and the children safe. After all, wouldn't you sacrifice your life for theirs? Of course, you would, don't deny it. As we both know, she is an independent woman who may think giving herself to him will stop bloodshed. You've now told her it wouldn't in no uncertain terms. Let that sink in; I'm sure she will make the right decision. You can rely on me to watch Lynne and, if called to, help talk her out of doing something silly.

****

During the morning, Susan began her editing job, ensuring she had dotted the i's and crossed the t's, as she put it, before emailing it back to the publisher when completed. That job done; she would have a clear desk to face whatever that night brought with Doctor Bart. Lynne intended to do some laundry and housework, saying it wouldn't do itself. Dave suspected she was looking for ways to stay busy and away from him while she thought through the implications of their conversation over breakfast, and he had decided that Susan's advice was sound.

Dave spent the early morning going stir-crazy, trying to find some jobs in the garden to keep occupied. Around nine thirty, he was pruning the rose bushes when his cell phone chimed; it was Matt Smith. "Matt, hi, any news?" he asked, making sure he was out of earshot of the house, suspecting the call would go badly.

"Dave, no good news, I'm sorry. We're not getting much help from the airlines. Not that they are being uncooperative, but we cannot find that Marlon Flanders flew back into New York. You and I both know that if he wanted to be devious, he could get here any one of a hundred ways. He could have taken a train to Chicago or another major city, flown here, or gotten a hired car and driven. Gotta say he is either one devious sick son of a bitch, or, and here is what the boss thinks, it's not him."

"What about the text messages?"

"Creepy as all hell, but we spoke to your carrier, and I just got the report back. Pay-as-you-go number, bought in New York three months ago, cash, no record of the buyer. But there is no way to tell where the messages originated from. It could have been local, but just as likely not. It could have been sent by phone or a computer, and therefore, routed from anywhere in the world. It would have been a different story if he had used the phone to call. Then, we could triangulate from the towers but not from a text message. The only good news is that nothing detrimental is coming out of IA. A friend of mine's wife is with the department, and as a favor, asked around. So far, they can't turn up anything to suggest you're crooked. But of course, for them, it's early days, and they aren't about to drop the investigation for a long while yet."

Dave sighed; it was as he had expected. It would take time to clear his name because it was almost impossible to prove a negative. Meanwhile, what could he do besides go to Barbados for two weeks? Of course, he would have to explain how and why he was going overseas, as that would make IA think the worst. He intended to get a letter from Dorothy Flanders to show his boss and the investigators. Hence, they knew the trip was legitimately given to his wife because of her career advancement and not by his ill-gotten means. But then there was Susan's appointment with Bart later. What would he say? If he could help her, that would hold up going away. Lynne would not leave Susan to face whatever treatment alone, assuming that there was a treatment that could help, which Dave hoped there was. Come to that, he didn't want to leave Susan to face an uncertain future either, so any trip to Barbados hinged on Susan.

"Thanks, Matt. Looks like I'm playing with a stacked deck. I appreciate you doing what you have, even if it is hopeless."

"For what it's worth, I believe you. I know you to be a straight shooter, so IA is barking up the wrong tree as far as I'm concerned. So, what does it leave if we take some form of underworld payback out of the equation? A psychotic stalker intent on taking your wife and children. Yeah, it sounds like a plot for a B-grade movie, but hey, if all the logical reasons pan out, we are left with illogical ones. And there is enough circumstantial evidence here to suggest Flanders is the problem. The issue is that until he shows himself, we're flying blind. I'm on your side, Dave, and I will keep searching."

"Thanks, Matt. I owe you. I'm coming in to work for the IA grilling; that will not be fun."

Dave's first stop was his office, which he shared with two other detectives trained in hostage negotiation but worked in different areas until their skills were called upon. Dave was the lead negotiator on the permanent day shift, which suited his family's lifestyle. This meant his weekends and nights were usually free unless he began a job before shift change when he would continue until there was a resolution.

The small office was unattended, which Dave was

grateful for as what he was about to do was technically against the rules. No officer was permitted to search databases for personal reasons, though, in these circumstances, Dave felt justified. He sat behind his desk and switched on his computer, then spent the next hour in what turned out to be fruitless searches. He could find no properties in New York State owned by Flanders, which meant when Flanders said he had a house arranged for Lynne to live in with him and the children, he was either lying or had access to a home through a different identity, possibly a corporate body. Or, of course, it was in another state; either way, it didn't help Dave's cause. He turned the computer off and went to the next floor to the detective's squad room to find Matt Smith. "Hi, Matt," Dave said as he sat in the chair before his desk. "What's new?"

Matt looked up, and Dave noticed he didn't smile. "Not good news, Dave; I'm sorry. So far as I can tell, Marlon Flanders did not return to the US, at least not by any commercial airline. I've checked with immigration, too, and nada."

"Why am I not surprised? What about the origin of the text messages yesterday?"

"No way to tell. We could find out if he called, but a text won't let us triangulate."

"Could he have someone, a family member or friend, who would have sent it for him while he hides in the States?"

"Anything is possible, Dave. There is plenty of technology to route calls and text messages through servers in other countries, but it still assumes he is here, and there is no evidence he re-entered. Okay, sure, I know there are backdoor ways he could get in, and his family is loaded, so maybe they even have a private jet he used, and he avoided immigration. The problem is proving it."

Dave shook his head, frustrated. "Have you read the messages? Can you see not only is he completely delusional, but dangerous too? He says he will take care of me and get me out of the picture. How's he going to manage that from Canada?"

"I'm with you, bud; I get it. My point is the boss will only be able to act with proof. We've put out a BOLO to every cop in the State, so if he shows his head, we'll get him, though I'm not sure what we can charge him with. But if we could find him, we would know he is here in New York."

"Yeah, he's mad but also clever. Matt, thanks for sticking with this; I appreciate it and owe you one. I better go and see the boss and face IA."

"Good luck with that."

****

Dave was interrogated by two detectives from The Internal Investigations Department for the next hour. It was clear to him that Detectives Royale and Lemmon did not believe Marlon Flanders was the culprit for the break-ins; therefore, to their thinking, Dave had done something to bring the troubles on himself either through underworld connections or a previous case gone wrong, such as a wrongful conviction. When they couldn't wear him down with relentless questioning, they told him he was on paid suspension leave and could not return to work without their permission. In the interim, they would interview Dave's family, friends, and work colleagues, and Dave was forbidden to talk to them, which suited him fine. He did not have to hand in his badge and gun but was forbidden to investigate. If he was found to be doing so, the detectives believed that would be proof positive of illegal behavior.

"Detective Margolis, you will be arrested if we discover you are interfering in this ongoing investigation, which will lead to you being fired and facing a criminal conviction," Royale said sternly.

"I don't need to investigate; I know who has done this, and I can tell you now, he won't stop. He is obsessed with taking my wife and children. You guys are so focused on finding crooked cops that you can't see the obvious when it is in front of you. You have zero evidence against me; for God's sake, I am a hostage negotiator, not involved with drugs or organized crime. I reported the break-in; why would I do that if I was responsible?"

"If you've done nothing wrong, Detective, you have nothing to fear from us investigating your past cases and connections."

"Sure, and while you're screwing around and wasting time, Marlon Flanders will come back and create havoc for my family, and if you think I will stand by and let that happen, think again."

Dave stormed out of the interview room.

****

"So, I'm suspended?" Dave complained to his boss, Mark Brennan. "I get targeted by a madman, and Internal Affairs refuse to believe my version and suspends me."

"Dave. what can I tell you? I've known you for years, and I'm having trouble believing you because dere is no evidence dis Flanders has done anything you say he has. I know you to be a straight shooter, but dis story, surely you can see how hard it is to believe?"

Dave shook his head in utter frustration. "But Boss, don't you see that's how smart he is? He's like some psycho maniac but clever like a fox."

He held his hands out in a placating way. "Think of it dis way. You're on full pay with permission to stay home and protect your wife. I ain't askin' for your gun and badge; if dis Flanders has snuck back in the country and tries anything, you will be in the right place to do someting about it."

Dave silently agreed; he had a point.

****

As Dave was interrogated, Susan Bodinski couldn't remember a time since her wonderful trip to Africa when she felt so happy and content. She sang a song to herself as she worked on Dave's computer, using the thumb drive in the USB socket to finish her edits on Seymour Styles' book.

Two hours later, Lynne placed her hand on Susan's shoulder and said, "Hey." Susan was so lost in the story the sudden touch startled her, and she jumped and shrieked, which made Lynne do the same, almost spilling the coffee she'd made.

They looked at each other and simultaneously giggled. "Oh. I'm so sorry, Sue," Lynne gasped, then laughed again. "I thought I'd bring you a coffee and didn't think to warn or whistle as I approached."

Susan wiped the laugh tears from her eyes. "It's fine, thank you so much. I got lost in this tale and am nearing the end. It's awfully good. I think it would make an excellent movie. I'm at a terrifying spot, so when you touched me, I thought I'd jumped through the ceiling." She reached for the mug in Lynne's hand. "You're a lifesaver. I've been gasping for a drink for ages but was trying to finish this."

Lynne nodded toward the screen. "What's it about?"

Susan sipped gratefully. "It's a suspense horror story about dreams. The protagonist has a recurring dream each night that starts precisely where the previous night finished, exactly one minute apart. It has this awful gray cat seemingly spawned from hell, intent on stopping our hero from reaching his destination as he walks through a park just after midnight. The man has to work out if the dream is real, and therefore a warning of things to come, or if he is going mad. I'm almost at the end, and it's a cracker involving a black magic ceremony, including the appearance of the Devil incarnate."

"Way too scary for my nighttime reading. Okay, I've finished my chores. I'm going to jump in the shower, and then I thought we'd go shopping. Then, I can tell you about my conversation with Dorothy Flanders. Sound good?"

She nodded. "I think, given twenty minutes, I can finish this novel, submit it to Wildgate, and then my time is my own until the next project comes along."

****

"Looks like rain is coming later," Susan nodded toward the weather through the large window overlooking the fruit and vegetables in the market, and Lynne nodded in agreement as she chose a large cantaloupe.

Susan told Lynne she had finished the manuscript and emailed it to the publisher so the author would receive his first contract in the coming weeks. "I enjoyed his book and look forward to what else he might write, but enough of that, come on, fess up. How did it go with Dorothy Flanders?"

Lynne exhaled loudly. "In a word, overwhelming. She wants me to start my training with her in two weeks. At first, she said next week, but I insisted I wanted two to get over the trauma of the last few days, get my head right, and hopefully make sure her husband leaves me alone and stays in Canada."

"Sounds fair. Do you think Flanders will stay in Canada?"

Lynne slowly gazed at her friend, then shook her head. "Nope. I think he is here, waiting to pounce. I don't know how he snuck back into the country, or maybe he never left. I can't imagine why he is fixated on me; I know I'm nothing special."

"Don't put yourself down, Lynne. To me, you are exceptional, and anyone who meets you would agree with that. And, of course, Dave thinks the sun rises and sets in your eyes."

"You're biased, but thank you for the compliment." She blushed. "I believe Marlon mainly wants me because of the children, as Dorothy suggested. I remember back when he first approached me. Now that I think about it, he wasn't so much interested in me as a woman, not at first, anyway. He wanted to know all about the children. The flirting came later. His whole behavior since he first tried to seduce me is so unreal; I mean, he has thrown everything away over me. Why am I so special? I'm a housewife with two kids and a husband who loves me. After all the drama I've heaped on him, thank goodness Dave still loves me."

"Dave's a keeper for sure. You're a very lucky woman. I can see how much he loves you." Susan sighed sadly as she remembered Mark and how he had abandoned her when the going got tough. She thought

Dave Margolis could teach him a thing or two about love and loyalty but didn't say it out loud. "So, can you see yourself as a powerful executive, running a million-dollar business?"

"Mmm, well, that's the thing right there, right? I can, and I can't wait for the challenge. I know the people, and mostly, they are good, decent, hard-working staff, whom Marlon used to bully to get them to do what he wanted. I always thought you caught more flies with honey than vinegar, though I agree, I must be tough when needed so staff don't think I'm a pushover. Fair, but tough is how I see my management style."

"Captain of the ship."

"Commander of the submarine."

"General of the troops." Susan giggled, and Lynne joined in, their heads almost touching as they laughed.

After a pause when they caught their breath, Susan said, "Apple of the pie," which set them off again.

Dave called while they were wandering up and down the aisles. "Hi, Dave," Lynne answered, "How's it going?"

"I'm suspended and under investigation," he responded, and Lynne could hear his barely concealed rage radiating from her mobile phone.

"Oh, Dave, I'm so sorry. This is all my fault."

"That would only be true if, back when this started, you could foretell the future. Otherwise, none of this is your fault; it's Marlon-fucking-Flanders' doing." He sighed. "Sorry for the language; I'm just so damned angry."

****

They went to lunch to meet with Dorothy Flanders, which Lynne had agreed to during the morning phone call. All three had little appetite, but Susan was keen to thank Dorothy in person, and Lynne thought it would be good to confirm she was accepting the offer in person. Lynne had promised she would not do anything about Marlon Flanders without Dave's knowledge, though he still harbored some doubts she might. Dave knew he had to trust her rather than lock Lynne up, which seemed the only alternative. Dave knew he had to have faith in her, but in his darkest moments, because she hadn't confided in him earlier, Dave still found that difficult.

Dorothy Flanders stood and smiled as they crossed the busy restaurant, guided by the hostess. Dave introduced Susan, who immediately hugged Dorothy and whispered frantically, "Thank you for helping me."

"You are very welcome, Susan. May I call you Susan?" Susan nodded eagerly. "When Dave told me what had happened to you and your plight to find a cure, I couldn't stop myself from offering what help I could. For me, it is money, and we make lots of it; for you, it's life. I hope that no matter how successful I become in business, I never lose sight of that distinction. So, Susan, thank you for permitting me to help."

While the hostess held Susan's chair, Dave held Lynne's for her, smiling at how Dorothy had made Susan feel at ease. He knew the money was a drop in the ocean to her considerable family wealth, but he was impressed that she didn't flaunt it and seemed genuinely humble.

"I took the liberty of ordering wine, a French Chablis. I hope that's okay with everyone. If not, of course, feel free to order what you like. I assume you'd like a beer, Dave? I ordered you one of those Italian ones you had at my condo the other day, which you seemed to enjoy." Dorothy asked with a smile. "I do love a man who knows what he wants."

Dave thought it was good that he had told Lynne about his visit to Dorothy. How she just spoke could be misinterpreted, such as how Dorothy said he had a beer with her, though Dave did not believe she did it with any malice, merely stating a fact and being considerate. "Thank you. I'm driving, so a beer or two will be fine. We are seeing Susan's specialist later, so I need a clear head to battle the evening city traffic."

A waiter appeared with a pewter bucket full of ice containing a wine bottle sticking above the rim and a tall glass with a freshly poured beer for Dave. Everyone stayed silent while the wine was poured and the pail placed in a matching stand to the side of the table. He bowed and discreetly left.

Dorothy picked her glass up and raised it as a toast. "Here's to a long and healthy life for you, Susan, and a long and happy career with Bond Corp for you, Lynne."

Everyone touched glasses and sipped.

"Mmm," Lynne said, which surprised Dave as Lynne had never been much of a wine lover. "That is delicious; you certainly know your wines, Dorothy."

Dave smiled inwardly as he realized Lynne was already working on building a respectful working relationship with the woman who was to be her boss. He had to admire Lynne for her people skills. *Maybe that's another thing Dorothy sees in Lynne,* he mused as he took a long draught of beer.

Dorothy nodded her approval of the compliment. "Lynne, I can't tell you how pleased I am you've decided to join us. I look forward to working with you and helping you build a career. Even though the episode with Marlon has destroyed my self-confidence as a woman and wife, my father says I am glowing. He says it is because of you. He calls it my *mothering, nurturing nature*. Whatever it is, I want to turn this experience into a positive outcome for us all." She pointed her glass again toward Lynne. "You, Mrs. Margolis, are going places, and it will be my great pleasure to help guide, train, and mentor you to be the best you can be."

Dave watched Susan grip Lynne's hand for support while Lynne blushed bright red. *Two peas in a pod, my God, they really are like twins. They are so close as if they know exactly what the other is thinking and feeling.* Dave thought back to his childhood and the loneliness that being an only child had brought. His mother had suffered severe complications during his birth, so she could not have a second child. Both parents had heaped all the love in the world upon him growing up, but Dave had often wondered what it would have been like to have a brother or sister to confide in. That was what Lynne had now in Susan, a *confidante*, something he could only imagine.

They ordered their meals, which were served with a speed that surprised Dave but also reinforced to him the kind of power a wealthy family like Dorothy's meant to a restaurant such as this. The staff were all over them, ensuring they got first-class service. Dave was sipping his second beer as the women enjoyed their desserts when Lynne's phone chirped from inside her purse. She glanced across the table at him, a forkful of pineapple cheesecake halfway to her mouth, and Dave's heart sank as he suspected the worst. Lynne placed her fork carefully on the plate, dug her cell phone out, looked at the screen, and then sharply at Dave. She resembled a deer caught in the headlights. Wordlessly, Lynne turned the phone so he could read the text message:

Unknown Number

—Hi beautiful, I hope you're enjoying lunch. It won't be long until we are enjoying lunches together. Be patient; plans are in place. We will be a family soon.

I love you—

Dave stood up, knocking his chair backward as he scanned the room, looking for Flanders. Through the red veil of his rage, he heard Lynne sobbing and turned back to see Susan standing alongside Lynne with her arm around her shoulders. "How does he know we're here at lunch, Dave?" Lynne cried.

Dave shook his head. "He couldn't possibly be that stupid." But Dave was trembling with rage and worry. Did the message mean Flanders was in New York, spying on them, and had watched them enter the restaurant? Or was it just a calculated bluff from Canada because it was a reasonable assumption they would be at lunch at this time of day? Flanders wouldn't be stupid enough to be inside right then, but that didn't mean he hadn't watched them from outside, if he was, after all, in New York. *How the hell did he know we would be here? Maybe he followed Dorothy. That makes sense…unless it is just a lucky guess.* It was the not knowing that Dave felt tearing him apart.

The remainder of lunch with Dorothy Flanders passed without interruption. Dorothy once more apologized for her part in creating the monster her ex-husband seemingly had become. At the same time, Dave and Lynne explained they did not blame her for her husband's erratic, obsessive behavior.

Dorothy understood that the date Lynne would start in her new position needed to be clarified. "I don't want you to worry, Lynne," Dorothy explained. "I've taken over the role and will continue to do so until the mess created by my husband is over and you are comfortable returning to work. As you said earlier, let's hope it is within two weeks, but if you need longer, just let me know. I have amended your position already with HR and informed payroll to begin paying you at your new salary. Whether it is a week or a month before you rejoin us is irrelevant so far as I'm concerned. I want this mess behind you so that when you return to work, you are one hundred percent mentally ready to take up the new challenge."

Lynne smiled faintly. "Thank you for the support. This is a nightmare I wish I could wake up from."

"Don't forget your trip to Barbados; just give me the dates, and I will make it happen. Susan, I can see how close you've become to this wonderful couple; how about you go with them and use the time to recuperate?"

Susan nodded. "Thank you. Dave and Lynne did ask if I would go with them if you agreed, and I said I would. It was to be my last farewell, but now I hope it is rest and recovery. And I have you to thank for the chance." She raised her glass as a toast, which Dorothy returned.

"Susan, Dave tells me you are a freelance editor. Have you ever thought of writing rather than editing others?"

Dave noticed Susan blushed brightly. "Umm, yes, as a matter of fact, I have. In my spare time, I have been working on an idea. It's a modern take on a classic love story, a thriller. I know it's a trope that's been done before, but I thought I had an unusual take on it."

"Well, if you don't mind my suggestion, you should write the story of the three of you. It would make for a fantastic story, one I'd like to read, but more than that, publish it for you if you do. Do you know part of our empire is a significant ownership in one of the *big five* publishing houses? I can guarantee it will see the light of day with a substantial advance if well written. And, of course, we own one of the largest public relations and marketing companies in New York. You are good friends with the new General Manager, and you will have my support as president to take you and your book through the stratosphere. But there is one condition."

Susan closed her mouth long enough to ask, "What would that be?"

She smirked. "No real names. You must not let anyone know that me, my ex-husband, or my organization are the real culprits in this story."

****

Ilene Whittaker was waiting for them and welcomed them into the waiting room. "Come, in, come in, come in." She smiled warmly, firstly at Dave, then Lynne, and finally, Susan. "Bart won't be long. How are you feeling today, Mrs. Bodinsky?"

Susan smiled worriedly. "I'm more nervous than anything else, Ilene; thanks for asking."

"Well, I've always found worrying doesn't make things better, only worse. Not that it's easy, no, I'm not saying that, but in my experience, the things you worry about the most come true the least. You know what they say? Stress is a killer. I can tell you that Doctor Bart is brilliant in his field. Secondly, he's had me working my butt off on the phone today on your behalf with your insurance company, and I know he's been hard at it too. Can I get anyone a coffee or iced water?"

Each shook their head. "We had a big lunch; thanks,

Ilene," Dave added.

"Grab a seat, and I will let him know you're here." She turned to her phone, but Susan interrupted.

"Did you have any success with the insurance company, Ilene?"

Dave noticed the receptionist stiffening and realized the answer was no. "Please forgive me," Ilene replied, "but I can't comment. Doctor Bart will explain everything to you. I shouldn't have even mentioned I'd been on the phone, but I was trying to reassure you that your case has Doctor Bart's highest priority."

She turned away, picked up the handset, and spoke into it. The three sat down and almost immediately stood up as the door to the doctor's consulting room opened, and Bart Chisholm beckoned to them. "Hello, Dave, Mrs. Margolis, and Susan. Please come through. I assume, Susan, you want Dave and Lynne with you?"

Try and stop us, Dave thought as he clasped Lynne's hand in his, knowing the next few minutes could be hard on his wife, almost as hard as it could be for Susan. As silly as that seemed, Dave could see Lynne's feelings for Susan as if she had replaced her long-dead twin sister. If the news were terrible for Susan, it would decimate Lynne to lose someone she had become so close to. They filed in as Bart held the door, with Dave bringing up the rear, and sat at the three chairs in front of the desk.

Bart sat down, tented his fingers with elbows on the desk, and began. "I know how anxious you are, so I won't beat around the bush. We've spoken to your insurance company, Susan, at length. I've gone as high as I can and pleaded your case. They have declined to honor a claim for an illness contracted in Africa. They say even if you sued them, they have sought advice, and there is a clause in your contract that excludes any medical issues arising from your vacation outside the United States. They say categorically, and I spoke with my attorney to confirm, they are not liable for any treatment or drugs for this claim."

Susan shrugged as if to say that was no more than she had expected. "I understand," she said quietly. "Is there anything at all you can do for me? Thanks to my wonderful friends here, I can access $50,000."

Bart paused, and silently, Dave urged Bart to get his obvious further bad news out of the way. His demeanor reeked of disappointment, and the suspense was killing Dave; he could only imagine what it was like for Susan and Lynne. "Susan, you must understand there has never been a case like this. No similar disorders matching your symptoms that I can find have ever been reported; believe me, I have spent all weekend researching."

Susan stood, choking back tears, and Lynne grabbed her arm. "Thank you for trying as you have. I knew I was a lost cause; these two wonderful people gave me hope, but I understand there is nothing you can do to help me."

"Wait, Susan." He stood and held out his hand as if directing traffic to stop her from running out of the room. "I didn't say there was nothing I could do. I explained that your case is unique and that there is no guarantee of success with anything we do, but that doesn't mean I can't try. I believe there is better than a twenty percent chance I can cure you with time and patience. And, I am afraid, with all that money you have, and possibly a touch more, though, it's impossible to know how quickly or slowly you will respond to the treatment I am proposing. There is no quick fix; you have several things going on in your body simultaneously, which complicates things. Please sit down and let me try to explain."

"You really can help me?" Susan asked, with a childlike, almost begging tone of voice as she fell back into her chair.

"Oh, my God," Lynne broke in, tears streaming down her cheeks. "I don't have the words to thank you, but Bart, thank you, thank you, thank you for giving Susan a chance. She is the most awesome, amazing woman I've ever met. And if ever someone deserved a break, it's her."

Bart smiled. "I can see how close you are, and Susan will need support and plenty of it. All right, let's get down to it. The first problem has shown up in the blood tests and biopsy results. Are you ready?"

Susan nodded; Dave let out a breath he hadn't realized he had been holding, and Lynne slid her chair closer to Susan and hooked her arm through hers.

Bart opened the folder in front of him. "Susan, you have a very rare form of auto-immune disease, and that will be our initial focus. Your body's way of fighting the bacteria in your blood is to cause the sores on your back. Firstly, at the sight of the first infection, and then spreading out from there. Usually, when parasitical bacteria invade the body, the body fights and slowly builds immunity. This is why we have flu and COVID-19 vaccines; giving humans a small inert dose can build immunity, so when a full-blown infection occurs, a patient has already grown the antibodies to fight it. That's not happening with you. Your body's defense is to aid the growth, not fight it. I have prescribed some powerful drugs to help curb your detrimental reaction to infection and hopefully raise your resistance to the intruding bacteria."

"How did I get such an immune disease, and why have I never discovered it before?"

Bart shrugged. "It may be nothing more than luck. You've always been healthy and never had to fight such an invasive bacterium, which was permitted to mutate because of inferior broad-spectrum antibiotics given to you in Africa. Perhaps, if they had tested further and used a specific targeted drug, the bacteria could have been destroyed there and then. Sadly, the doctors gave you a generic, cure-all type that can be effective in some simplistic cases, but your case was far from simple. You felt better, continued your vacation, then returned to the US.

Meanwhile, inside your body, a war was raging for control, aided by the very drugs that were supposed to help. Next, your auto-immune problem raised its head, which allowed it to grow inside your blood cells, which in turn permitted the bacterium to take hold in your skin. Rather than make you feel unwell, it manifested into skin ulcerations and took root. If we can defeat the infection, some of your sores will require severe excision and skin grafts to remove and rebuild. For a good long while, you will resemble a patchwork quilt. I'm sorry to say that even assuming we succeed, your back will show deep scarring, making wearing a bikini at the beach potentially embarrassing for you."

"If you can save me, Doctor, I won't care about that."

"Good. Susan, once we get on top of this, exposure to the sun will be something you must avoid at all costs. I didn't just mean for vanity's sake but for your recovery. With your skin in its state, prolonged sun exposure, even with sunscreen applied, would be catastrophic. Skin cancer would be fatal because of your low immune system."

"I understand. So, a trip to Barbados lazing on the beach would not be advisable?"

"Alaska, wearing furs would be better." He grinned, unaware of the proposed West Indies trip.

Dave shrugged, not bothered about losing the planned luxury vacation and knowing Lynne would feel the same. They could do it later. For the time being, Susan's recovery was far more important. "What else will Susan have to go through, Bart? Seems like you're holding back," he asked.

He nodded, firstly at Dave, then turned his gaze back to Susan. The drug I mentioned will aid with the auto-immune problem, but we still need to fight the bacteria and halt creeping ulcers. For that, I have been able to get you enrolled in a trial of a very potent, new antibiotic. According to the literature I've read, it should help. You will be on a three-week course, and make no mistake, the pills will knock you around and make you wonder if it's all worthwhile. There are some potential side effects. You will likely feel tired and nauseous. You will lose your appetite and possibly your sense of taste, though everyone reacts differently. You may experience all or none of those side effects or have something else, such as itchiness and rashes. This is an experimental drug in the final stages of testing that has had some extraordinary successes with skin disorders, though, of course, no one has had a condition like yours before, so we are flying blind. And then will come radiation and chemotherapy. We must destroy the bacteria growing sores on your back, and we will only have one chance to get it right.

Only when that's done can we begin skin grafts to repair the damage."

Susan stared at him, and Dave could almost hear her mind evaluating what Bart had told her. He hoped it wasn't too much for her, that the cure was worse than the cause, and Susan would climb back out on the ledge. Eventually, she nodded her acceptance. "And you give me a twenty-percent chance of surviving?"

"If you push me for my honest opinion, I think it's closer to thirty, but as I said, there is no literature on your condition. You must be aware that there are risks that the treatment I propose won't work. Possibly, it could go badly and hasten the advance of the sores or cause some other hitherto unknown problem. I will be donating my and my practice's time for free, but make no mistake, the costs will mount up. And you, Susan, you need to be on board with putting yourself in my hands and going through hell for a while in hopes that you come out the other end of the tunnel cured. But please understand there is no guarantee. Can you take several weeks off work?"

"Yes, she can," Lynne replied. "Susan will be staying with Dave and me for the duration. I will not begin my new job until Susan is back on her feet."

Dave realized that his marital problems with Marlon Flanders suddenly paled into insignificance, and Lynne was committed to Susan's recovery. His darkest fears had been Lynne would run off to be with Flanders to save Dave from being hurt or killed, but now she had said that she would devote herself to helping Susan through her darkest times. He looked from one woman to the other, reveling in their evident emotion. It was the kind of love and caring that only two women could feel, he mused.

Sometimes, help with a problem can come from unlikely sources. He felt more assured that with everything going on in their lives, Lynne was staying for the duration no matter what, and whatever Flanders did or didn't do, Lynne would be by his and Susan's side.

"Susan," Bart interrupted Dave's thoughts, "I've painted what I consider to be the worst-case scenarios. I don't believe things will be as bleak as I've suggested, but you must be prepared for all eventualities."

Susan smiled. "Doctor, it was only a few days ago I was about to end everything until this wonderful man entered my life. And then, he introduced me to Lynne, and I feel blessed to know them both. I'm in this one hundred percent. I will not weaken or give up until you tell me all hope is lost. I owe it to these two who have gone out of their way to make me feel like life is worth living. I've never had two friends like these guys, and I'm not going to give up for them and me."

Chapter 12

Loss

"Falling down is not a failure. Failure comes when you stay where you have fallen."
Socrates

"It's not what happens to you, but how you react to it that matters."
Epictetis

Tuesday
Dave woke to his cell phone ringing, which he had left on the dining table the night before. He grabbed his robe and put it on as he swung out of bed, hurrying to get to it before it went to his message bank. He sighed as he reached the table just too late. The screen showed it was a missed call from Simon. Dave hit the dial button but got the busy signal just as he heard Lynne's phone chiming its musical ringtone.

"Good morning, Simon, it's Dave; what's up?" He answered Lynne's phone.

"Dave, thank God you're there. Did you come and pick up the kids early this morning while we slept?"

Dave felt an icy hand reach into his chest and squeeze. "No, we haven't; why? What's wrong?"

"They're gone. We've searched high and low, but they're not here."

Dave urged Simon not to touch anything and hung up before waking Lynne to tell her the devasting news. The calm way Dave instructed his father-in-law masked the apoplectic terror he felt inside. Someone had kidnapped his children! Would he ever see them again, read them bedtime stories, hug them when they hurt themselves, or do a million other things a parent loves to do? His mind raced before he forced himself to calm down. He had to be strong because he knew Lynne's guilt for sleeping with Flanders, which now seemed to have led to their children's abduction, would be overpowering. He needed to push his rage and feeling of living in hell to the side and be strong for her sake.

Lynne was hysterical when he woke her and told her of the call. Her screams brought Susan running, and Dave explained what had happened. Susan launched herself at Lynne, hugging her tightly, crying tears of understanding and grief at the pain her new best friend was experiencing. Dave was grateful that Susan came running when she had. She comforted Lynne, helped her dress, and reassured her repeatedly, her soothing voice helping to keep Lynne from an anxiety attack or worse. Despite his misery and utter devastation, Dave took charge and told the women to prepare so they could leave for Westbury as soon as possible.

Dave left them to dress, called his captain, told him what had happened, and said they were going to the scene immediately. Captain Mark Brennan took charge and launched the highest possible media alert to publish the children's abduction and the suspected perpetrator, Marlon Flanders. An *amber alert* was designed to bring as much publicity as possible when a child went missing because, historically, in the US, seventy-five percent of children abducted by strangers were murdered within three hours.

Lynne called Flanders' cell phone continuously as Dave drove with lights flashing and siren blaring but got an *out-of-service announcement* with every attempt. She left vitriolic voice messages threatening not only would she never be a part of his life, but she and Dave would hunt him down to the ends of the earth if necessary to bring their children home.

****

Fifty minutes later, they arrived. Dave parked on a grass verge at an acute angle thirty yards before Lynne's parent's home because police officers had blocked the road off either side. Dave saw uniformed officers conducting door-to-door interviews to find witnesses. Forensics officers combed the gardens, path, and street for evidence while a helicopter hovered above them.

Warning messages and pictures of Ben and Molly, supplied to his captain by Dave via email before they left home, were repeatedly broadcast on TV, radio stations, mobile phones, and social media. Dave desperately hoped that his children would not be a part of that statistic because while Marlon Flanders was a stranger to them, he believed Flanders wanted to take the children and raise them as his own, not abuse them sexually. Dave recalled Dorothy insisting her husband was at his happiest when with children but was not a pedophile.

An officer visited Dorothy Flanders to obtain a recent picture of her husband, which would join the *Amber* broadcast to the public, all police officers, and the media. She immediately called Lynne and expressed her deepest sympathy and regret for the events.

For the first time, Dave saw what it was like to be a

victim rather than a police officer. Dave felt it worsened his fears because he knew he would not be permitted to participate in the investigation. Naturally, his captain would state Dave was too emotionally involved and impossible to reach calm, rational judgment calls. Dave agreed that if he ever came face to face with Flanders, he would not be able to stop himself from attacking the man, and if that led to Flanders' death, he would not lose any sleep over it. The logical part of his brain knew he should not be a part of the official hunt, but he also knew he would be front and center of his *unofficial* search as soon as he could get free.

Dave, Lynne, and Susan were led through the cordon and discovered the inside of the house was a hive of activity of more forensics officers inspecting the children's bedroom. The speed and extent of the investigation surprised Dave, but then he knew that when one of *their own* was in peril, all cops went the extra mile, knowing they could one day, too, require assistance. The fact that it was a cop's children missing heightened the universal sense of urgency. They were a brotherhood, and no one understood a cop's life more than another.

Dave's boss, Captain Mark Brennan, was already in attendance because he lived in Westbury, only four blocks away. He sat at a table with Simon and Beryl, sipping coffee, looked up when they burst in, stood, and tried to soothe the frightened pair. "Dave, Lynne, we're doing everything possible. I'm sorry for what has happened and for doubting your suspicions about this, Marlon Flanders. Flanders gained access through a rear window and used chloroform to ensure your children didn't wake. We found traces of it on both pillows. We can take comfort that he hasn't used violence, and from what you've told me, it seems he means no harm to come to them. We will catch him, and it's just a matter of time before we bring your children home. You have my word."

Lynne listened intently while wringing her hands together, then went to her mother, and they cried on each other's shoulders while Susan stayed near the doorway. In a frantic, quivering voice, Simon said, "We're so sorry. We never heard a thing. I checked on them around eleven when we went to bed, and everything was fine. But they were gone when we got up at seven."

Dave could see the guilt radiating from the elderly couple and knew he had to try to help them feel better. "We know; please don't blame yourselves; it's not your fault. I'm glad you didn't wake up and confront this man. He may have hurt you both, or worse. Marlon Flanders has become completely obsessed with Lynne and our children and will stop at nothing to make his sick fantasy come true. We don't blame you, don't feel bad; honestly, it's *not* your fault."

Mark Brennan stood and nodded to Dave to follow him. "Dave, I need to ask you some questions, and Mrs. Margolis, I need your phone, please, so we can organize a trace on any incoming calls; our tech boys are on their way. If Flanders expects you to go to him, he will be in touch, and we can pinpoint his location by triangulating the signal when he turns his cell back on." Lynne nodded, too distraught to speak. She opened her clutch purse and handed her phone over.

"I feel like a third wheel here; how about I make everyone tea or coffee?" Susan suggested. Despite his inner turmoil, Dave again realized she was a wonderful woman. He smiled and nodded a yes, hiding that he felt so enraged he could punch a hole through a wall. "Susan, you know how I like mine; yes, I'd love one; this could be a long day." He followed his captain out of the room.

****

The number of officers attending the abduction site quickly swelled to over fifty. Under Captain Mark Brennan's direction, uniformed patrolmen visited every house in the street and questioned the occupants, hoping to find a witness. Back at headquarters, officers were pouring over traffic CCTV camera footage to locate the car used by Flanders while others tried to contact his family in Canada.

Maurie Wiscowski, a widowed shift worker at a steel mill who lived seven houses away, was initially angry at being woken up but offered the first breakthrough when told the reason for the intrusion. Around four fifteen a.m., Maurie had entered the street and drove toward his home, a block past Simon and Beryl's residence. He noticed a white American brand sedan pull away from the sidewalk. Though he couldn't identify the specific make, he thought the model was vaguely familiar and was sure he'd seen it on the street before. Maurie thought it odd but admitted being tired after a twelve-hour shift, so he didn't consider it sinister, just unusual. The witness became agitated and blamed himself when he realized the car was most likely driven by the man responsible for taking the children.

The patrolman radioed in and requested a senior officer attend. Four minutes later, Matt Smith, who had just arrived to help when he heard the news, even though it was his day off, ran to question the witness further. Matt, too, blamed himself for not doing what he'd have disappeared in a puff of smoke. "Susan, I knew you would say that, and I understand your thinking. But I would like to ask you for some favors, okay?"

"Anything, you know that."

"All right, here goes. No matter what happens, I want your word of honor you will keep going with Bart's treatment plan. If he can help, I want you to take it. You have the money; you must promise me this; it's non-negotiable."

She stared at him, and comprehension dawned on her. "Why are you saying that? Where will you be? Why can't you come with me after the police catch Flanders?"

"Oh, I hope to be with you, don't worry. But all I am asking is that if I'm not, you will continue anyway."

"What are you not telling me, Dave?"

Dave sighed; she's *far too clever.* "I need to ask you a huge favor, Susan. I understand why you think you should return to your condo, But I'd like you to stay for a while and keep Lynne from going crazy. I need to check out something, and I'm unsure how long it will take."

"You can't take off and leave Lynne to deal with this alone. She's frantic now but will be apoplectic if you go."

"She won't be alone; she'll have her mother, father, and you." He glanced around to ensure they were not being overheard by one of the nearby officers. "Lynne told me something a few days ago that probably means nothing, but I need to check it out. Flanders told her that when he was trying to get her to go to Chicago so he could seduce her, his family had a vacation lake house in the Hudson Valley. Maybe he's taken the kids there."

"So why do you need to do it alone? Why not let the

police do it; they have the manpower?"

"I checked for his address when I went to work because I wanted to visit him and have a one-on-one chat with him about the problems he was causing, like the break-in, killing our cat, and everything else. But then I was told he had returned to Canada, so I let it slide and didn't check further. The thing is, I couldn't find a property in that area owned by anyone with the surname Flanders. So, I think it could be in a corporate name if it exists at all. Let's face it: it may have just been a smokescreen to lure Lynne away. At this point, we don't even know if Flanders has taken our children for sure, though I can't see any other alternate scenario that fits. His family in Toronto will surely close ranks to protect him, and then we might not be able to get a warrant to search their records. If Flanders is there, with Molly and Ben, and we flood Lake Mahanna with cops door knocking, he may get wind and do something unthinkable if he feels backed into a corner. Suppose I sneak away and check out first with Dorothy to see if she knows about the place. If not, I can go to the lake on the QT and ask around. If Flanders is there, I will call in the SWAT team."

Susan got that look of understanding again. "No, you won't. You'll kill him."

Dave stared back. How he felt, he knew she was right; Dave doubted he could stop himself from ending the fiasco.

Chapter 13

Patience

"It is easier to find men who will volunteer to die than to find those who are willing to endure pain with patience."
Julius Ceaser

"To lose patience is to lose the battle."
Mahatma Gandhi

Later that evening, Dave coaxed Lynne into leaving the house for a walk. He felt they were both stir-crazy and needed to speak privately with her about his plan. They walked, with his arm around her, hugging her to him. At first, she had been reluctant to leave. Lynne was desperate for news, not only because it was their children who had been abducted, Dave knew, but also because she felt so guilty that it was her actions in seemingly encouraging Flanders that had caused him to become obsessed with her and the make-believe fantasy family life he envisioned with her, Ben and Molly. Dave assured her that any news whatsoever would be conveyed to his cell phone immediately, and eventually, she relented.

Logically, nothing made sense, Dave knew. But he also acknowledged the futility of using logic to understand illogical acts. As a police officer, he had encountered hundreds of cases where an act of violence or criminality beggared belief in the cold light of day. Yet, to the perpetrator, the reasons had been crystal clear. Sure, sometimes, drugs had been the cause, but in others, there seemed no rhyme or reason, and this seemed like one of those times. He waited until they reached the end of the street before he began. "Lynne, I need to get away for a while and check something out."

She stopped dead in her tracks. "What?" she almost screamed.

"Shush, love. As I recall, you mentioned a few days ago that Flanders told you he had a house on a lake, Lake Mahanna, and wanted you to spend a weekend with him there. I wonder if he has used that as a bolt-hole and taken Ben and Molly there."

She searched his face, which he deliberately kept deadpan, not wanting to upset her. "Yes, he did make that offer, but he didn't say where on the lake it was. Why don't you tell your captain that? He can flood the area with a SWAT team and check it out."

"Okay, let's explore that. Are you sure it was Lake Mahanna he invited you to?"

She cocked her head to one side, remembering the conversation. "Y-y-yes, I'm pretty sure that's where he said."

"But not a hundred percent?"

"Almost. I'm positive that's the lake. Ninety-five?"

"Did he describe the house in any way?"

She seemed to Dave to be exasperated by her tone of voice. "No, Dave. I wasn't paying attention because I had no intention of spending a weekend with him. So, maybe he knew that, and he was lying about a house there, but my opinion was he was bragging about how much money he and his family had and how he could make my life complete if I went away with him."

"It's all right, Lynne. I'm not criticizing; I'm just trying to point out one of the reasons why I don't think we should waste valuable manpower checking out a maybe. If the captain sends a squad there, he has to take officers from elsewhere, and I don't want him to do that."

She nodded thoughtfully. "You said that's one reason, what's the others?"

"Well, we have to consider his state of mind if he is there. A bunch of cops questioning house to house is bound to be noticed. He may do something unthinkable if he believes they are closing in and he feels trapped."

She gasped and visibly shuddered at a thought too terrible to contemplate. "What do you want to do?" she whispered.

Dave slipped his arm through his wife's, causing her to walk with him again. "Lynne, I'm worried. I think the only way he returned to New York under the radar was by a private plane, which he now has hidden at a small airfield somewhere. With the *Amber alert*, they will all be monitored, so Flanders needs somewhere to hold up. When the cops stop the search, which sooner or later they must, he can fly our kids to Canada in his jet, and from there, he has the money to disappear. From what I surmise, it looks like he would relish the life of a single father, though we know he wants you to join him. But even without you, he has two children he can call his own. I don't want to stop the hunt for him, but I do want to go and quietly check out the lake houses and see if he is hiding out there."

"And if he is?"

Dave paused. "Then I will bring our children home."

****

Just after midnight, Dave checked on Matt Smith and sighed in relief when he saw by the dim light filtering through the blinds that the cop was asleep on the couch. At Mark Brennan's forceful suggestion, Matt had insisted on returning to Dave and Lynne's home with them and spending the night. Dave wasn't sure if it was to protect them or keep Dave from taking the law into his own hands and hunting Marlon Flanders. But he acceded to the barely veiled order from his captain because he realized if he didn't, it would be like an advertisement he intended to do just that.

Susan and Lynne were on board with his intention, and when they made the pretense of going to bed earlier, the three sat in Dave and Lynne's bedroom, planning in quiet voices what he would do. Dave intended to sneak out of the house and drive to Lake Mahanna to be there early in the morning before he was noticed missing. Lynne and Susan would distract Matt as much as possible to give him time to search for Flanders without interference. He told his wife and new best friend that, at some point, they would have to admit where he was and why because otherwise, they could be charged with an obstruction of justice offense. Dave hoped that, at the very least, they could distract Matt until lunchtime so he would have a few hours to try to find the house if it existed. Dave would take his cell phone and promised to call Lynne every chance he got to report in and tell them of his progress, if any. Lynne had handed her cell phone to Mark Brennan, but it had been returned and paired with an investigator's for monitoring for further calls or texts. Dave wasn't concerned with that as he could not hide what he was doing for long.

He had no real plan other than to ask if anyone knew

of the Flanders family. He had the picture of Marlon Flanders and would show it anywhere he could, such as cafés, restaurants, and markets. He would use his police ID in hopes that people would be more forthcoming with information.

Seeing Matt on the couch, Dave quietly returned to the bedroom and said his goodbyes to Lynne and Susan. "Susan," he began, "I can't thank you enough for staying with Lynne and helping to keep her sane. You know I appreciate it, don't you?"

"Dave, you, and Lynne have saved my life; this is the least I can do to thank you. Do what you need to do; don't worry about anything here. Lynne and I will hold off your colleagues as long as possible." She flung her arms around his neck and hugged him tightly. "Godspeed," she whispered. "Find this madman and bring your beautiful children home." Susan stepped back away from him, and he turned to Lynne.

"Baby, are you sure you're going to be okay?" he asked his wife, who was struggling to hold back tears.

She swallowed. "I brought this misery on us with my stupidity. Please, Dave, find them and bring them home. If you have to, kill him. Don't you dare let him hurt you. I've lost Ben and Molly; if I lost you too, I'd have nothing to live for."

Dave nodded, then took her in his arms, and she sobbed softly into the nape of his neck. He wanted to hold her forever but knew he had to make a move. "I love you, Lynne Margolis. If Flanders is there, I will find him, I promise."

****

Dave slipped out of the back of the house, over the rear fence, and around the corner to his car. When they arrived home earlier, he had left it unlocked and had turned the interior light off, knowing he would return in darkness and didn't want a sudden flashing light to wake anyone. He intended to quietly slip away into the night, and Dave thought he was successful knowing Matt Smith was asleep. When he reached the vehicle, Dave gently eased the door open and slid inside, softly closing the door behind him.

"Where are we going, Dave?" Matt Smith asked from the back seat, startling Dave out of his skin.

"Jesus Christ," Dave exclaimed. "You frightened the crap out of me."

"Sorry, bud, but you made it obvious you planned something. Seriously, Dave, all those furtive glances between the three of you, I'm not dumb. Now, you can either share it with me, and I help you, or you don't, and we stay here, or, of course, I tell the boss you are hiding something. Trust me, I'm on your side, and what you tell me won't go any further unless I decide it's too dangerous or illegal. It would mean my badge if I didn't report something of a criminal nature you intended to carry out, and I know you well enough you wouldn't want to drop me in deep. So, I ask you again, where are we going?"

Dave slowly shook his head, angry with himself for telegraphing his intention and Matt for letting him play into his hands. Dave sighed, knowing he had no choice, and he had to admit that if Matt had confronted him with his suspicions, Dave would have denied it. "Lake Mahanna."

"Why there?"

Dave told him, taking great trouble to explain that it might be nothing and that he hadn't wanted to cause a false alarm to derail the search. Dave further explained that he thought he could be discreet and call the cops if he found something worth reporting.

Matt nodded. "Good call, Dave. You're right, but two can finish the job in half the time. Let's go; I'm coming with you. The boss told me not to let you out of my sight. I agree this is slim, so I won't report to him until we find out if Flanders is there.

****

The drive was long and tedious. Neither cop felt much like talking other than the logistics of what they would do when they arrived. They had agreed that if he were in hiding there, Flanders would not broadcast it. He would know there was an alert for him and the children, so all he could do was lie low and wait for the hunt to die. So, they decided they would ask around the town to see if anyone knew the Flanders family, as well as Marlon, because if the house was a family property, it could have been years since he was there, if ever. Flanders had invited Lynne for a dirty weekend, which inferred he was at least familiar with the place. He was a big man, so theoretically, someone should remember him; at least, that was Dave's fervent hope.

Earlier that evening, Dave had called Dorothy, who was distraught at the thought her ex-husband had abducted their children and offered anything she could do to help, including a massive reward for information. Dave thanked her and said he would suggest it to the captain. He wanted his questioning to seem casual, so he asked, almost offhanded, "Dorothy, can I ask if you guys had a holiday home? Maybe a weekend vacation place at the beach or a cabin on a lake, somewhere he may have taken the kids to lie low for a while?"

"Not that I can think of, Dave, no. We always went to my family's place in the Hamptons or the house on Long Island. But my father is currently at the Hamptons, and my sister and husband are at the Long Island home while they build a new house."

"What about his side of the family? Do they have somewhere here when they come to stay from Canada?"

"Good question. I've only visited with Marlon's family in Toronto, so I'm unaware of anything here. When we got married, they all stayed in a hotel in Manhattan. I vaguely recall Marlon saying his father was looking to purchase something here several months ago, but I don't recall him saying they did. Of course, his family has closed ranks and won't talk to me now. I'm the bad one in this opera, not Marlon. Are you thinking he is in hiding here somewhere?"

Dave hesitated for a moment too long. "I don't know what to think, Dorothy. Lynne and I are going insane with worry, so I'm just clutching at straws."

"Police officers were here earlier, asking me a thousand questions, but I don't think I was any help to them. Everything Marlon has done has taken me completely by surprise, and I don't know what to think. He is a focused and self-assured man, but I never thought he would become obsessed to the point of kidnapping. I suppose, once I kicked him out, it tipped him over the edge to the point where he lost his self-respect, along with his marriage. Maybe if I had given him a child of our own, none of this would have happened. I'm so sorry, Dave."

"It's not your fault, Dorothy; don't blame yourself."

The conversation wound down. Dave felt frustrated she had been unable to shed any light on the Lakehouse and wasn't in the mood for small talk. Deep down, a part of him did blame her for not keeping her husband on a tighter reign, but the problem with that thought was if he started blaming her for her partner's behavior, then he had to apportion blame to himself for Lynne's.

****

Their first stop was at the largest gas station on the outskirts of Mahanna, just as the sun was rising and a new day was beginning. Mahanna was a vacation town, primarily servicing the tourists or people who owned homes or vacation rentals on the shores or close to the third biggest lake in the state. Dave knew there were around three thousand residents, but that number swelled four times that during the popular seasons.

Matt turned in his seat. "Dave, you fuel up; I will go inside, pay for the gas, and buy us a coffee. I will also ask if Flanders has come through recently. When we are together, please let me take the lead; after all, you are still serving your suspension, so you have no official standing. When we split up to cover more territory, you're on your own, though we will communicate by cell if one of us gets any information. For now, please stay in the background. I'm risking my badge letting you carry out any form of investigation; I know you understand."

Dave nodded, opened the door, stepped out in one motion, and then stretched the cramp out of his back after the long drive. Matt repeated the movements before heading inside. Five minutes later, Matt returned. Dave reached across to open the door for him and took a paper cup filled with black coffee, steam rising out of the small opening in the lid. Matt slid in and passed a paper bag he'd been holding between his teeth. "I got you a bagel, too," he uttered.

"Thanks. Anything?"

"Nah. Curly headed young guy by himself inside only does the night shift. He's not seen Flanders but suggested returning later in case Hank, the day shift manager and owner, saw anything."

Dave nodded, put the cup in the holder in the consul, started the engine, and drove to the parking area to the side. He left the engine running but put the transmission in park, then took a sip from the cup. "Matt," he began, haltingly, as if embarrassed. "When you shocked me earlier by waiting for me in the car, I may have acted like I was pissed at you…"

"Because you were."

"…Yeah, well, there is that. But I want you to know, mostly because you took me completely by surprise. I had this plan in mind: the women would distract you long enough for me to come here, carry out discreet inquiries, find out I was an idiot, and then sneak back before anyone was the wiser. The point is, I appreciate your support and help; you're a good guy, and I thank you."

Matt stared at Dave for two minutes above his cup before sighing profoundly and lowering it. "Okay, I accept that, as far as it goes. But we both know that if you came here alone and found Flanders, you would not have called in the cavalry. You'd have gone Rambo or Dirty Harry and killed him to rescue your kids. While that is understandable, it's also dumb. It would be a premeditated act of murder, and you'd have spent years in the State Pen. Dave, you're a seasoned cop, and the DA would have argued successfully that you should have known better despite the fear for your kid's safety. Even us coming by ourselves is pushing the envelope, but I can assure you, if we can prove Flanders is here, we *will* be calling in the troops. We are clear on that, aren't we?"

Dave knew Matt was correct; that is what would have happened, and yes, he could have spent years in jail for murder despite the justification he may have felt he had. But, damn it, it was his children, and he was frantic with worry. But Matt had stuck his head in the noose for him, and he couldn't let a good man down. "Yeah, Matt. We will call it in."

They stared at each other, gauging their sincerity until Matt broke the deadlock. "Don't make me cuff you to the steering wheel because I will if I have to."

Dave smiled at the mental image of being handcuffed inside the car. "We're good," he said finally. "We will report in if we find him here." He opened the bag and took a bite of his bagel, hoping Matt would believe him, even though Dave knew if given half a chance, he would shoot Marlon Flanders dead without hesitation if it meant saving Ben and Molly.

****

Around eight a.m., Dave drove to the main street and parked at one end. They both exited the car in unison, and Matt held his hand out for the keys. The main town road was six to eight hundred yards long, with businesses on both sides. Most were tourist shops selling clothing and gifts, while others were offices, supermarkets, realtors, and cafés. There was even a tiny second-hand car yard. Some shops were starting to open, and people were milling around, looking in windows for breakfast diners. "Dave, not that I don't trust you, but guess what? I don't trust you. So, I will take the car and park at the far end, and we will work toward each other. We stay in touch by cell, and if one of us gets a clue, we immediately communicate it to the other. Are we clear?"

"Yeah, we're clear," he replied, tossing the keys, which Matt caught deftly. Let's check in with each other every hour, on the hour, news or no news?"

"Deal."

Matt drove away, and Dave turned and walked into the Mahanna Café and began his search for any mention of the Flanders family.

****

Three hours later, Dave was frustrated. He'd spoken to a couple of hundred or more people and came up with nothing. He knew Matt Smith had the same lack of results until their last check-in. He'd also called Lynne to pass along the lack of success and noted she seemed to be barely hanging on to her sanity. Dave tried to comfort her and understood that while he was doing something, all Lynne had was to wait around, and every minute of no news brought more heartache for her. He promised he would be back later that night if nothing came up, and if he and Matt did discover something concrete, she would be the first to know.

Dave left the hardware store after more unsuccessful interviews when his phone chirped; it was Matt. "Hi, Matt, anything?"

"Probably not, but I have a long shot, which I will check out."

Dave immediately straightened up; any chance, no matter how slim, was something. "What have you got?"

"Don't get your hopes up; it's probably nothing. I just happened to notice the busboy at the market loading bags of groceries into a van for delivery. I questioned him, and apparently, it was a phone order made by a man who said his name was Wilson. It's a cash-on-delivery order, so I couldn't check if it was a fake name. I noticed some kids' candy on top of one of the paper bags, and as we know, it's not vacation time, so kids should be at school, not here at the lake. Now, it's probably nothing; apparently, phone orders for delivery are commonplace, but I offered to make the drop-off for him. I showed my ID, gave the guy a ten-dollar tip, and paid for the groceries. He jumped at it, so I will be the delivery man instead and check it out. The house is on Maddison Pool Road, number 1012. I will call once I've checked it out, but as I said, it's clutching at straws, so don't get excited. If it is Mr. Wilson, I hope he gives me a bigger tip than the ten dollars I gave the real driver."

"I'm striking out here, so let me come with you."

"Dave, for you to be able to sleep tonight, you and Lynne need to know you checked out every possibility. How far away from the Market are you? You should be able to see the sign from where you are; it's called SAVE-AWAY MARKET."

Dave looked up the street and noticed the yellow and black neon sign. "Did you do both sides of the road? If so, and you did the pawnbroker's shop, I've got about ten businesses to stop at."

"Okay, so let me check out the Wilson house, and you finish interviewing here. If we both blow out, we can head back and get home by nightfall; Lynne will be glad to have you back home. If either of us uncovers anything, call the other, and we will make a plan from there. Sound good?"

Dave shrugged, knowing Matt's suggestion made perfect sense. He understood he just needed to feel like he was doing something. The ache in his heart for his missing children threatened to swallow him, and he knew he had to get back to Lynne soon because she would be worse. "Okay, I'll finish these last few places; you check out the lead; please call me the minute you know something."

"Will do, but, Dave. So that you know, I'm going to turn my cell off. If I'm talking to Flanders, I don't want my phone ringing and giving away the fact I'm a cop, so don't call me. I will call you when I'm done."

Dave finished the interviews, continually glancing at his watch, wondering what was taking Matt so long, and at the one-hour mark, decided he could not wait any longer. He pulled his cell phone from his jacket pocket and made the call. He cursed silently when he received a recorded message saying the phone number he was calling was switched off or not in a serviced area. Agonizingly, he waited fifteen minutes and tried again but got the same result.

He sat on a low brick wall and thought about the situation. He was stuck in town, without a car, and could only contact Matt once he surfaced again. Granted, that could happen at any moment, but he wondered, what if it didn't? *What's the worst thing that could have happened? Matt has found Flanders and is in trouble. Okay, so assuming that has occurred, what are my options? Call it in and get a swat team out here. Can't. We don't have a warrant to search the house because there is no evidence to show cause. If I call it in, and Matt is not in trouble, just delayed, or he's damaged his phone somehow or has a flat battery, he will face the captain's wrath and could be suspended for coming here with me. I can't risk it, so what's left? Go to the house and look for the car. That would be a start.*

It took him a further ten minutes to track down a cab, and in a town of its size, he considered himself lucky at that. He gave the driver the address on Maddison Pool Road but added a few house numbers so the cabbie would drive past the house of interest. The street followed the shoreline around a huge lagoon on the lake's western side with large, exclusive-looking homes, each set on acreage blocks. As they drove slowly past 1012, Dave could see no sign of life, which worried him as he'd hoped he'd see something so he could stop worrying. The house was huge, made from white stone and timber construction with a gray slate roof and high-security walls and gates protecting it from the street. Dave again noted the lack of life, but there was no obvious sign of that with other houses. Dave guessed that any living areas inside the homes would face the lake, not the street, so unless an owner were gardening, it would be normal not to see anyone from this side. That thought didn't help the helplessness and worry he felt.

Dave thanked the driver, gave him a decent tip, and asked for his direct phone number if he needed to be picked up later. He had no definite plan now that his car was nowhere to be seen, but he realized he might need to get out of the area if no one was home and he couldn't find Matt. It was early afternoon as he watched the taxi go back the way it had come, then Dave turned the other way and began walking until he came to a tree-filled park from the street to the lake. Comprising bar-b-que areas, children's play equipment, and a small pier for tying up boats, Dave thought it quite beautiful. He headed to the jetty to get a view of the back of the house.

Dave could make out the gray slate roof, but that was all. His view was blocked because of the angle of the lake and by a series of willow trees that bent their branches and leaves to the ground and followed the shoreline. He was eight houses away from his target but noted a gravel path that followed the waterline he could use to get closer, and by utilizing the willows, he thought he could get unseen nearer to the back of the house. He switched his phone to silent, then took off at a trot, feeling nervous that he might soon find his children.

Chapter 14

Vengeance

"Vengeance is in my heart, death in my hand. Blood and revenge are hammering in my head."
William Shakespeare

"There is no satisfaction in vengeance unless the offender has time to realize who it is that strikes him and why retribution has come upon him."
Sir Arthur Conan Doyle

Matt Smith believed he was on a wild goose chase, but if only to appease Dave, he was determined to try, knowing that they would have no regrets if they did all they could between them. He'd almost not mentioned the Wilson grocery angle to Dave, but he realized it gave Dave some hope if it achieved nothing else. Even if that was soon dashed, at least for a while, he had something to hold onto. Matt knew that because of the number of hours that had passed since the abductions, statistically, the children were most likely dead. That theory assumed the kidnapper took them for sexual reasons, which was the leading cause of child abductions in America. Of course, if it was Marlon Flanders, which Matt seriously doubted could be, then there was every chance the kids could be alive and hiding. It was that slim possibility that made Matt take a chance and investigate.

He parked with a slight skid on the gravel at the gated entranceway of 1012 Maddison Pool Road. Matt took a deep breath, trying his best not to look like a cop but a delivery man, and stepped out of the car. He glanced at the CCTV camera mounted on a stone pillar and pressed the intercom call button.

"Hello?" came a male voice from the tiny speaker.

"Save Away Market grocery delivery," Matt replied while holding the button again.

Silence followed until the speaker crackled to life again. "Where's the usual guy and the van?"

Matt felt a chill run down his spine. *Could it be Flanders?* He thought. *If it isn't him, why sound so suspicious?* "He's off sick with COVID. Marty, the owner, is my brother, and I'm visiting from Florida; he asked if I could help, so here I am." He smiled his best. *I'm not a cop, just a guy helping his brother* smile at the camera.

"Thanks for doing that. Okay, leave the bags at the gate. I will grab them shortly."

"Can't do that. I was told it was cash. There is one-seventy-five to pay."

"Yeah, that's right, sorry I forgot. Drive on up to the house." There was a loud click, then a whirring noise and the gates began to move.

Matt slid back into the car, waited for the gates to open fully, and debated whether to call Dave and tell him of his suspicion. He decided against it, thinking that Mr. Wilson may still be genuine. *Besides, there could be other cameras, and I'm being watched. I'll drop the stuff off, leave, then call Captain Brennan if it's him.* Matt started the engine and drove through, then down the long, curved, white gravel driveway to the house. Grand stone steps led up to the verandah and front door. Matt picked up two of the four shopping bags, put one under each arm, and climbed the steps. The door opened, and a tall, well-built man beckoned him inside. Matt recognized instantly that he was face-to-face with Marlon Flanders. Trying not to show surprise, he nodded a greeting and stepped through the doorway.

"Straight through, please; the kitchen is down the hall to the right."

"Gotcha," Matt replied, then heard the front door close behind him and walked where he'd been directed.

The following noise he heard coincided with a sense of falling, and for a split second, he couldn't understand what the *"thunk"* noise meant or why he was suddenly lying face-first on the marble floor. Everything was spinning around; he felt nauseous and struggled to stay conscious.

Marlon Flanders stood above him and brought the aluminum baseball bat down again and again on the back of Matt's head until he stopped squirming and lay in a puddle of blood and brain matter.

With each blow, Flanders screamed: *"You're."* *Thunk. "Not." Thunk. "Taking," Thunk. "My," Thunk. "Kids."*

****

Dave edged closer to the white house, using what cover he could but trying to look like a guy out for a carefree walk around the lake, not a cop looking for his partner. He passed a middle-aged couple beaching their canoe who eyed him suspiciously. "Hi," Dave said as he passed them, hoping they would not ask him his business. The woman raised a hand in greeting half-heartedly, and the man nodded. *Not a very friendly neighborhood,* Dave thought and kept walking.

At the next mansion, a man was using a ride-on mower, trimming the immaculate Bermuda grass, but he ignored Dave if he even saw him. Dave assumed that the locals didn't appreciate tourists visiting their piece of paradise, which he supposed was understandable as the homes would be valued in the millions. He walked on, edging ever closer to his target, now only three houses away.

****

The rear of the Flanders Lake House, as Dave thought of it, even though he didn't know if that was correct, had terraced gardens leading from the raised stone rear veranda and the outdoor entertaining area down to the path he stood on, hiding behind a willow tree. On the lake, behind him, tied to a small jetty, sat a bright orange ski boat named *BOLLERO.*

It looked like the entire rear of the building was tinted glass, making it difficult for Dave to see inside but possibly easy for someone inside to notice him. Dave knew he had to be careful. Flanders knew what Dave looked like by Lynne's family picture on her desk at work. He dared not spook Flanders if he was inside because there was no predicting what he might do if he felt cornered, so he needed to try to get closer without being seen.

He took his phone out and called Matt again. Once more, the phone was switched off or not in a service area. *Fuck, fuck, fuck. Maybe Matt is back in town looking for me, and his phone has died.* Somehow, though, Dave didn't believe that. He wasn't entirely sure what he thought, but his internal radar warned him to expect the worst. *Okay, let's workshop it. Matt finds Flanders and is inside the house, either interviewing him or he's been neutralized somehow. Locked in a basement or something. But where is my fucking car? Matt was delivering supplies, so he drove to the front gate, and Flanders buzzed him in. Then what?* That was the question, and Dave did not want to face the ultimate truth but knew he had to. *If I'm thinking of the worst-case scenario, Flanders recognized Matt as a cop and somehow immobilized him. He would know he'd have to hide the car, but he'd also know if Matt were a cop, he would need to run because others would follow. So maybe hiding the vehicle was only required to be temporary…the garage.* Dave had noticed earlier what looked like a three, or perhaps four-car garage at the front right-hand side of the property. *Surely, there is enough room to hide a car from view. Then, maybe later tonight, Flanders plans to take Ben and Molly and run again.* Dave sighed; he knew it made sense, but only if it was Flanders in the house.

He dialed Lynne's cell phone. And she answered almost immediately, "Dave, what's happening?"

Dave knew Lynne and could tell she was close to breaking point by her near-hysterical voice. "Lynne, calm down, listen please, baby. I need you to stay calm." He quickly told her where he was and why.

"What do you need me to do?" she asked.

"Have faith and trust me. I want you to wait fifteen minutes and if you don't hear back from me, call my boss and tell him what I suspect. He will, of course, tell me to stand down until he can send a SWAT team if I call him, which would mean ignoring a direct order. But I'm afraid they will be too far away and take too long to get here. If Flanders has done something to Matt, he will slip away…or worse, make a stand and put our children in danger. I need to confront him if he is in the house. So be it if he isn't, and it's a false alarm. It will probably mean the end of my career, but I have to do this for Ben and Molly's sake. I just wanted to tell you before I go inside and face…well, whatever I'm going to face. Possibly nothing, and I'm only guilty of breaking and entering. But maybe Flanders is waiting for me, and then, whatever will happen will happen."

Lynne stayed silent, and he heard her sobbing, knowing she carried a world of guilt for allowing the sex with Flanders to grow into an obsession for him. "Lynne, I need you to listen to me. Can you do that?"

Lynne moaned, and in his mind, he could see her biting her lower lip, which was her habit when she tried to stop herself from crying. "Dave, I love you so much and am so sorry for this mess; it's all my fault."

"Lynne, shush, okay? What's done is done and can't be undone. I need you to know that I forgive you. You are only guilty of an error in judgment, that's all. The rest? Well, you can't be held responsible for the actions of an unhinged man. As Dorothy says, something inside him snapped once he lost everything: his company position, wife, and you. He wants to blame everyone else but himself. That's not your fault. I need you to hold on; I love you and don't blame you for what has happened, okay?"

She didn't reply, and Dave knew it was because she was beyond being upset. But he couldn't let her mindset stop him from doing what he needed to do. "Lynne, pay attention, please. I'm going into the house soon, and I need you to know that I love you; you have always been the only one for me. I hope to be able to call you back and put Ben and Molly on the phone if they are inside. If Flanders is there, I have to do whatever it takes to get our children from him, do you understand?"

"Please, please, please be careful. I don't deserve you. Yes, I understand; it's either you or him. Just make sure it's you who comes out, and please bring them home."

"I will. I love you, Lynne. Wait fifteen minutes, then call Mark and tell him I believe Flanders has done something to Matt Smith and is holed up inside 1012 Maddison Pool Road, Lake Mahanna. If you don't hear back from me within fifteen minutes, make the call, Lynne."

He ended the call because he knew if he didn't, she would say something more, and he would reply; she would say she loved him, and he would say it back, and the conversation would continue. No, it was better to end the call and do what he needed to do. Dave took a deep breath, unholstered his gun, clicked off the safety catch, and chambered a round. The sun was low in the sky behind him, which might make it difficult for anyone inside the house to see him approach.

Dave shrugged, stepped out from behind the tree, and then sprinted up the hill, aiming for a large flowering bush in the first terrace bed. Nothing happened; shots didn't ring out, which gave Dave hope. He glanced around the bush, looked for his next hiding spot, climbed the stone wall, and ran in a zig-zag path to another bush on the next level.

So far, so good; two more terraces to go. Dave didn't wait around to catch his breath; he climbed the stone retaining wall, then, with a crouching gait, angled his approach to the left toward a maple tree. As he approached the house, Dave expected the sound of gunfire any moment, but thankfully, it didn't come.

He peered around the tree trunk and noted no sign of life from the house. Despite his belief Flanders was inside, the silence gave him doubts. Dave decided, and instead of running to the glass doors from the alfresco area to the inside, which was his original plan, he kept going left to what he believed was the rear of the garage. He flung his body against the stone wall, panting from nerves and exertion, and inched his way along to the window, tucked the pistol into his belt, cupped his hands over the sides of his face to keep the glare off, and looked through the dusty glass inside the garage.

Slowly, his eyesight adjusted to the gloom, and Dave could make out two cars. Dave gritted his teeth with a mixture of ice-cold anger and despair, seeing that one of the vehicles was his. Flanders had done something to Matt Smith and put the car out of sight. Dave took his phone out and hurriedly sent a text message to Lynne:

—*Make the call now; tell the captain I need urgent assistance. Flanders is here, and Matt Smith has been hurt.*—

****

Alongside the window was a wooden door. Dave tried the handle, but unsurprisingly, it was locked. He took a deep breath and shouldered it. The door rattled on its hinges but didn't give. Dave stepped back and did it again, harder, and this time, it flew open as the latch fell on the floor and skidded across the concrete. Dave took a moment to consider that he had broken the law he swore to uphold for the first time in his life. He crossed to the driver's window of his car and looked in. The keys were dangling from the slot, but everything else seemed normal. For a moment, Dave second-guessed himself that this was his car, but he knew it was without checking the license plate. He removed the keys, went to the trunk, and popped it open. He turned his head just in time as vomit projected from his mouth in an arc to splatter on the floor.

Dave staggered back, weak, wiping his mouth with his hand. "Oh, Matt," he whispered as he gazed down at the dead body crumpled inside the trunk. He didn't need to look for a pulse but did, as if on autopilot. Matt's body was cold to the touch, his head a bloody pulp. There was no doubt he was dead. Dave berated himself because Matt had believed Dave's hunch and chose to support him rather than turn the information over. Matt would be alive now if he'd followed protocol, as he should have. Dave doubted he would ever be able to forgive himself.

He did what he should have done before. Dave phoned Mark Brennan, who answered immediately. "Dave, what the hell is going on? I just had a call from your wife; she is frantic and told me to send you help. I just got off the phone with the local cops there. They are sending a patrol car. Now tell me what the hell is happening."

"No time, Boss. I've found Matt; he's been murdered and crammed into the back of my car inside the garage at the address Lynne sent you. Flanders killed him. I have to go now and get my kids; they are in the house with Flanders. You've got probable cause because when I saw my car was inside the garage, I broke the door down and found Matt's body."

"Dave, do not go inside the house; that's an order."

Dave took the cell from his ear, stared at it momentarily, and ended the call, not bothering to reply.

He took a deep breath, looked around, and saw the door he thought would lead inside the home. Dave could not see any sense in being quiet; Flanders must have heard him breaking into the garage. He strode purposefully to the door and yanked it open; he would save his children, and nothing would stop him, especially a madman.

The door swung wide and led into a huge kitchen with large stone benchtops and gleaming appliances. Dave froze halfway to the breakfast bar when he saw Flanders. He was sitting on a leather modular couch that faced the expanse of windows overlooking the lake, which, on any other occasion, Dave would have stopped to admire. Ben and Molly were on either side of him, cradled in his arms, crying softly, obviously frightened. Dave could see a knife in each of Flanders' hands, no doubt from the magnetized strip on the wall above the meal preparation area in the kitchen. Each blade gleamed in the reflected evening light shining off the shimmering surface of the lake, and each point pressed into the skin on Ben and Molly's neck.

"You're not taking my kids from me," Marlon Flanders said, and at that moment, Dave knew all semblance of sanity was gone from the man holding his children hostage.

He weighed up his options. From side on, he could not shoot. Ben was on Dave's side of Flanders, mostly obscuring the target. Dave knew he was nowhere near a good enough shot to hit Flanders' head, especially at that range, which was about all Dave could see. He knew he had to get closer, but his heart sank deeper when he realized even if he could take the shot, both children were awake and would witness not only a death close-up but the man's head exploding if his bullet hit its mark.

Dave doubted they would ever recover emotionally, but then again, with knife blades to their throats, what choice did he have? Dave didn't speak in response to Flanders' ludicrous statement but began walking again. He intended to get closer so that if he had to take the shot, he could at least hit what he was aiming for before Flanders had the chance to stab the children.

"Your friend tried to steal my children, so I had to stop him; he won't be stealing any more kids."

Dave took a deep breath, trying to keep calm, and kept walking. "Ben and Molly are not your children but Lynne's and mine. I fathered them, and Lynne gave birth while I held her hand. You weren't there, Flanders."

"Daddeeeee save us, pleeease!" Molly screamed, and Dave saw Flanders squeeze her to him harder.

Before Dave could answer her, Flanders did. "I will save you, baby; this man is not going to harm you or take you from me. Remember what I told you: we are together for life, and soon, your mummy will join us." Flanders turned his dead eyes to Dave. "Don't come any closer."

Dave was now directly in front of the three on the couch, a dozen feet from them, his back to the windows with the million-dollar view. He raised the gun so that the barrel lined up with Flanders' chest. "Lynne will never join you, and you are not Ben and Molly's daddy; I am. Let them go, or I *will* shoot."

Flanders shrugged, and as he did so, the tips of the blades pierced the children's necks, causing a spot of blood to appear and a scream from each. "No, you won't. You won't do it because, you know, even if you shoot me, the last thing I will do before I die will be to kill these two bundles of joy. You won't take my kids from me if I can't have them. Drop the gun, kick it away, and sit on the floor, cross-legged, right where you are."

"Why are you doing this, Flanders? Why was Dorothy not enough for you? Why did you have to try to steal my wife and my children?"

Flanders didn't reply, just stared at Dave, obviously waiting for him to comply. Dave sighed, dropped in a squat, then folded his legs under him to sit as he had been told. Next, he slid his Glock across the floor back toward the kitchen, not wanting to send it nearer to Flanders than him. "That's better. Do you want to know why I did it all? Because I am an alpha male, and I take what I want. I'm a businessman; I run multi-million-dollar companies and make strategic plans every day of the week. That's what I do and why they pay me the big bucks while you're just a cop. Lynne deserves better than you, and she's going to get it. Dorothy? She had her chance, and it's over. She belittled me, denied me children, and favored her daddy over me while Lynne beckoned. Lynne wanted a better life away from you, so she chose me; we love each other."

"She didn't choose you, you idiot. You forced yourself on her, threatened her, fabricated a theft, and extorted her to have sex. That's not love; that is an obsession, a sick, perverted obsession. Then you raped her when she discovered your lies, and then to cap it all off, you abducted her children. That woman you say you love is home, frantic with worry, terrified you will hurt our children, and look at you, holding a knife to them so they can't run to their real father: me. Call yourself a man? An alpha male? Well, if you are, send the children away to another room, then take me on, just you and me, or are you too scared of what this real man will do to you? Alpha male? Don't make me laugh."

Anger flitted across Flanders' face. "You want mano-a-mano? You're just a dumb cop. I fought heavyweight golden gloves and MMA in the Octagon. Oh, I'm going to make you eat your words and beg for your miserable life. Kids, go to your rooms at the top of the stairs. I will be up soon and read you both a story." He removed his arms from around them, and simultaneously, they ran across the room crying and jumped onto Dave's lap.

Dave sobbed as he clung to them. "It will be okay, guys, I promise. I love you both so much." Dave whispered.

Flanders raised his voice and stood up. "You're both being disloyal; I will punish you for that later; now do as you're told; go to your room."

"Molly, Ben, please, go. Let me take care of the bad man, then I will take you home to Mummy."

Slowly, they disengaged their arms from him and, sobbing, stood up. Ben, ever the big brother, took his sister's hand. "C'mon, Molly." They shuffled away, constantly looking over their shoulders until they got to the wooden staircase, then ran up it. Dave watched them all the way, relieved that the children would not witness it no matter what happened. In the distance, Dave heard an approaching siren; help would be here soon.

He turned back to Flanders, who had silently crossed the room and now towered about Dave. Without warning, he kicked Dave in the side of the face, snapping his head to one side, breaking his jaw, and smashing three teeth against the inside of his mouth. Dave felt himself flying backward and his head hitting the parquetry flooring. Dazed, the room spun, and he tried to hold onto consciousness. Molly and Ben, they were depending on him, and he had been sucker kicked. He could not, would not let the fight be over before it started.

Dave was vaguely aware Flanders was laughing, and worse, was laughing at him. He raised his left arm as if stopping traffic, his hand flat as if at a stop sign, trying to ward off further kicks or blows, while his right hand moved from the outstretched position to his side. In his foggy brain, he wanted Flanders to think he was trying to stand. He turned his head to the side and spat out a mouthful of blood.

"I told you; I'm the alpha male, and no one will ever take my kids from me; I will kill them first. It sounds like sirens are coming closer, but getting through the gates will take a while. You called the cops, didn't you? Let's end this, then I will get Ben and Molly. The boat is tied to the jetty; I will have enough time to get across the lake and be gone. Don't worry, I will take good care of them and Lynne when she joins us."

Flanders dropped, so he knelt astride Dave's body. He raised the knife in his right hand while Dave groped inside his jacket pocket.

"This one is for ruining my marriage to Dorothy." He screamed and drove the blade down and into Dave's chest. Then he raised his left hand, which held the second knife. *"This one is for ending my career."*

Dave fought to hold onto consciousness. He was in shock and could not feel any pain from the knife wound, but he knew it was probably fatal. His hand finally closed around the handle of Lynne's new pistol. He had no time to remove it from the jacket pocket, so he lifted his hand at an angle and pulled the trigger. The bullet blew through the tweed material and hit Flanders in the armpit of his raised left arm, holding the knife, which spun out of his hand as the shoulder smashed.

Flanders screamed and lowered his eyes to meet Dave's with a smoldering hatred Dave had never witnessed. Dave took a rasping breath. "Alpha male? Go to hell." He re-aimed and fired again, this time hitting between Flanders' top lip and nose. The bullet trajectory traveled up into his brain and blew a hole out of the back of his skull.

Chapter 15

Serenity

"Serenity comes when you trade expectations for acceptance."
Gautama Buddha

"Wake up, Dave. Please, wake up."
The voice seemed to come from far away as if the breeze carried it. Dave tried to focus but then gave up. *I'm dreaming,* he thought and let the darkness retake him.

****

A faraway voice was back again. Fuzzy, indistinct, echoing. It reminded him of sonar beeps for some inexplicable reason. "I'm sorry, Mrs. Margolis. There is no change again today." Dave was aware of movement beside him but could see nothing. *Where am I?* he thought, but he had no idea. Then, a memory crept up on him as a beautiful smell hit his nose. *What is that smell?* It reminded him of something happy, something extraordinary, someone he loved. A perfume worn by…he couldn't remember. He drifted away again, but the scent lingered in his nose and mind as it tried to recall who it reminded him of.

"Please, please, Dave, wake up," Lynne said as she hugged him.

****

Lynne Margolis stared down Susan Bodinski using her most serious expression. "You *will* have that operation, Susan. You know it's what Dave would have wanted: for you to get better, and you've come so far on the drugs. Bart was right; your autoimmune disease was the main problem, and the drugs are allowing your body, along with the antibiotics, to turn back the tide. Have the operation, let Bart remove the worst scarring, and perform the skin grafts. If Dave were with us, you know he would want you to."

Susan could not hold it back any longer; she cried, heart-wrenching sobs from somewhere deep inside. Lynne hugged her, still wary of touching the sores, which, though the weeping and creeping ulcerations had stopped spreading, still caused Susan pain and discomfort. "I know I'm stupid, yes, I know Dave wanted this, but he's not here, is he? I miss him so much."

Lynne wiped away her tears. "Please, Susan. Have the operation anyway."

****

Four months after shooting Marlon Flanders dead, Dave Margolis was still deep in the coma that had held him in its clutches.

Lynne sat by his bedside, as she had every day while Ben and Molly were at school. Then she would leave to pick them up and deliver them to her parents. During Lynne's absence, Susan would sit with Dave. Then, Lynne would return to the hospital to sit with him until ten p.m. when the nursing staff hustled her out of his private room. Each day, they had spoken to him, telling him everything he was missing while he slept. They never knew if he could hear them, but the experts said that often, coma patients were aware of their surroundings and could listen to conversations. That was enough for Lynne; she spoke to him non-stop, and Susan, who had become a mirror image of Lynne, as if they really were twins, did too.

Susan told him how successfully her treatment was going and how grateful she was to Dave for making it happen. Knowing how Dave hated to be thanked, she did it in hopes she could reach him with emotion and words. She told him about the books she was editing, even reading him passages that were sometimes humorous, sometimes exciting, and once, even naughty. She told Dave about her life, living with Lynne and helping with the children, and she loved it. Mark had tried for reconciliation unsuccessfully once he heard on the grapevine that she was recovering. "Not in this lifetime," she told Dave as she ruffled his pillows, hoping he could pick up that she was wearing the same perfume as Lynne now. He's done his dash with me. I do not need a fair-weather husband. Since meeting you, I know the kind of man I want. The kind who would fight for his wife and children and risk dying for them, not run away when times get tough."

Dave didn't stir. He never did. The doctors said it was from blood loss and shock. He had received facial reconstructive surgery, though Lynne or Susan didn't mind the minor scarring he was left with; Susan thought it added character, and for Lynne, it was a constant reminder of how much Dave loved his wife and children.

****

"Dave," Susan said ten minutes before Lynne arrived to take over. I don't know if you can hear or see me, but I will show you something. Oh, and by the way, I have Lynne's permission to show you, so there's no need to fret. She stood and turned her back to his bed. "Dave, I'm going to take my top off so you can see the fantastic work your friend Bart has done on my back. He thinks two more operations should do it, but oh my God, wait till you see his handiwork. Okay, are you ready? It's still too uncomfortable for me to wear a bra, so I'm going to be topless; I hope you won't mind. I honestly don't care if you see my breasts; if it would wake you up, I'd show them to you every day."

****

After Susan left for the day, Lynne spoke to him about how the children were doing at school and that the victim support counselor, Colin, had greatly helped their well-being as they were now back on track with their lessons. Colin was happy to cut the visits back to monthly, which she believed was a fantastic improvement for them. It seems Molly and Ben realized their father rescued them, and the abduction and Marlon Flanders were becoming fading memories.

Lynne turned to Dave and said quietly, "Please wake up, Dave. The kids miss you and want to thank you for being their hero and saving them. Come back to us, please; we all miss you."

She glanced at Dave, but as usual, there was no sign he could hear. She held his hand in hers, but he had no return grip. "Susan tells me she pranced around you topless. What did you think of how well her back is coming? It's okay, Dave; I know you enjoyed looking at her front, too." Lynne giggled and looked at his face—still nothing.

"I can't tell you what having Susan with me is like.

She has helped me so much. I think you were right when you said there was some deep connection between us because my twin sister died when we were kids. Well, that explains my feelings for her, but freaky, isn't it that she feels the same about me?" Lynne paused, wanting his opinion on something important and hoping he could hear her. "Dave…I want you to know something. Susan and I both love you. I mean, she loves you as much as I do, and in the same way, and I am not threatened by that. We talk about it at night; I've told you before, we sleep in the same bed, and no, nothing like that happens. Get your mind out of the gutter; neither of us has a gay bone in our body. We both love you, and umm, when you get better and come home, what we really would like is if you would agree to us living together. Dave, I mean *really* living together, the three of us in the same bed, and umm, you make love with us both."

She felt it; suddenly, he squeezed her hand. "Oh, my God, oh my God, oh my God." She grabbed the nurse call button and pressed it repeatedly. She looked at his face; his eyes were open! "Oh, Dave, I love you so much."

He croaked a reply, but no words came out. He was back.

Epilogue

A gentle breeze stirred the white sand as the relentless Caribbean sun beat down on the beach umbrella, which shaded Dave as he dozed. He wasn't sleeping, he'd told Susan and Lynne, just resting up. He adjusted his sunglasses and looked toward the ocean while absently stroking the white scar Marlon Flanders had left him with on his chest. Ben held Lynne's hand while Molly held Susan's, her "other mom," which was what the kids had come to call Susan as they paddled in the gentle waves. Lynne wore a stark white two-piece bikini, while Susan wore a long T-shirt over bikini bottoms, still cautiously protecting her back. Susan looked back and saw him and waved; he waved back and heard the two children giggle as a larger-than-normal wave crashed on the sand and crept up their legs. Life was good; in fact, Dave reflected that life was incredible.

Lynne had been working for Dorothy for over three months, starting a month after Dave woke up. She hadn't wanted to leave him and return to work, but Dave insisted. He had rehabilitation to go to, but he had resumed work on light duties, and when his vacation time was over, he would start back as a negotiator, which had always been his first love.

Lynne seemed to be thriving in her new role as General Manager. Dorothy had been correct in recognizing Lynne had qualities far above being a manager's assistant, and they worked together nonstop, with Lynne being a sponge and soaking up all she could learn. Dorothy trained, guided, and mentored each step of the way. On the three-month work anniversary, Dorothy had given Lynne a sizeable bonus. She insisted she, Dave, Susan, and the children take advantage of the school break and take the long overdue trip to Barbados. They had been in residence a week, and Dorothy and her father were due to arrive later that night when, Lynne believed, her position as permanent CEO would be formalized over dinner.

Dave closed his eyes, edging closer to sleep, when he heard muffled giggling from his children as they approached, the sand hiding their steps. The next moment, four pieces of cold, wet kelp seaweed were dumped on his stomach, making him leap up, suddenly wide awake.

"Come on, *stick in the mud*; come and swim with us," Susan said, laughing as Dave wiped off the weed.

At that moment, he knew she was the instigator, as she often was; her sense of humor was like a breath of fresh air and always made them smile. He dipped his head, grabbed her, and lifted her onto his shoulder. Susan squealed and wriggled her legs, but that would not stop him. Relentlessly, he marched toward the azure-blue ocean.

"Don't you dare throw me in!" She giggled, but he knew that she realized that was precisely what he was going to do.

Susan had become radiantly more beautiful than the first day he had seen her perched on a ledge, forty stories up. And since her treatment with Bart Chisholm, her self-confidence had grown, and every time he looked at her, she took his breath away. That she loved him with a passion rivaling Lynne's staggered him, and Dave often wanted to pinch himself that it wasn't all just a dream. Susan was a part of his family now. They had spoken endlessly about their *living arrangement* and that during the four months, Dave had been unconscious, Lynne and Susan had become inseparable, sharing their mutual tragedy. As Bart restored Susan's health, beauty, and mental well-being, both women knew they had Dave to thank. Perhaps that was a part of the reason for the blossoming three-way love affair, or maybe the relationship that had developed between Lynne and Susan while Dave was in the hospital. Dave didn't know or care. It worked; boy, did it work. He often recalled the first night they shared a bed, and with Lynne coaxing and urging, he made love with Susan, always being careful not to hurt her back. Lynne had held Susan's hand throughout, murmuring encouragement and whispering how beautiful they looked together. There was no jealousy or ill feeling. Not then and not since. Sure, they sometimes had differences of opinion, but they never argued.

Ben and Molly seemed to blossom because they had two moms to love them, and Susan became a natural mother, which amazed her because when with Mark, they had no desire for children. While she was incapable of conceiving, Susan thought now, looking back, that Mark had guided her and that deep down she had wanted them, but because she loved him, she consented to his desire and way of life, and they never spoke of adoption.

"Dave, don't. Don't you dare," Susan squealed once more.

"Go on, Dad, dunk her," Ben chimed, and Molly laughed loudly.

He waded into the waves while Lynne smiled and held her children's hands, biting her lip because she wanted to cry. She had some news to share with Dave and Susan, and she intended to tell them later, after dinner, when they retired to bed, although she suspected Susan already knew. They were so in tune Lynne thought it was impossible to hide something so monumental from her.

"Arghhhhhhhhh!" Lynne heard Susan scream as Dave lowered her gently into the surf. Lynne laughed, knowing her life was complete. She had her husband, the best man in the world. She had her sister, who completed the other half of herself that had been missing for so many years. Two beautiful children, recovered now from their trauma, and the best news of all? She was pregnant again.

Author's Note

This book has taken me three years to write, rewrite, and edit with my wonderful editor, friend, and mentor, Melanie Billings.

I first pitched this idea to Mel as a collection of short stories with a central theme, focusing on the things (sometimes extreme) people will do to find and keep love. As always, Mel was supportive, and while she said it was something the publisher might not be keen on, she offered to read it when completed. To put that in context, dear reader, getting a senior editor of a publishing house to read a manuscript in its entirety, knowing it might be something that would probably be rejected, is no small thing.

So, off I went to write the first story about a NY police Negotiator who, on the day he discovers his wife's infidelity, climbs out onto a forty-story ledge to stop a beautiful woman from killing herself. As the story grew 'legs,' I realized I could achieve my goal of focusing on different aspects of love revolving around the three central characters (four if I include the dreadful nemesis, Marlon Flanders). This is why each chapter has a title and famous quotation featuring that theme.

Did I achieve my goal, dear reader? Well, ultimately, that is up to you. I hope you enjoyed Dave, Lynne, and Susan's journey to hell and back. But I do want to stress that none of this tale would have been possible, or anywhere near as readable, without my dear friend Melanie Billings.

Thank you, Mel. I hope you know how sincere that thank you is.

Stephen King

Perth, Western Australia.

A word about the author…

I was born in the UK, what seems like an epoch ago, and moved to Australia at age 16. I was a long-haired rock guitarist and poet/songwriter before real life got in the way, and I gave it all up for love.

I've always felt I had tales to tell. I won short story competitions and wrote poetry in my wilder, younger days, but always wanted to write novels. I've now published eighteen books. While some are Police procedural thrillers, mainly focusing on Serial killers, all my stories have a love theme running through them.

I believe love and family are everything. Anything else you gain in life is a bonus.

I live in Perth, Western Australia, and am fiercely patriotic. My wife is amazing in that she not only puts up with living with a writer but encourages it. I've been blessed with five children, and I adore them all. Check out my website at: http://stephen-b-king.com

Thank you for purchasing
this publication of The Wild Rose Press, Inc.

For questions or more information
contact us at
info@thewildrosepress.com.

The Wild Rose Press, Inc.
www.thewildrosepress.com